"Who's going to help you when the baby comes?"

His playful look was gone.

Her heart thudded heavily within her breast. The bottom line, the end of the road she traveled, and he'd nailed her right where she was most vulnerable. "I don't know yet. I haven't decided what I'll do when the time comes."

His brow lifted. "Seems like that would have been the first thing you thought of."

No, the first thing had been escape. Finding a place to hide, where no one could seek her out. A sanctuary for herself and her child.

"Erin?" Quinn tasted her name, relishing the breathless sound of it. His gaze appreciated the look of her, his mind wondered at the unexpected appeal to his senses. He hadn't looked for this attraction, and yet it could not be denied. She was the quarry, he the hunter, her capture the goal....

Dear Reader,

Entertainment. Escape. Fantasy. These three words describe the heart of Harlequin Historicals. If you want compelling, emotional stories by some of the best writers in the field, look no further.

Carolyn Davidson is one of those writers. Critics have described her books as "moving," "explosive" and "destined to delight." Her latest, *The Tender Stranger,* is no exception. It's the touching story of a pregnant widow who flees from her conniving in-laws to a secluded cabin in Colorado. Alone and frightened, Erin welcomes the handsome, caring stranger who appears on her doorstep—not knowing that he's the bounty hunter her in-laws have hired to bring her back. Don't miss it!

Rory by Ruth Langan, is the terrific first book of Ruth's new medieval series, THE O'NEIL SAGA. In it, an English noblewoman falls madly in love with a legendary Irish rebel. And Ana Seymour returns this month with a heartwarming Western, *Father for Keeps,* about a wealthy young man who returns to Nevada to win back the woman who secretly had his child.

Be sure to look for *Robber Bride* by Deborah Simmons. In the third DE BURGH story, the strong, arrogant de Burgh brother, Simon, finds his match in a free-spirited runaway bride who is hiding from her despicable would-be husband.

Whatever your tastes in reading, you'll be sure to find a romantic journey back to the past between the covers of a Harlequin Historical.®

Sincerely,

Tracy Farrell
Senior Editor

Please address questions and book requests to:
Harlequin Reader Service
U.S.: 3010 Walden Ave., P.O. Box 1325, Buffalo, NY 14269
Canadian: P.O. Box 609, Fort Erie, Ont. L2A 5X3

Carolyn Davidson
The Tender Stranger

HARLEQUIN®

TORONTO • NEW YORK • LONDON
AMSTERDAM • PARIS • SYDNEY • HAMBURG
STOCKHOLM • ATHENS • TOKYO • MILAN • MADRID
PRAGUE • WARSAW • BUDAPEST • AUCKLAND

ISBN 0-373-29056-X

THE TENDER STRANGER

Copyright © 1999 by Carolyn Davidson

Books by Carolyn Davidson

Harlequin Historicals

CAROLYN DAVIDSON

Reading and writing have always been major interests in Carolyn Davidson's life. Even during the years of raising children and working a full-time job, she found time to read voraciously. However, her writing consisted of letters and an occasional piece of poetry. Now that the nest is empty, except for three grandchildren, she has turned to writing as an occupation.

Her family, friends and church blend to make a most fulfilling existence for this South Carolina author. And most important is her husband of many years, the man who gives her total support and an abundance of love to draw on for inspiration. A charter member of the Lowcountry Romance Writers of America, she has found a community of soul mates who share her love of books, and whose support is invaluable.

Watch for her next Harlequin Historical novel, *The Midwife,* a September 1999 release. She enjoys hearing from her readers at P.O. Box 2757, Goose Creek, SC 29445-2757, and promises to answer your letter.

Men with the quality of tenderness in their emotional makeup make wonderful heroes, and the woman who is fortunate enough to be truly loved by one of them is indeed blessed. I am married to such a man, and have found that each of our five male offspring has, in some way, inherited their father's nature. And so this book is dedicated to my sons, Bobby, Michael, Jon, Larry and Tim, because each of them, in his own way, is a hero to the woman he loves.

To my granddaughter, Erin Elizabeth, whose innocent and loving spirit was the inspiration for my heroine, and who shared with me the days and weeks spent in the writing of this book, I give my appreciation.

But as always, and with deep devotion, this story is for Mr. Ed, who loves me.

Chapter One

October, 1875
Pine Creek, Colorado

They'd told him she was easy on the eyes, and that her hair was darker than midnight.

Quinn Yarborough peered through the spyglass at the woman so aptly described. A grunt of aggravation marred the silence and he shifted, seeking a more comfortable spot. The rock beneath him was ungiving, and he settled for edging closer to the rim of the flat, over-hanging cliff.

She was all they'd said, at least from the rear view. Her hair hung free, a black curtain, reflecting and yet somehow absorbing the tantalizing light that comes just before dark shrouds the land. Erin, for that was her name, he reminded himself, was slim but rounded, her hips womanly.

And then she disappeared behind the barn door, and he settled down to wait. It wasn't a barn, actually, more of a shed. Probably didn't have more than two or three stalls, from what he could tell.

Quinn tilted his hat to shade his eyes and focused his vision, then waited. He'd been on her trail for almost three months, from New York City to St. Louis and westward. She'd been smart, changing conveyances often, hiding behind other names. But not smart enough to thwart his prying and prodding. Buying this cabin, having her legal name put on the deed, had been a grave error in judgment.

Erin Wentworth, widow of Damian. Wanted by her former father-in-law, wanted enough to warrant the hiring of Quinn Yarborough, obtaining exclusive rights to his time in order to find her. Time he should, by all rights, be spending running the profitable agency he owned in New York City.

In years past, Quinn Yarborough had been known to haul men back from their hiding places when others had long since given up the search. But those were the early years. Now he had men working for him, highly trained, ruthless in their diligence, and usually successful at their job.

That this case was unusual went without saying. He'd long since given up the personal touch, sending others out in his stead. The price of success involved sitting behind a desk these days, he'd found.

Until now.

He didn't think he'd have much problem nailing one small woman. And with that thought in mind, he watched as the shed door slid open.

They'd told him she was just a bit of a thing, a slender woman, innocent appearing. They hadn't been specific about their reasons, only that it was imperative she be found.

And once she was found, he was faced with the task of persuading her to return to New York City with him.

Since he considered this job to be along the lines of fulfilling an obligation, he was prepared to be most persuasive.

A chicken squawked loudly, the sound carrying to where he lay, and he chuckled as it half flew, half scrambled from the shed. The woman burst through the door in its wake, bent over, arms outstretched, as if to catch a stray leg or wing.

With a yelp of anger, Erin Wentworth stood erect, one arm bent, the hand resting on her hip. Through the spyglass Quinn watched her lips move, and he grinned, the curse all too apparent to his knowledgeable gaze.

He set the glass aside and blinked, then put it to his eye once more. Focusing again on the feminine figure, he growled his own oath. They'd managed to give him all the facts he'd needed to seek out and find this runaway female. All but one.

They hadn't told him she was pregnant.

Erin clutched at her side, the hitch catching her unaware. Chasing the stupid chicken away from the door, then across the width of the shed, had been a mistake. The crafty hen loved a challenge, and these days most anything, even a squawking chicken, was swifter moving than Erin's pregnant self.

"Stay out here and go hungry, for all I care," she muttered, watching the truant hen, who had stopped to peck at a stray bug. "I've got better things to do than play nursemaid to a dumb chicken."

She turned back to the shed, reaching inside to pick up the milk pail, frothing with warm milk. She peeked inside the dim structure before she slid the door closed, then nodded with satisfaction. Her saddle horse, packhorse and the small Jersey cow she'd hauled up the mountain at the end of a leading rope were nosing their allotment of hay. Across the shed, five laying hens, clucking softly to themselves, pecked lazily at the handful of feed she'd spread before them.

By the time she took care of the milk, it would be just about dark, and supper was almost done in the oven. Her stomach growled in response to that thought, and she grinned, rubbing her side reflectively.

"If nothing else, I'm feeding you well, baby of mine. With fresh milk and eggs every day, you should be growing like a bad weed." Before long the child within her would respond to her words. The thought was cheering.

She carefully made her way across the grassy clearing toward the cabin. Along with the small meadow she used for pasture, it was the only level spot on this side of the mountain. The rough cabin held almost everything she needed to get her through the coming winter. One more trip down to Pine Creek and she'd have supplies enough to last till spring.

The chicken clucked as she passed it by, cocking its head to one side to keep her in view, and Erin laughed aloud. "You'll be ready to scoot inside by morning, I'll warrant," she said to the frisky hen. "If you don't freeze overnight."

And that might not be a bad idea. She'd have chicken for dinner three days in a row should that happen.

She climbed the two steps to the shallow porch and opened the door, inhaling the scent of baking cornbread. Carrying the milk pail to the farthest corner from the stove, she covered it with a clean cloth and headed back to latch the door for the night.

From the shed a whinny pierced the air. An answering call resounded from beyond the clearing, and Erin held the door in place, only a crack allowing her to peer outside.

"Hello, the house!"

It was a deeply masculine voice, rough and forceful, and she drew in a quick breath, sensing danger there in the twilight. Beneath the trees edging her property she could barely make out the horseman, silent now, mounted upon a horse so dark it almost blended into the dusk.

"May I come closer?" the man called.

Erin's heart was pounding at a rapid pace, and she felt a moment's dizziness as she leaned against the barely opened door. Then with a deep breath she forced strength into her words.

"What do you want? I have a gun."

"I'd be surprised if you didn't, ma'am." The horse stepped from the trees and walked toward the cabin, the man a shadowed figure, hat drawn down, shoulders wide, seemingly at one with the animal he rode.

Erin reached for the shotgun she kept in the corner, then pushed the door open a bit farther.

He'd almost reached the porch, and she shivered at the unknown danger he represented. It might be more sensible to shoot first and ask questions later, she supposed. Still, if he were set on harming her, he probably wouldn't have ridden up so openly. Besides, it would be a mess she'd rather not clean up if she didn't have to.

"Ma'am? I'd like to talk to you. Can I come in?" His rough tones were more like a west wind in the pines, not rasping as she'd first thought. It was as if he hadn't spoken in a long while and his words had grown rusty in the meantime.

"Stay where you are, stranger," she said forcefully, the gun barrel in full view. "Speak your piece."

"I need a place to harbor for the night. It's settin' to storm out there and my horse is averse to getting wet. Can I use your shed for shelter?"

Erin squinted in the twilight, unable to see his features. "Take off your hat, mister."

He obeyed, his fingers long against the wide brim. The other hand rose to sweep through his hair, combing it back with a casual movement.

Her gaze swept over him, the long length of his body apparent even astride the big horse. He was deeply tanned from what she could tell, dark hair hanging to his collar, a somber look about his features. A long gun in a scabbard alongside his saddle was the only visible weapon, though she doubted if it was the only one he carried.

"Get down, mister. I'll leave a plate of cornbread on the porch for you. You can stay the night, but I don't have an empty stall. Your horse will have to be tied to the wall."

He nodded. "Much obliged, ma'am. I'll appreciate the meal. It's been a long time since noon."

"You come up the mountain from Pine Creek?" she asked, suspicion rife in her tone.

He shook his head. "No, across from Big Bertha on the other side."

The mine was about played out, but there were still men working it. Maybe he'd been let go, like so many others, once the mother lode had ceased to produce in any measure. The clerk in the store at Pine Creek had filled her in on the surrounding territory when she arrived, and Erin had listened avidly. It paid to know her surroundings.

"All right, you can stay the night," she repeated abruptly, closing the door as he turned toward the shed.

Drawing the pan of cornbread from the oven, she cut a large square, centering it on a thick plate, one of the two that had come with the cabin. A dollop of butter at the edge of the plate, along with a knife and fork, completed her offering. She opened the door slowly and bent to place the food at the edge of the porch, once ascertaining he was not in view.

"On second thought..." she said after a moment, turning back to the stove. Her common courtesy demanded more, and she filled a mug with steaming coffee from the pot resting on the back burner.

As she opened the door again, the visitor looked up from the edge of the porch, his hand reaching for the plate. His eyes were dark, narrowing as the light from inside illuminated his face.

"Ma'am? Something wrong?" he asked. And then his mouth twisted into a one-sided smile as he spotted the cup she held.

She stepped warily from the doorway, holding the coffee in his direction, and he took it from her, his fingers careful not to infringe on her grip.

"Thank you. It's most appreciated." His eyes widened a bit as he scanned her form, then hesitated as his gaze came to rest on her swollen belly.

"You all right, up here by yourself?" he asked quietly.

"What makes you think I'm alone?" she asked, backing into the cabin. Her heart was thumping, her cheeks felt flushed, and she leaned against the doorjamb.

"Dunno. Guess I took it for granted. Didn't see a man around. Not much room in there to hide anybody, is there?" His smile was wider, but his look was unchanging, dark and piercing.

"I do all right, mister. Just go eat your meal." She

closed the door and leaned against it, her head back. This wasn't what she'd bargained for, this stranger at her doorstep.

She'd hoped for solitude here, prayed for safety and expected to be ignored. No one back east knew where she was. Even the man at the store thought she was a widow lady named Mrs. Peterson. That he also probably thought she was a bit eccentric, maybe even unbalanced, living alone on the side of a mountain all winter, could not be avoided.

Her cornbread tasted flat, the coffee strong, and the milk she drank was too warm to be refreshing.

"You ruined my supper, mister," she muttered, turning down the wick on the kerosene lamp before she readied herself for bed. Her flannel gown was big, bought large enough to accommodate her increasing bulk, and she wrapped it around herself as she curled in the middle of the bed.

The window allowed moonlight to cast its glow against the floor, and she watched as shadows flitted across the glass panes. An owl, from the size of it, then another night bird. Leaves from the hardwoods at the edge of the clearing would be on the ground by morning, what with the wind blowing up a storm.

Her eyes closed and she opened them with effort, hearing a horse call from the shed. Maybe the chicken would cluck outside the door and he'd let her in. Probably wasn't cold enough to freeze the creature, anyway.

The morning dawned with a red glow, the sun behind hazy clouds, barely peeking through. It hadn't rained much, but there was a storm still brewing out there.

Erin dressed quickly before she turned to the stove, shaking down the ashes and stoking the fire with three chunks of wood. She set six thick slices of bacon in her skillet and placed it on the back burner, the coffeepot, freshly filled with water and ground coffee, at the front.

She broke an egg into the pot, added the shell and closed the lid. The thought of a stranger coming had taken on a lesser feel of danger. He probably meant well. Coming at twilight, and being built on such a grand scale, he'd appeared to be a threat, right off. He might look less forbidding in the light of day.

She separated the milk and put a pitcher of cream on the table, then poured the skim into the bucket. It broke her heart to pour it on the ground, but the little Jersey was a good milker and she had more than she could use. The cream she shook in a jar for butter, and she managed to drink over a quart of whole milk a day. Still, some went to waste.

At the rate she was going, she'd be fatter than a pig by the time the baby came. Her hand pressed against the familiar rounding of her belly, and a small foot shifted, meeting her touch. A smile nudged her lips and she acknowledged the possessive thrill that shivered through her at the evidence of the miniature being inside her flesh.

He didn't move much, not as much as she'd expected or hoped, but each twitch, every tiny kick, was a reminder of her reason for being alive. She was bearing a child, a living extension of herself.

Her mouth drew down. That it should also be a reminder of the man she had married could not be helped. Damian Wentworth had been a two-faced—

She shivered. Better that she not think of him.

Her warm sweater buttoned up to the throat, she lifted the pail and set forth. First to the edge of the clearing, where she poured the leftover milk upon the ground.

Then to the outdoor pump, where she rinsed and scrubbed out the pail.

Finally she turned to the shed. The door was open, and she blinked in surprise. Surely it had been shut when she ventured from the cabin.

"Good morning, ma'am." From behind her, near the outhouse, came the voice of her guest.

She turned, a bit awkwardly, and faced him. He was even larger than she'd realized from her vantage point on the porch last night, with him on the ground below. He towered over her and she watched warily as he waited, unmoving.

"I didn't know you were stirring already this morning," she said after a moment. She watched as a half smile curved his mouth. He needed a shave, dark whiskers hiding half his face, suddenly making him appear a danger once more.

"I tend to be quiet, I suppose," he said, apparently in lieu of an apology for startling her. His eyes met hers and he cleared his throat. "I'd be more than willing to help with the chores. Maybe I could earn another cup of coffee."

"You know how to milk a cow?"

His grin turned wry. "Afraid not, ma'am. But I'm handy with horses. I could probably even gather up the eggs, if you like." He chuckled. "That scallywag of a hen of yours woke me up before dawn, wanting back in the shed."

Erin felt a smile crease her face, unbidden, but perhaps welcome. "I usually give the horses a good measure of hay at night. I try to stake them out in the morning, when the weather's good."

"The cow, too?" he asked.

She nodded. "After I milk her. The chickens can run

free for the morning. They won't go far. I don't feed them till afternoon. When they hear the feed rattling in the tin pan, they come running."

"You come from farm folk?" he asked, turning to lead the way to the shed.

"No, from city people, actually."

At least she told the truth there, he thought with satisfaction. Best to keep your story as straight as possible, he'd always felt. Less confusing that way.

"How long you been here on your own?"

She looked up at him, then glanced away, as if not willing to answer his query.

"A while," she said finally, reaching to open the shed door. It creaked mightily and she shoved at it.

"Here, I'll do that." He eased her to one side, and she stiffened at the touch of his hand on her arm, then backed away.

The cow lowed impatiently, looking over her shoulder as the young woman approached. It was time and past for milking, her solemn expression said, and in answer Erin went to her, speaking softly, her hands touching the pretty face.

"I'm here, Daisy. Did you think I forgot you?" Her low, musical laugh was misplaced here, he decided. It belonged over a tea table, or better yet, in a bedroom. That image flashed in his mind unbidden, and he suppressed it quickly, irritated with himself, even as he admired her dark hair and elegant features. He'd been too long abstinent when a pregnant woman held this much appeal.

"The cow's name is Daisy?" he asked, steering his mind in another direction.

She nodded. "I've named most everything. The mare is Socks and the gelding is Choreboy."

"Not the chickens?" His voice held a touch of humor, almost as if he expected an affirmative answer.

She cast him a look over her shoulder as she moved to put the milking stool in place. "I'm not that lonesome, mister. I can refrain from calling chickens by name."

"What shall I call you?" He ventured the query as she settled herself on the low stool, and he watched warily lest she tip the three-legged seat.

Her hesitation was minute, but he noted it, making a bet with himself on her degree of honesty. She was having a hard time keeping her stories straight. Between New York and Denver she'd used six different names.

"I'm Erin Peterson," she said quietly, her forehead leaning against the soft brown hide of her cow.

Make that seven. "Are you?" he mused.

She glanced up at him, her eyes watchful.

"Pretty name." His nod was friendly, his smile bland. "You have a name, I assume?"

He nodded. "My mama called me Quinn Yarborough, after my pa."

"Really? Where was he from?" Her fingers were adept at the milking chore. He figured she'd had three months to perfect the task. The milk squirted in a satisfactory manner against the walls of the pail and the odor was almost sweet.

"Pa came from Scotland. My mother was a farmer's daughter in New York. They settled in upstate New York, where I was born."

"What are you doing in Colorado?" she asked, shifting on the stool a bit, her dress tucked between her legs, making room for the pail. She lifted a hand to wipe her forehead, where wisps of dark hair had fallen from place.

"Gold." It was as good an answer as any, he decided. Probably better than most. Gold miners were scattered throughout the mountains like ants on a rotten log, running every which way, looking for sustenance.

She peered at him over her shoulder. "Find any?"

His grin was automatic. "Sure enough. The mother lode, as a matter of fact."

His smile faded. She wouldn't appreciate the humor of that statement, should she know of what he spoke. The money he would gain from her capture was minimal. The satisfaction would far outweigh the monetary gain.

Damian Wentworth had been his boyhood friend, both of them living in the same household. And there the similarity ended.

The Wentworths were high society. Quinn Yarborough's mother had been their housekeeper, a job she found after her farmer husband died at a young age and left her to raise a son on her own.

In those early years, Damian had shared his toys, his pets and his waking hours with the housekeeper's son. Then, when the time came, they had parted, Damian to attend a fine university, Quinn to make his own way in the world.

They'd lost touch, only an occasional article in the newspaper keeping Quinn up to date. First the notice of Damian's wedding, then three years later, an obituary. Sudden death was always suspect, in Quinn's book.

The young woman frowned at him, her tone dubious as she questioned his claim. "You found the mother lode? I don't believe you."

He shrugged. "When you're working for someone else, you don't get your proper share, you know. I made a bundle, and since I wasn't lookin' to be a rich man, it was time to skedaddle. Men have been known to be killed for less than what I carry with me."

"Aren't you afraid to spread that news around?" Her fingers were brisk, stripping the milk from the small cow's udder, and she concentrated on her task.

"The only person I've told is you, and somehow I don't think you're about to rob me blind."

She laughed, a short, humorless sound. "You're probably right, Mr. Yarborough. I'm not much of a threat to anyone."

She rose from the stool and bent to pick it up, placing it by the wall. Her hand snatched the pail from disaster as the cow shifted position, one back hoof coming precariously close to the bucket.

"What would happen if you got hurt out here, all by yourself?" he asked quietly, aware suddenly of her risky situation.

"These animals are no danger to me," she answered. "I tend to fear more the two-legged variety that happen this way."

"Like me?" He took the bucket from her and carried it to the doorway. She followed, into the daylight where he could see her better.

She leveled a glance at him, unsmiling. "You could have hurt me already, if you'd a mind to, Mr. Yarborough. Let the chickens out and stake the horses and cow, will you? I'd like them to graze a bit before the storm hits."

She took the milk from his grasp, making her way to the cabin, slowly, lest the milk slosh over the edge of the pail. Daisy had given more than usual this morning. Jerseys were not known for quantity of milk, rather the richness of the cream. She'd have plenty for rice pudding today.

"I didn't plan on having breakfast, Mrs. Peterson." He'd managed to put away two bowls of oatmeal, swimming in rich cream. The bacon was a little old, but better than none at all. She must be about ready to go to town for supplies.

He said as much.

"Winter's coming on," she admitted. "I'll need to stock up. Things will keep better once it gets colder out."

"I'd be happy to give you a hand with supplies before I move along." He leaned back in his chair, the casual suggestion coming as if it were of no account one way or the other.

She looked at him across the table, her face flushed from the heat of the stove. "You mean, go to town with me? And wouldn't that make me the talk of Pine Creek?"

His jaw tightened, and he felt the clench of it narrow his gaze. "Not with me around, ma'am. I'd not treat you as anything but a lady. Any man with eyes in his head could see that you might need a hand, getting ready for winter."

"I'll be fine." Her mouth thinned, and she bent over her bowl.

"You sending me on my way?"

She looked up, and her eyes skimmed his features, as if she looked for assurance of his credibility. "Not till after the storm," she said finally, waving her spoon at the window. "It looks like it's going to blow up very soon now."

The sky had indeed darkened, the trees being whipped by the wind. He rose and walked to the door, opening it to look outside. The chickens gathered in a clutch near the shed, pecking away at anything that moved, clucking softly as they stepped carefully about in a tight circle.

A shimmering flash of lightning lit the sky across the valley below, and a crack of thunder met his ears. The cow lifted her head from the edge of the meadow and lowed impatiently. The horses shifted their ears, grazing as if they must eat their fill before the rain came down.

Behind him, Erin stirred, her chair scraping across the rough floor. He set his jaw. Getting her to town was taken care of. From there to New York promised to present a multitude of problems.

The cow would be left on her own, but it couldn't be helped. He'd take the horses and enough supplies to get them through the mountain passes. It would take a couple of days to reach Denver, with her being a good size already.

Ted Wentworth was a sly one, all right. Not one word about the girl being in the family way. Whether that would have made a difference or not was a moot question, Quinn decided. He was here now. And if he were making a guess, he'd say she was well past the halfway mark.

"Mr. Yarborough?" She was behind him, and he turned to face her.

"Don't you think the animals should be brought in? I'd not like them to be hit by lightning." She moved to the window and looked outside. Her hand was pressed against her back and she wore the trace of a frown.

"I'll get them in," he told her quickly.

"I'll help." She turned away from the sight of lightning, and winced as the thunder clapped overhead.

"You stay indoors." There was no sense in her trotting to the meadow and back, hauling animals around. The dumb chickens would no doubt be glad of the chance to get inside once he opened the door. The rest he could handle in ten minutes.

She didn't argue, and he left with a last glance in her direction. She was pale, biting her lip, and if he was any judge at all, he'd say she was hurting.

The pain was back, this time a little harder, spreading from her front to the back, where it gripped with a tenacious hold on her spine. She'd had it several times lately, but this was the worst, and without any reason she could see. No bending, stretching or lifting to bring it on. Just a sudden hot flash of pain that took her breath.

She sat down carefully and leaned her head forward, cradling it with her arms against the hard table. The baby hadn't moved much lately, and it worried her. Her eyes were damp with tears, and she held them back ruthlessly. She would not cry, not now, not with that man here to see.

She stood, the pain easing a bit. The dishes were a small matter, barely taking up space in the dishpan. Her utensils were sparse—only a skillet, a stew pot and a tin for pone. They soaked in warm water from the stove, her big kettle always heating. She'd had to pack lightly, coming here, but fortunately, old Mr. Gleason had left behind everything he owned.

None of his belongings had been clean, but she knew how to scrub and scour, and the place was as tidy as she could make it. She'd bought lye to make soap and followed the directions from the storekeeper's mother.

Quite a pioneer she'd become, she thought with a smile. There, the pain was gone. Just a random hitch in her back, she decided, relieved as she bent and twisted a bit, only to find it vanished.

Another flash of lightning lit the inside of the cabin, and she shivered as the thunder cracked ominously on its heels. From outside a sharp whinny sounded, and she caught sight of Quinn Yarborough striding across the meadow with two horses in tow. They were cavorting, their ears back as they reared against the restraint of the lines he held.

He drew them in, and within seconds had them close to the shed. As he opened the door, the hens fluttered and squawked, fighting to get inside. He followed them in, the horses eager to be out of the weather.

Erin moved to the porch, looking anxiously to where her cow was staked. Quinn's big stallion tugged at his tether just beyond Daisy, and in no time at all Quinn had run across the yard and onto the meadow to snatch their lead ropes from the stakes he'd driven into the ground.

The stallion pranced sideways and Daisy lowed piteously, both of them apparently fearful of the coming storm. The sky opened and a cloudburst hit the man and beasts without warning. One moment it was windy and dark, bulging clouds scudding across a lowering sky. The next, they had opened and poured out their burden.

Within a minute, Quinn had hightailed his charges inside the shed and the door had slid shut. And just that quickly, the rainstorm changed, turning to a steady but softly falling shower.

Quinn opened the shed door and looked across the yard at her. She'd backed up against the house, only the shallow porch roof sheltering her, and he frowned, waving his hand.

"Go on in the cabin," he called. "I'll be right in."

"Bossy!" She sniffed her irritation at the man. They were all alike, wanting to tell the women around them what to do. Almost as bad as Damian Wentworth had been. Certainly as bad as his father.

Just stay here, with us. It's what Damian would have

wanted. We'll take care of you, he'd said, his arrogance matching that of his late son.

And take care of her they would have. But all they wanted was the baby, of that she was certain. She'd have been out in the cold once the baby was born, had she stayed.

And if she knew anything about it, they were probably scouring the country for her, even now.

Men! It would be forever before she was ready to allow another one to run her life. The memory of harsh hands and cruel words was too fresh to be forgotten, and she had determined to put the past behind her and form a new life for herself and her child.

The sight of Quinn Yarborough's long legs jumping over the worst of the low spots in the yard brought her to herself, and Erin opened the door for him. He paused at her side on the porch, glaring at her damp cheeks, where an occasional raindrop had blown beneath her shelter.

"I told you to go inside." He stripped off the soaking wet shirt he wore and shed his boots, picking them up to carry them within. Then he waited for her to step through the doorway ahead of him.

"So you did. I don't take orders well."

His look was shot with wry humor. "I noticed." He moved to the stove, pulling a length of twine from his pocket. A line from one wall to the other was quickly strung and he laid his shirt over it. His boots stood in front of the oven door, and he looked at Erin with the first trace of uncertainty she'd seen on his face.

"I want to strip off my pants to dry. Do you mind?"

She shook her head and walked to the window, giving him the privacy he'd asked for. She'd lit the kerosene lamp earlier, and now its glow permeated corners of the small room.

It wasn't until she'd gazed for several moments out into the rain that she realized the window was acting much like a mirror, and his every move was apparent to her view.

Quinn was stripping her quilt from the bed to wrap around himself, and she caught a glimpse of his tall frame and an abundance of pale flesh as he did so.

Her cheeks flaming, she closed her eyes, bending her head forward to rest against the glass pane. "Oh, dear!" The whisper was soft but fervent, barely discernible.

"Mrs. Peterson? Erin? Are you all right?" His murmur was low, the warmth of his big body directly behind her, and she drew in a deep breath.

How had she gotten into this mess?

Chapter Two

She watched his approach in the windowpane, as he moved behind her in the room. Then warm hands gripped her shoulders and Erin stifled the urge to relax beneath their weight. For too long she had been building her courage to remain isolated from the world. She could not allow the presence of this man to make her soften, dependent once more on others.

"Erin?" He repeated her name and his fingers shifted, turning her to face him.

She shrugged, a gesture meant to rid herself of his touch, but to no avail. Her feet moved at his bidding and she looked up into eyes that searched hers.

"I'm fine, just worrying about the animals, I suppose."

He laughed, a muted chuckle, and shook his head. "They're about as well off as we are. The shed's pretty weathertight. You'd do better to worry about yourself. That wind's blowin' rain under the eaves. It's my guess our feet'll be getting wet before we know it."

She glanced down to where the door met the floor. A thin line of water had formed along the crack and begun to invade the room. Even as she watched, it widened and seeped forward, the boards darkening from the dampness.

"I'll get a towel," she said quickly, tugging herself from his grip.

"Hold on! Tell me where to look. I'll take care of it."

He pulled a chair from the table and lowered her onto it, allowing no excuse. His hands were firm, and Erin subsided quietly. She'd not had anyone show this degree of concern for her well-being in longer than she could remember, save for the storekeeper in the town below.

"In the box beside the bed," she directed. Probably one towel wouldn't do the trick, she decided, watching as the water crept into the room. "You might have to use more than one."

"You got that many to spare?" he asked, bending to locate the designated box.

"Four, but I'd rather keep at least one of them dry."

"There were some burlap bags in the shed. Too bad you didn't store them in here."

"They were here to start with," she said with a downturning of her mouth. "In fact, this whole place was cluttered with more junk..." She shook her head as the memory filled her mind. "The former owner was something of a pack rat, I found. I cleared his trash out the first day I arrived."

One hand held the quilt high off the floor as he pushed the towel against the threshold with the other. Then he turned to face her. "How long have you owned this place?"

She hesitated, wary at his interest. "Three months," she said reluctantly.

"I'm curious. You're a beautiful woman, living on the edge of nowhere all alone. Why..."

"You're old enough to know how to contain your curiosity. Didn't your mother ever tell you it isn't polite to ask personal questions?" She attempted to insert a note of humor, but the words sounded stark and ungiving to her ears.

He nodded. "Yes, and she probably would be ashamed of my manners right now. I beg your pardon, ma'am. There are more of us, people like you and me, than I could begin to count, living in the present and trying to forget the past. The West is full of folks looking for a new life."

"I'd rather not speak of the past," Erin told him, more gently, since he'd deigned to apologize.

"Your choice." His nod was almost genteel, and she answered it with a like gesture.

She felt the heat of his gaze as he faced her, his eyes skimming her face before his mouth twitched in an admiring grin. "Is there any coffee left in the pot?" he asked, turning to the stove. "Let me get you some."

Erin rose, needing respite from those eyes that regarded her so freely. She shook her head, denying his offer. "I'll get it. You need to hang your britches over that line. They'll never get dry, there on the floor. Either that or drape them over the chair in front of the oven door."

"You're right. My other things are in the shed, and I don't think the weather is going to break for a while. I'm reduced to the quilt, it seems, for now." He bent, picking up the pants he'd shed, and spread them across the back of the second chair. The underwear he draped on the line, which by now was drooping precariously close to the stove.

"I'll add some wood," Erin said. "I need to put my soup on to cook for dinner." She poured a cup of steaming coffee for Quinn and motioned to the cream. "There's plenty if you'd like some to lighten up the flavor. It's pretty strong."

He nodded and splashed a dollop into his cup, watching her as she dug potatoes from a sack she'd hung from the rafters. "Don't you think we sound pretty formal for a pair of refugees from a storm, sharing your cabin, me wearing your quilt?"

She looked over her shoulder at him. "You're the refugee. As soon as the storm is over, you'll be gone."

He sipped his coffee, watching her over the rim of his cup. "I've been thinking about that. You know, I'd feel a lot better if you agreed to let me stay on at least long enough to help you with the supplies, like I mentioned before."

She turned back to the potatoes, considering his offer. To all appearances, he seemed to be a gentleman, though what such a creature was doing roaming the mountains of Colorado was another puzzle. Perhaps he was a miner. Perhaps.

"Did you work the mines for a long time?" she asked, depositing three potatoes on the table. Knife in hand, she began peeling them, awaiting his reply.

"Long enough to know it wasn't what I wanted to do for the rest of my life." His tone was dry, his mouth twisted in a grin. Leaning back in his chair, he allowed the quilt to slide from his shoulders, freeing both arms. "How about you? Were you born in Denver?"

She shook her head. "No, back east."

"St. Louis?" he prodded.

The man was downright irritating, she decided. Him with all his talk about good manners. "No." Her reply was a single syllable, firm and to the point.

He ducked his head, hiding a grin, almost.

"I'm a widow. I'm going to have a child, and I like living alone. Does that answer all your questions?"

"No, ma'am, it sure doesn't. But I suspect that's all I'm going to get, isn't it?"

"If I wanted to be neighborly I'd have found a place with houses on either side of me," she said quietly. "I came here to be alone, Quinn."

"Just one more question, Erin? Please?"

She looked up at him. He was about as persistent a man as she'd ever met up with. "Just one," she said finally.

"Who's going to help you when the baby comes?" His playful look was gone. Even the admiring light was dimmed as his eyes darkened with concern.

Her heart thudded heavily within her breast. The bottom line, the end of the road she traveled, and he'd nailed her right where she was most vulnerable. "I don't know yet. I haven't decided what I'll do when the time comes."

His brow rose. "Seems like that would have been the first thing you thought of."

No, the first thing had been escape. Finding a place to hide, where no one could seek her out. A sanctuary for herself and her child. And of all the godforsaken spots she could have come up with, she'd ended up on the side of a mountain west of Denver. How ironic.

She laughed, a strained sound that made him wince.

"Erin?" Quinn tasted her name, relishing the breathless sound of it. His gaze appreciated the look of her, his mind wondered at the unexpected appeal to his senses. He hadn't looked for this attraction, and yet it could not be denied. She was the quarry, he the hunter; her capture the goal.

Yet for the life of him, for whatever reason, he'd lost

any incentive he had to cart her back to New York. For the first time in years he found himself willing to put his own needs and concerns on the back burner. All in the interests of a pregnant woman who had a past—but not much of a future, from what he could see.

Erin moved quickly, rinsing the potatoes at the pump, then slicing them into a pan, ignoring the sound of his voice speaking her name. The last of the bacon was cut into small pieces, then dropped into the skillet to fry up. An onion, chopped with rapid slashes of her knife, joined the bacon and sizzled in the grease.

"Erin? I have an idea. Why don't you hear me out?" So quickly his thoughts had spun out of control. Watching her, listening to her, he'd already juggled his plans twice. Now Quinn was about to commit himself in a new measure, perhaps allow a time of grace in which to consider the woman.

She stirred the bacon in the skillet, her back straight, only the proud tilt of her head making him aware that she listened to his words.

"I'll take you to town and help you get supplies, then bring you back here. That'll give you a bit of space to maneuver, not having to do it on your own."

"You've already made that offer," she said crisply.

"But you never gave me an answer," he reminded her.

"Let me think about it."

He drained the coffee cup and rose, walking to the window. "It's not going to let up much. I think we're stuck inside for a while."

"Do you like rice pudding?"

"My mother used to make it for a special treat when I was a boy," he said, his memory of that time fresh in his mind as he spoke the words.

"I've got a lot of milk and eggs to use up. We'll have some for dinner."

"I hope the rain lets up in time for you to milk Daisy tonight. She won't be happy if she has to wait till morning."

Erin turned from the stove. "I'll have to go out there, rainy or not. I couldn't do that to the poor thing. I can't imagine anything more cruel."

Which was what he'd had in mind earlier, he reminded himself. Leaving the cow to fend for herself while he hustled her owner down the mountain and back to the big city. He traced a circle on the steamy glass of the window. It seemed that this issue was going to be more complicated than he'd thought at first.

Even if he went through with his original plan, there would be no carrying her off from here without a bit more forethought involved. She wasn't in any shape for him to instigate a battle. In fact, fighting with the girl was not what he had in mind. That image brought a sense of shame to the surface.

If he were to follow his baser instincts, Quinn's hands would touch more than her shoulders. His eyes would do more than take in the beauty of her profile, the soft, tempting fall of hair that caught shimmering highlights from the lantern.

How he could so easily overlook the rounding evidence of her impending motherhood was beyond him. He'd never thought to find a woman in her condition so all-fired appealing. And yet she was. More so, in fact, than any other female he'd come across in years.

If Ted Wentworth could only see him today, within arm's reach of his quarry and unable to commit himself to her capture. Forty-eight hours ago, two short days past, he had been hot on her trail and ready to roll back to Denver, Erin Wentworth in hand.

Quinn's common sense told him he'd had no concept of a woman in Erin's condition. He could no more sling her on a horse and head down the mountain than he could flap his arms and fly. There didn't seem to be any way out of it. He'd have to let Ted Wentworth know what was going on, and then make plans to winter here. At least until Erin had the baby and they were both ready to travel.

Would he be ready to earn money at her expense then? Or ever, for that matter?

The rain let up just before dark. His clothes were as dry as they were going to get, Quinn decided. He hurried to put them on as soon as Erin left the house to go to the shed, wearing boots that came almost to her knees. They'd been a legacy of the old man who lived here before her, and although she scuffled along to keep them on, they served the purpose, she'd told him.

His trousers were still damp, but usable, and his boots were hot on the inside, curling his toes with the stored-up heat from the woodstove. He slapped his hat on with haste and headed out the door, dodging raindrops as he ran for the shelter.

Erin had made a detour to the outhouse, and he met her halfway between the cabin and the shed. His hand took her arm and he held her steady as they trekked through the mud.

The cow was making anxious noises when Quinn pushed the door open, and the horses nickered softly in greeting. The hens were settling in for the night and looked impatiently at the intruders as they entered.

Quinn found the lantern and lit the wick. Erin had

already settled herself to milking, obviously able to find the cow without benefit of light. He smiled as he watched her work, grinned as he listened to her softly crooning assurances to the pretty little Jersey.

"For a city girl, you sure caught on fast to taking care of stock, didn't you?"

She laughed softly. "When it's a matter of food, you learn or go hungry. I depend on the animals for transportation, eggs, and milk and butter. In turn, I feed and tend to them. Works out pretty well, I'd say."

"You got your list made up for the general store in town?"

"Pretty much. Flour, sugar, lard and cornmeal are the heavy items. I can't carry much canned goods, so I'm limited there. A farmer down below will be bringing up feed for my chickens. The young man at the store said he'd try to get up here during the bad months and bring supplies once in a while. I'll shoot some game for myself."

"You? Shoot a deer? What would you do with it then?"

She made an impatient noise. "Probably not a deer. Maybe rabbits. There are traps overhead in the cabin, too. One way or another, I'll survive."

The thought of her setting a trap sickened him, the image of it closing on her fingers as she struggled to pry the cruel jaws open a harsh picture in his mind. He set it from his thoughts.

"You know how to gut a rabbit?"

"I'll manage. I watched the cook clean chickens when I was a child. It can't be much different with a rabbit."

His admiration for this fragile woman increased. She was not what he had expected while heading across the country with one goal in mind. And now, in one short day, she'd managed to turn his life in another direction.

"Let's plan on going down to town tomorrow," Quinn told her. A door at the back of the shed provided a place to pitch the badly soiled wood chips from the stalls and he opened it wide. The pitchfork he found on the wall had a tine missing, but it would do for now, and he bent to with a will.

"All right." Her words were slow, as if she considered the matter even as she agreed to his plan.

"You want to feed the chickens tonight?" he asked.

"I'll do it first thing in the morning. They've gone to roost already." She leaned her forehead on the cow's flank, almost as if she communicated somehow with the animal. A soft lowing met his ears as he watched the two of them, the woman and the animal she tended.

"She's talking to you," he said softly.

Her look was distracted, surprised, and she grinned, the first real humor he'd seen. "Of course. We understand each other."

The hay was tossed to the horses and Daisy, the hens were ignored, and the lantern turned off within minutes. Quinn carried the pail of milk, closing the shed door with one hand, then reaching to grasp Erin's arm as they headed to the cabin.

The trip to town hung in abeyance for two days. The trail was too wet to travel in safety, Quinn decided, and Erin had to agree.

"I didn't plan on going down the mountain for at least another week," she told him after three days of watching him take over her chores, with the exception of milking. He'd shot a pair of rabbits and skinned them out, gutting them at the edge of the woods, then washing them in the creek.

She'd been pleased, frying the small pieces in the skillet and cooking rice atop the stove. "They sure don't carry a lot of meat on their bones, do they?" she'd said over supper.

"Run it off, probably."

"Do you think it will snow before long?" she asked, her thoughts darting ahead to the long winter months.

"I'm surprised it hasn't already." He licked his fingers and reached for another piece of meat. "We're pushing it, waiting till tomorrow to head out."

"I'll be ready early," she told him. "I got out my heavy cloak and a pair of britches I bought to ride in."

"You're sure you'll be all right? Riding, I mean?" His look was dubious.

She glanced up. "Of course I will. I'm healthy." She forced from her mind the harsh pains she'd suffered through twice since he'd arrived.

"We'll leave as soon as we take care of the animals."

She gave him a nod, rising to clear the table and clean up the dishes.

The sky was cloudy, but the mud had dried considerably. Leaves covered parts of the trail and Quinn rode slowly, keeping Erin behind him, lest the mare lose her footing and send her rider tumbling.

"It's going to take all day to get there if we don't move faster," she complained behind him.

"Then we'll stay there overnight if we have to," he said patiently. "There's no way to hurry when you don't know what's under the leaves, and the ground is still mushy in spots."

She subsided, aware of his greater knowledge, and

tried for good humor. The jolting when the mare broke into a trot jarred her back and made her bite her lip, but there was no way she would snivel. The least she could do was ride along without complaining.

They gained the edge of town well after noon and spent an hour in the general store. The storekeeper wanted to talk, and Quinn was hard-pressed to be polite. Only the advent of the sheriff bursting in the door to haul the merchant away to help fight a fire on the outskirts of town halted the man's stream of conversation.

"Do we need to stay and help?" Erin asked, looking over her shoulder at the red blaze in the sky. They rode in the opposite direction, and she felt somehow guilty for leaving while others might be in peril.

"The sheriff said the woman was safe, and it was too late to do anything for her husband. We need to be out of the trees before it gets full dark, Erin. I don't want to be straggling around looking for the trail at midnight." His words sounded sensible to her, but the urge to remain and offer aid was strong within her breast.

She subsided, following him down the rutted road, the trail climbing quickly once they passed the last of a long string of houses. "The farther from the middle of town we go, the shabbier the houses get, Quinn. Did you notice?" she asked.

"Folks out here can't afford much," he said. "They need room for a garden. Most of them can't get everything store-bought."

Just beyond the last dwelling, a woman dug determinedly beside her home, and Erin slowed down. "Do you think she'd have any extra potatoes? I'll bet that's what she's digging."

Quinn pulled his horse up, the packhorse halting behind him. "Could be. You want some?"

She nodded. "I'm almost out. I've been pretty stingy with them. They weigh too much to carry."

"My horse can handle them," Quinn offered, riding to the side of the fenced-in area that held a small house where several children played near the doorway.

He paid rather more than Erin thought the potatoes were worth, but the woman looked surprised and pleased at her good fortune as she provided a sack to contain them, and Erin didn't have the heart to scold Quinn for his generosity. She smiled a last time at the bedraggled creature, waving at the children, before she turned forward to follow his lead.

The trees enclosed them in a cocoon of stillness, the wind muted by the tall trees and dense undergrowth. They rode for hours, mostly in silence, Quinn holding up a hand once as Erin would have spoken to him.

And then she understood as he slid his rifle from the scabbard and motioned again with a finger against his lips. Just ahead, a buck deer stood in the middle of the trail, its spike horn antlers proudly angled. She almost called out, dreading the sight of the elegant creature lying on the ground, its life's blood draining.

Her good sense prevailed and she only winced as Quinn's shot went home, downing the buck without any flurry. He keeled over as if he'd been struck on the head, and Quinn was off his horse in an instant, looping his reins over a branch.

"This won't take long," he assured her. "I'll just gut it out and hang it. I can come back in the morning and haul it to the cabin." Taking off his coat, he hooked it on the saddle horn and drew his knife.

She watched in awe and with more than a trace of reluctance as he cleaned the deer, finally tying its back feet together and throwing the rope over a branch. He

hauled the carcass high, with what looked like a mini-
mum of effort to her, yet his muscles strained against
the gray fabric of his shirt. The end of the rope was tied
to a second tree, and they were on their way once more.

The rest of the ride was a blur in her mind, her body
weary, her eyes yearning for slumber. Finally, the cabin
a shadowed haven before them, Quinn came to her, lifting her from the mare and holding her shoulders while
she gained her balance.

"Thank you." She looked up at him, savoring the
warm touch of his hands, which penetrated the heavy
coat. Then, as if she could not meet his gaze any longer,
looked over his shoulder where the moon chased the last
of the twilight from the sky. "I can't thank you enough
for your help," she said softly, moving from his touch
to reach for her saddlebags.

His big hands halted her attempt, and he shook his
head. "You go on in the house and get washed up for
bed," he told her. "I'll be done in no time. I'm going
to try milking Daisy. If I can't get the job done, you can
come out and finish. Is that a deal?"

She nodded, too tired to argue, too weary to be pride-
ful. "I'll cut some cheese from the round I bought and
slice some bread."

"Put the coffeepot on the front burner. There should
be enough left from this morning to heat up," he told
her. He watched as she made her way to the porch, then
up the two steps to the door.

She lit the lantern, fed the ever-hungry stove and
found warm water in the big kettle. The cloth was rough,
but the warm, clean water was refreshing, and she closed
her eyes at the pleasure.

She was asleep when he came in, the lantern over the
table flickering at its lowest level. The simple food was

ready for him and he ate it, washing it down with coffee.

He eyed her for a moment, curled in the center of the bed, boots off, but still clothed. Her body weighed less than he expected, he thought as he lifted her and pulled the quilts down. He placed her back in the spot she'd already warmed with her body heat and covered her with care.

So easily, he'd come to appreciate the quiet strength of the woman, her ability to cope with circumstances, even the long ride today. With not a moment's complaint.

She'd been foolish to come to this place, this deserted cabin, where her existence was riding a fine edge. And yet he couldn't help but admire the courage of her choice, even as he wondered why she had shunned the help offered by the Wentworths.

He wasn't surprised that Ted and Estelle Wentworth wanted her back in their home. She was a daughter to be proud of. Perhaps not their daughter, he amended silently, but the next thing to it. And the chances were good that the child she carried would be equally as fine.

But how Damian had ever wooed and won this prize was beyond him. From all he'd heard, the boy Quinn had known had come to be something of a scoundrel, chasing women as if it were more important than his studies, back at university. He'd been handy at gambling, and whiskey had been his downfall, so the stories went. Strange that this fine-featured woman, with so much to offer a man, should have settled for Damian Wentworth. And even stranger that her beauty and strength of character had not been enough to keep him faithful.

Perhaps it was the money that had wooed her to his

cause. No…not likely, he decided. If hard, cold cash—and what it could buy for her benefit—was her priority in life, it wasn't readily apparent now. Although she wasn't hurting for money. Somewhere she'd gotten a nest egg.

He'd looked the other way as she unearthed the box from beneath the floorboards of the cabin earlier. But his glance had encompassed a pile of money before he'd turned aside.

It was a problem he stood no chance of solving tonight, he decided, catching a yawn with his open palm. And leaving the warm cabin now for another night in the cold shed was less than appealing. He cast another glance at her, there beneath the covers, her hair tangled around her face, her eyes deeply circled with weariness.

She would never know if he stayed inside. He could be back out in the shed before she woke. He lifted a quilt from atop her, replacing it with her heavy cloak. Another yawn made him shake his head in weariness.

He'd leave early to bring the deer back. He'd rise before dawn and be gone before she stirred.

Chapter Three

"Mr. Yarborough!" Her words bore more than a trace of shock.

He rolled over, tangling the quilt around him, and struggled to his feet. "I thought we'd decided on 'Quinn,'" he growled. The quilt fell to the floor and he turned to look at her.

The image was one of early-morning sensuality. One cheek creased by her pillow, hair as black as a raven's wing and eyes blinking away the residue of sleep, she stood by the bed, wrapped in the second quilt.

"'Quinn' was when I thought you were a gentleman."

"Hell, sleepin' on your floor didn't turn me into an outlaw, Erin," he muttered, bending to pick up the quilt that threatened to trip him. He folded it, aware that her look scorned his attempt.

She held out a hand, baring her arm to the elbow, and his eyes narrowed as he handed her the bundled-up quilt. What she was wearing beneath her own bulky coverlet was anyone's guess. She must have discovered his presence while she was getting dressed or undressed.

"I planned on being out of here before you woke up,

Erin.'' Although he'd have hated missing the sight of her, all sleepy eyed, with that halo of dark hair shimmering around her face.

''I'd planned on you using the shed.'' She dropped the quilt on the bed and wrapped her own covering around her a little tighter, her arm disappearing beneath the protection of patchwork.

''I beg your pardon, ma'am.'' It was the best he could do, being all primed with his usual early-morning problem, and the sight of her adding to it by leaps and bounds.

''Well?'' She watched him impatiently, her nostrils flaring, her chin high as she waited.

''I'm goin'…I'm goin'.'' Quinn snatched at his boots and struggled into them, hopping on one foot at a time as he slid his stockinged feet into place. At the sink he pumped once and caught the water as it ran from the spout, splashing it over his face and neck, running his fingers through his hair.

He'd hung his coat over the back of a chair in front of the stove last night and it was warm when he slid his arms into it. At the door he shot another glance in her direction. She hadn't moved, just stood there like a statue, all full of indignation.

Made a man want to give her something to be mad about, Quinn thought with a twinge of exasperation. About one more day with this woman and he'd be more than halfway to forgetting what he'd come here to accomplish.

Damn! What a way to start the day.

Erin drew in a deep breath. She'd stripped almost to the skin in front of the man. Down to her drawers and chemise anyway, ready to dig into her carpetbag for a clean dress. And then she'd heard him grunt as he shifted about on the wood-planked floor.

That it didn't frighten her was a miracle. Heaven knew she wasn't used to finding a man sleeping in front of her stove, but some inner awareness identified the culprit even before she peered around the table to where he lay.

The coverlet had been handy and she'd hidden quickly behind its concealing folds, then called his name with the proper amount of indignation. She'd almost smiled when he'd staggered to his feet, his hair every which way and his eyes blinking at her.

She sank onto the edge of the bed. That look he'd given her...that knowing light in his eyes as he scanned her well-covered form, his gaze alert after only a moment... She'd felt warmed by it. Still did, if the truth be known.

Yet, despite that, he was a gentleman. She owed him an apology for that remark. He'd only sought a warm spot to spend the night, and borrowed a quilt to add to his comfort.

And that gentleman would be looking for breakfast before too long, if she knew anything about it. Bending to her carpetbag, where she stored her clean clothing, Erin drew forth a dress and donned it quickly. Her soft shoes were by the stove and she made her way there, buttoning her bodice as she went.

And then waited.

The sun was over the meadow by the time she heard his horse whinny. She was at the door in an instant, drawing it open to seek his whereabouts. Across the yard, just beyond the shed, Quinn rode at an easy trot, the carcass of the deer across his horse's haunches.

He raised a hand to wave at her and she lifted hers in

response, trying in vain to suppress the delight that would not be denied.

For over an hour she'd thought he was gone, that her fit of pique had sent him on his way. If she'd used her head she'd have remembered his promise to head out first thing and bring back the deer he'd shot.

"The coffee's hot," she called out, and smiled at his answering wave.

"Give me fifteen minutes," he answered. "Have you milked yet?"

"No, I knew you'd done it late last night. I found the pail in the corner, so I knew she'd be all right for a while."

Quinn nodded, dismounting and leading his horse to a tree near the cabin. "I did. Just let me hang this deer and I'll wash up."

She'd baked biscuits earlier and kept them warm on the back of the stove. Her skillet was full of gravy, made with freshly ground sausage she'd bought yesterday. The gravy had thickened, and Erin dipped milk from the pail he'd brought in last night to thin it out.

She was pouring coffee when he came in the door.

"That buck's a young one. Should be tender," he told her, scooping soap from the crock she kept on the sink-board. He washed up, then dried his hands, his gaze pinning her in place.

"You still mad at me?" The question was blunt and to the point, and she felt a flush sweep up over her cheeks.

"No." She motioned to the table. "Come sit down. I've made gravy for the biscuits. I suspect you're hungry."

"Never thought I'd be tempted by raw meat before, but that deer was lookin' pretty good by the time I got back with it.'' Quinn's voice held more than a hint of good humor, and Erin chanced a look at him.

He was opening biscuits, three of them making a circle on the chipped plate. The skillet of gravy was in the middle of the table and he took the handle with care, holding it with her dish towel.

''Looks good,'' he said, and then glanced up. ''You ready for some?''

She nodded and he ladled a generous portion onto her single biscuit. The steam rose and he inhaled sharply, sniffing the spicy aroma with appreciation. With the first forkful on its way to his mouth, he remembered his manners.

''Thanks for cooking, Erin. I appreciate it.''

She felt the flush return. ''It was the least I could do...Quinn. You've been more than generous with your time.''

He shrugged. ''Seems to me we're about even on that score. You let me take shelter from the weather, and I returned the favor another way.''

Her question, burning in her mind for three days, could wait no longer. ''Where are you headed, Quinn? After you leave here, I mean,'' she asked cautiously, knowing it was an infringement on his privacy. She'd heard in town that one never asked questions in the West, but took folks at their face value.

''Nowhere for a while,'' he said with a grin. ''I've got a deer to butcher and take care of.''

She made an impatient gesture. ''You know what I mean. Where were you going when you showed up here? Where will you go when you leave here?''

His smile vanished, and his look was that of a man who didn't relish explaining himself. ''I've been looking for someone,'' he said finally.

"Up here?" Her brow rose and her heart beat just a bit faster.

"In this general direction."

The thought that had been nudging at her urged her on. "Will you still be looking when you leave here?" she asked carefully, a sudden sheen of perspiration dampening her forehead. Would Ted Wentworth have gone this far, sending a man to find her?

Quinn bent over his plate and ate, allowing her words to hang between them. Another pair of biscuits found their way to his plate, and he ladled more gravy with careful precision.

"Quinn?"

He looked up. "Probably not."

"Did the Wentworths..."

He hesitated, then nodded. "Yeah, they did. I've been on your trail for almost three months, Erin. You did some fancy footwork, but buying this cabin, using your real name, was a mistake."

The perspiration turned her clammy and she rose, suddenly unable to face the food before her. Her chair fell with a loud clatter and she hurried to the door, intent on gaining the porch.

She'd barely inhaled a deep breath, her lungs filling with blessed clean air, chilled by the early-morning frost, when he was there behind her.

His fingers held her shoulders with a firm grip and he was silent, as if he willed her to speak.

She filled her lungs again and felt the sweat on her forehead evaporating in the clear, crisp breeze. "I'm not going back."

His fingers tightened; she shivered, aware of his masculine strength, aware that he could easily bundle her atop her horse and take her down the mountain, to where the stagecoach line ran into Denver.

"Are you a bounty hunter?" she asked, despising the thready whisper her voice had become yet unable to strengthen it in the face of imminent disaster.

"I've been called that." He stepped closer, until the heat of his body sheltered her back with seductive warmth. "You're cold, Erin. Come back inside."

"You lied to me." Her words were bleak.

"No, I just didn't tell you the whole truth."

She shivered again, wondering at her foolishness, taking warmth from the man who would be her undoing. "You're not a miner."

"I've worked the mines."

"Not Big Bertha, I'd be willing to bet," she said, her words gaining strength.

"You'd win."

She watched a hawk circle over the meadow, then swoop to its quarry, rising with a shrill cry of triumph, claws grasping a small creature. She felt a sudden kinship to that rodent, her shoulders held in a grip not unlike that of the bird of prey she watched.

"Come inside. It's cold out here." It was a command this time, and she obeyed, unwilling to waste her small reserve of strength on such a useless battle.

Quinn sat back down and picked up his fork. "You need to eat."

"I've lost my appetite." The words were sharp with reproof.

His lips jerked as if they might curve into a smile and his dark eyes narrowed, as if he appreciated her sarcasm. "You need the food. The baby needs nourishment."

Erin sat down and pushed at the cold gravy with her fork.

"You'd do better to start fresh," he said mildly, taking her plate in hand and scooping the remains of her meal to one side. His big hands swallowed a biscuit as he broke it apart, then he spooned warm gravy over it.

"Try that," he suggested, watching her closely.

She nodded and accepted his offering. "Does the sheriff know that you're here, looking for me?" she asked.

He shook his head. "There wasn't any need to tell him. You're not a hunted criminal, Erin."

"Damian's father believes I killed his son." She ate, chewing and swallowing, as the words rang in her ears. She'd said it aloud, finally.

"Does he?"

She glanced up, her look impatient. "You should know. He obviously hired you to bring me back to New York. He must have decided that he can prove I pushed Damian down those stairs that night."

"Did you?"

Quinn waited, unaware that he held his breath, watching as her mouth twitched and trembled, just as her hands lifted to cover her face.

"Does it matter? I wished him dead. Perhaps that's almost the same thing."

"Not by a long shot, honey." He stood, still unsure whether or not she'd answered his question. He'd been hell-bent on hauling the woman back to New York, set on justice for the man he'd once claimed as a childhood friend.

Now, after less than a week, he wasn't at all sure what he was doing. Ted Wentworth's motive was less than honest, it seemed. For the first time, Quinn had begun a search without being fully aware of the facts. He'd had only Ted's insinuations to go on.

Quinn had been determined to give an elusive peace of mind to Damian's parents, in thanks for their kindness to the boy he had been. They'd been more than generous with their funds, and he'd assumed that Estelle truly cared for the daughter-in-law who'd run off.

Nothing added up at this point, he decided. The woman was not what he'd expected—not by a long shot. Never in his years of hunting down one criminal after another had he doubted his own judgment to this extent.

It had taken this little bit of a woman to stop him in his tracks.

"Ted Wentworth told me he and his wife want you to live in their home. He's worried that you can't take care of yourself."

Erin nodded. "He asked me to stay. I couldn't. And then when Estelle pushed and pushed, and said insinuating things about the night Damian died, hinting things…" She shuddered and looked up at him, her eyes bleak.

"I couldn't live in the same house with a person who hated me. Not again. Not ever again." She looked down at her empty plate and smiled, a sad travesty. "I ate it all. You were right."

"If he had proof, he'd have sent the law after you," Quinn said firmly, rising to take their plates to the sink. His fork scraped the residue of their meal into the pan she kept there for the purpose. "You need a dog around here, or a pig maybe," he muttered after a moment.

"Whatever for?" Her voice held a trace of surprise, much better than the calm weariness she'd assumed for the past little while, he decided.

"Dogs eat leftovers, and pigs eat most anything."

She laughed, a rusty sound. "I wouldn't know how

to go about butchering a pig. And I can't think of any other use for one. Maybe a dog would be a better idea.''

''I'll check in town next time I ride down. Maybe somebody has a litter of pups.''

She was silent behind him and he turned, leaning against the sinkboard. Her eyes were wary, the blue orbs shot with silver, dark lashes framing their distinctive beauty. She'd gathered her hair atop her head in a careless arrangement, and tendrils had escaped from the silken mass to fall against her neck.

Her aura of vulnerability, meshed with the graceful beauty of the woman herself, moved him, emotions he'd long since forgotten making themselves known. The need to protect her was uppermost, followed by a longing to touch the soft curve of her cheek, to place his mouth against her brow in a gesture of comfort.

Yet it was more than comfort he ached to offer, and that need rose in a tumult of desire that shamed him with its fierce strength. She was alone, vulnerable, and on top of it all, she carried a child beneath that enveloping skirt she wore.

''Next time you go to town?'' she asked quietly. ''You're not...''

''I'm not moving you from this place, Erin, at least not right now. The weather is changing, you're not fit to travel and I've got a lot of thinking to do.''

As if that settled the whole thing, Quinn levered himself from his position at the sink and headed for the door.

''Can I help with the deer?'' she asked, rising from the table.

''Bring out the biggest kettle in the house and I'll fill it at the pump outside. I'll want to wash the meat. Then you can cook the neck roast in the oven for supper.''

"There's a barrel in the shed. Maybe we could salt some of the meat down in it," she offered.

"You got enough salt for that?"

She looked puzzled. "I don't know how much it'll take, but I've got ten pounds."

He nodded. "We can put some of it in brine. In the meantime, I need to sharpen my knife."

With a vengeful reminder of her vulnerability, the pain returned, sweeping from her belly to wash against her spine in waves that took her breath. She'd only carried the kettle outside—certainly not a heavy chore—then returned to the kitchen to sort out her dirty clothes for washing.

Not that she had any amount to worry about, but two dresses were ready for a scrubbing, and probably Quinn Yarborough had an assortment of laundry she could wash out for him. It was the least she could do, with him furnishing meat for her table.

She'd bent to empty the box she kept the soiled laundry in when the steadily rising ache turned to pain, a clawing pain that took her breath and brought tears to her eyes.

Erin lowered herself to a chair and held her breath. Her head bent, she waited out the grip of harsh discomfort, then released the air within her lungs in a steady stream.

She slid her palm across the rounding of her belly and waited, but no answering pressure greeted her seeking fingers. Her brow furrowed as she concentrated. Surely the baby had moved this morning? But the hours since rising had been fraught with worry over Quinn's disappearance and the conflict he'd revealed on his return.

If the baby had moved, she'd been wrapped up in her

thoughts, unaware of the small shifting and wiggling it might have done.

Last night. Maybe she'd noticed it then. But her mind drew a blank, the long ride up the mountain a dim memory as she thought of the day past.

"Please move, baby." It was an anguished whisper, and Erin felt hot tears slip from beneath her closed eyelids.

To no avail. The firm swelling that was her child was unmoving, and she rose to her feet, unwilling, unable to consider the fears that pressed upon her.

The daylight hours were spent tending the deer and working at the stove. At noon Erin fried thin slivers of meat from its haunch in her skillet, making sandwiches from the leftover biscuits for their dinner. It was as tender as Quinn had predicted, and she cooked up three apples for a lumpy bowl of sauce to go with it.

At twilight they ate supper. The neck roast was juicy, the meat falling off in long strings, but easily cut. She'd baked potatoes in the oven with it, and they ate by lantern light. Quinn refused to allow her to milk Daisy, and told her that his talents had grown to include the care of the cow.

She smiled at his quip, and gave in gracefully. The walk to the shed for chores was almost beyond her strength, and she nodded as he told her to stay inside.

The pain had come again, over and over during the afternoon, each time increasing in force, until she thought she'd drawn blood from biting at her lip.

In the midst of eating his supper, Quinn noticed, his watchful gaze finding the small swelling.

"What did you do to your mouth, Erin?" he asked,

leaning across the table to lift her chin with his index finger.

She drew back, for months unused to a man's touch against her flesh. She'd borne—almost welcomed—the weight of Quinn's hands on her shoulders, felt their heated width through the material of her dress.

But this was different. Like a caress, it was imbued with a personal quality of caring she'd seldom felt in her life.

Certainly not in those three years past, while she'd lived in the same house with Damian Wentworth.

"Erin?"

"I must have bitten it," she said, turning from him.

He waited, unmoving. "Are you all right?" As if he sensed her discomfort, he touched her again, this time with the palm of his hand at the small of her back.

She closed her eyes, suppressing a groan. There, where his hand pressed with care, the pain had dwelt with harsh tentacles. Now her flesh felt as though it quivered, seeking the comforting presence of his palm.

"Are you all right?" His tone was genuinely worried now and he turned her to face him. "Erin?"

Another sweeping, drawing sensation began, centering in the depths of her belly this time, quickly spreading to release an avalanche of pain to the middle of her back.

"No, I'm not," she admitted in a thin, anxious wail. "I think something's wrong, Quinn. I don't know what it feels like to birth a child, but I think that's what's happening."

"How long have you had pains?" He clutched her shoulders as if he would squeeze the answer from her flesh.

"Today, since early on. Several times over the past

week or so, but just once in a while.'' She chewed at her lip, and he nudged her chin with his finger.

''Don't, Erin. You'll draw blood.''

''If the baby comes now, it'll be too early. He'll be too small!'' Her voice sobbed the final words and he drew her to lean against him, her head drooping to rest on his broad chest.

The pain surged, hitting her again, this time with the strength of a runaway train, and she almost collapsed under the sudden onslaught. Her groan escaped before she could close her lips against its release, and she reached with both hands for the tight rounding of her belly.

''Come on,'' Quinn told her, lifting her with ease. ''You'll feel better on the bed.'' In moments he'd pulled back the quilts and sheet, easing her down, watching as she curled on her side.

''Let me take off your shoes and stockings,'' he said quietly, as if unwilling to mar the silence of her misery.

She nodded, allowing his touch as he slid his hands up her calves beneath the folds of her dress to draw down the round garters she wore, bringing her knit stockings with them. His hands turned her to her back, and she complied.

''Do you think you should get undressed?'' he asked, clearly awkward at this stage of her disrobing.

Erin nodded, aware of the cessation of the pain. It had held her in its grip longer, much longer, than the last one and she feared its return.

''I'll put on my nightgown,'' she told him, swinging her legs in an awkward movement to the edge of the bed.

''Where is it?'' He watched her, and she realized with

a blend of embarrassment and relief that he was not going to leave her alone.

"Under my pillow."

He reached past her and grasped the gown, shaking it out and holding it up before himself. "Get your dress off," he told her, and his tone would brook no argument.

Her fingers were shaking as she unbuttoned her dress and slid it from her arms to the bed. The chemise was next, and she forced herself to tug it up, rising a bit from the bed to draw it over her head, then holding it against her breasts.

Her face flaming, she reached for the hem of the gown, hanging like a shield between man and woman. Quinn was there, just two layers of flannel from view, and she slid the gown over her head, tugging at it, until he lowered it in place.

She pushed her arms into the sleeves and he bent to straighten it on her shoulders, meeting her gaze. He smiled, a mere twitch of his lips, as if he would encourage her thus.

"Stand up and let me get rid of your clothes," he told her, and she obeyed, rising with his help, as if the process of birth, barely begun, had already robbed her of her strength.

He reached beneath the gown, his hands impersonal and circumspect as he drew her petticoat and drawers down with the voluminous fabric of her dress. Balancing herself with one hand on his shoulder, Erin stepped out of the rumpled pile of fabric, and drew in a deep breath.

The pain was returning. Too soon...too soon! Fear wrapped her in greedy arms as she bit against the bruised lip once more. Only the knowledge that Quinn Yarbor-

ough stood between her and the terrible night to come
gave her courage.

Only his quiet presence and his hands holding hers in
silent support allowed her to close her eyes, gritting her
teeth against the raging beast that consumed her.

Chapter Four

Quinn's hands were gentle, promising kindness, as did the warm glow of his eyes. Against her chilled flesh his fingers soothed, kneading the muscles of her calves as cramps beset her. His gaze comforted her, though how she sensed the compassion Erin could not have said. Yet there was, within his dark eyes, a generosity of spirit, a silent bathing of her pain, as if he would take it as his own.

And at the same time he was forthright, willing her with his soft-spoken encouragement to be at ease with his presence. For surely he sensed that she was totally unused to being viewed and handled in such a familiar manner by a man. Certainly not a man whose acquaintance she had made only several days ago.

"I'd say this is one hell of a time to get charley horses, ma'am," he muttered, his hands working to ease her pain. And as he spoke, he cast her a grin that could only be described as impertinent.

Erin bit at her lip, torn between embarrassment and gratitude. That this man would accept the task of delivering her child was more than she could imagine. If he'd hightailed it down the mountain and left her to fend for herself, she would not have blamed him.

Indeed, she'd been stunned speechless when Quinn had taken it upon himself to ready her as best he could for the imminent birth of her babe. He'd lifted her from the bed to deposit her in the rocking chair while he spread a piece of canvas from the shed over her mattress, then covered it with the sheet.

She'd watched, her body convulsing twice in the throes of labor before he finished his task. Quinn's eyes had watched her closely as she rubbed her belly and moaned at the peak of each throbbing pain. Then, with care, he had held her arm and lifted her from the rocking chair as she made her way back to the bed.

Giving birth was a messy business, she'd already discovered. Her water had broken midway across the floor, and only Quinn's easy manner had allowed her any degree of calm.

"Happens every time one of God's creatures gets ready to deliver its burden," he'd said cheerfully. Then as he cleaned up both her and the floor he'd told her about the various animals he'd helped into the world.

The cramps in her legs had begun soon afterward, and she shivered within the folds of her last clean nightgown.

"You've not delivered a child, have you?" Erin managed to ask, trying not to notice as his hands massaged her thigh, where another knotted muscle made her cry out.

"Would you feel better if I told you a tall tale?" he asked, and then smiled as she hesitated to answer.

"I've hauled calves and colts into this world. I've watched cats and dogs deliver more blind little creatures than you can shake a stick at. And in every case, things worked out as they were supposed to."

He eased his body straighter, tugging her gown down to cover her knees. ''There, that seems to have done the trick.''

''Thank you,'' she whispered, feeling the flush creep up from her breasts to bring heat to her face. ''I don't mean to be ungrateful. I'm just not used to...''

Quinn smiled again, and his eyes were crinkled at the corners. ''We're in this together, honey. I can't say it's what I'd have chosen, but I'm sure as hell glad I'm here. You'd be in sad shape if you were facing this alone.''

Erin nodded. ''I know that.'' And then she drew up her legs, turning her head aside as another pain began its assault. Again the tension mounted, and once more the muscles of her belly and back rebelled as her womb drew in upon itself. Erin closed her eyes and leaned her head against the wall, her fingers widespread against the hard surface of her abdomen.

''Try to relax,'' Quinn said, his own big hands covering hers, as if he would lend his strength to her endeavor.

She nodded, inhaling sharply as the pain reached a pinnacle. It began a downward slide, and she counted the throbbing beats of her heart as her body softened and relaxed against the sheet beneath her.

It was the middle of the night before the pain took a new twist, and Erin cried out for the first time as she was caught up in the vise that gripped her. Barely had she caught her breath when the onslaught began anew.

''Don't fight against your body,'' Quinn murmured, his fingers offering hers a place to grip. She clutched at him, abandoning all pretense of dignity as she was engulfed by the white-hot torture her body could only accept.

Whether it lasted for minutes or hours, she could not

have judged. Only the blurred edges of Quinn Yarborough's face remained in her line of vision, and she
squinted her eyes as she sought some measure of reassurance there. If his smile was strained, she ignored it.
If his brow was furrowed, she was too intent on her own
suffering to pay it any mind.

Survival was the issue, and Erin was determined to
find ease from the agony of this night. If that meant
using her muscles to push the baby into the cruel realities
of the world, then she would do as this man asked and
push with all of her strength.

"That's the way," Quinn said, his voice coming to
her in the mist of her misery. "Push, Erin. Push hard."

She heard her wail of despair as if it came from another's mouth, and cringed at the message it delivered.

"I can't. I can't do this anymore!" Surely that wasn't
her speaking those words of surrender. Her breath rasped
loudly as she inhaled and concentrated on the words
Quinn spoke once more.

"Yes, you can! Listen to me, Erin. Take a deep breath
again. Now, push.... Hear me? Push!" His tone was
filled with command now. He'd done with being kind,
she decided, and almost laughed at the thought. As if a
laugh could have been formed from her throat. As if she
could think of anything but the rending of her body.

And then there was a silence that threatened to swallow her whole, perhaps lasting for only a moment after
all, ending with the fragile wail of her child. Her mind
welcomed it as she was swallowed up by the bed beneath her.

Just so quickly, every bone in her body relaxed from
the strain of the battle fought and won. Just so brutally,
she felt an overwhelming weariness seize her, and she
could only reach a hand to the man who held her babe.

"Let me see." Erin's words whispered from between dry lips. She blinked, willing her vision to clear, only vaguely aware that tears flowed in a steady stream. And then she saw the tiny, wizened face of a being so minute, so infinitely precious, it came near to halting the beat of her heart.

"I'm going to put him on your stomach, honey," Quinn said quietly. "I'll clean you up a little here and then tend to him."

Erin felt a new series of tugging pains, felt Quinn's hands against her flesh, but knew only the joy of watching the movements of her child. Quinn had wrapped him in a length of flannel from her belongings, and only the tiny face was visible to her. But his body trembled beneath the covering and she felt an urgency to hold him.

"Give him to me," she whispered, holding up her arms, fearful of snatching him up from his precarious resting place, lest she drop him.

Quinn stood erect, his stance weary, and shot her a glance that pierced her to the depths. "Let me get rid of this first," he said, wrapping a bundle and depositing it near the door. He turned back, and she felt a moment's dread as he hesitated.

"What is it?" she asked hoarsely, lifting herself to her elbows to better see the mite of a babe.

"I fear he's not big enough, Erin. He's trying hard, but his breathing isn't too good." Quinn stepped quickly to where she lay and picked up the small bundle, cradling it in his two hands. He bent over her and she turned to her side, the better to hold his offering against her breast.

"He'll be fine," she said quickly. "Look, he's moving his mouth."

Quinn sat on the edge of the bed and leaned over her,

one big hand against her back, giving welcome support. "I see him, honey."

It was almost more than he could stand, watching this valiant woman cradling the poor little scrap of humanity against her bosom, as if she could pour strength into the baby she held. With blue lips parted, the child struggled to inhale, his efforts bringing harsh reality to the forefront.

"Erin…I'm afraid for him," Quinn said, bending low to turn the baby to his back. He leaned to touch the blue lips with his own and blew his own breath in tiny puffs of air within the boy's mouth. He watched as the miniature nostrils pinched in an effort to inhale.

Once more Quinn attempted to instill his own life force in the babe. And again he watched as the struggle worsened.

Erin's eyes widened, pinning Quinn in place with her gaze. Her hands loosened their hold and she gave full access to the baby he'd delivered. As if she placed her trust in his knowledge, she joined his vigil, inhaling as he did, breathing small bits of air in time with his.

The small body they watched shivered, and Erin cried out, a wordless agony of sound. Again the soft bundle convulsed, and Erin's cry was softer, desolate, as she sensed the end of the short, futile battle.

Quinn shook his head. "I don't think we can help him. He's so little, Erin. He didn't have long enough to gain strength for this world."

She was silent now, as if she accepted his words, and he shifted his attention to the pale oval of her face. Her eyes were no longer wet with tears, her lips barely trembled, as if she faced and accepted the pain of her loss.

"Poor little mite," she crooned, gathering the still,

silent bundle to her breast. She bent her head low, her mouth touching the soft, dark down upon his head.

Quinn felt the tightening of his muscles, long misused in the hours of bending over the bed, his back and legs taut with pain of their own. Yet his would ease with movement. His would be forgotten by tomorrow.

That Erin's hours of suffering should produce only more pain to come for this small, brave woman seemed hardly fair. And yet, during the years of his childhood, his mother had told him in no uncertain terms that no one had ever been guaranteed equality, that fair was a relevant word, that he could count on only whatever the Fates decreed.

He rose to his feet and backed to the rocking chair. If, for these few moments, Erin Wentworth needed to bid farewell to the babe she'd delivered, he could only grant her that. He'd spent the whole night waiting and watching. A few more minutes weren't going to make much difference now.

Quinn wasn't nearly so stoic in the light of day as he swung a pick and shovel at the hard side of the mountain. Such a tiny grave would have been simple to dig back in New York State. Here, the very roots of the trees wove together to thwart his efforts, and he began to reconsider his choice of a burial spot for Erin's child.

And then the pick broke through the root he had been chopping at, and he found the going easier. Even the harsh cold surrounding him could not touch him this morning, it seemed. The day was dreary, the sun hiding above the low-hanging clouds, but he felt the chill wind as if it mattered little. He was already cold to his depths, dealing with the sense of defeat he'd carried with him since before dawn, when the baby had struggled for his last breath and lain peacefully at last in his mother's arms.

Erin hadn't cried since. She, who had borne pain and suffering to a degree he wouldn't have believed had he not seen it himself, had seemed to wither like a flower without rain. She'd tucked that small body against her heart as if she could warm its fast-cooling flesh with her own.

Even when he bent to take the tiny mite from her hold, placing it in a wooden box he'd put together with a few nails, she'd shown no emotion. Only lifted sad eyes to his and watched as he wrapped a second piece of blanket about the still form.

"What will you name him?" he asked, fitting the lid to the box. No bigger than a shoe box, he held it in one hand, tucked against his side as he awaited her reply.

"Name him?" Her voice was thin, her eyes dark pools of pain.

"I'll baptize him, if you like, Erin." He'd never done such a thing, didn't even know if it was proper, but if saying words over the boy would comfort her, he'd sing hymns and recite a hundred prayers.

"Call him John," she said after a moment. "It was my father's name. I think his soul must already be in heaven, but I doubt saying the words over him would hurt anything."

Quinn nodded, silently agreeing.

"Quinn! Let me go with you," she cried, suddenly a bundle of motion as she threw back the covers. Her feet touched the floor before he could gain her side, and with one hand he reached for her, his fingers spread wide across her chest.

Beneath his palm her heart beat rapidly, and for that he was thankful. She was stronger than he'd thought, sturdier than he'd given her credit for. Her breasts rose and fell beneath his hand and he held her thus, shaking his head.

"No. It's too damn cold out there for you, Erin. I don't want to have to dig another grave." His words sounded harsh to his own ears, and he hesitated a moment. "I don't mean to be cruel, but I don't think you can make it, honey. It's bitter cold and coming up snow again."

Her protest was almost mute, only a small, wounded sound that might have been acquiescence as she crumpled beneath his touch.

He relented. "I'll pull the chair over to the window. You can watch from there," he told her, waiting until she nodded agreement. Placing the small box at the end of Erin's bed, Quinn pulled the rocker the short distance to the window and then returned for the woman who waited.

He lifted her, wrapped in a quilt, and placed her in the chair, tucking the warm covering in place. From the window, the spot he'd chosen was visible, though snow was now beginning to fall steadily.

"Will you name him? Or shall I?" he asked, returning to her side.

"You." The one syllable, harsh and borne on a breath that touched his hand with its warmth, answered him as she bent low over the box he held.

He lifted the lid and then placed his hand against the window, where moisture dampened the glass. He transferred the bit of water, touching the downy head with two fingers.

"I baptize you John Wentworth, in the name of the Father, the Son and the Holy Ghost...Amen."

Within his chest Quinn felt pain of his own, that he

should be the one to bury not only the babe, but the hopes and dreams of its mother, in that hole he'd dug. His gaze swept over Erin, pausing on the tender bend of her neck, her dark hair haloed in the light from the lamp on the table.

She pressed her index finger against her mouth and transferred the caress to her child's forehead, then sat erect once more.

"I'll not be long," Quinn told her, easing the lid back over the still form. Four nails were in his pocket, the hammer on the table, and he snatched it up as he moved to the door.

"Quinn…" Her voice halted him and he turned back.

"Thank you." Her lips barely moved as she spoke the words. Her eyes held immense sorrow, but no tears, and he nodded, closing the door behind him.

Strangely, he'd feel better about the whole thing if she'd weep, he thought, trudging across the small clearing. But from the looks of her, she'd shed tears enough, at least for today.

The snow fell heavily for two days, and then the sun came out, rising like a pale golden ball in the east. Quinn peered from the window, still tousled from sleep, his bare feet feeling half-frozen. His gaze turned to the small mound, covered with snow, just across the clearing. And behind him he heard the rustle of bedcoverings as Erin roused from sleep.

"Quinn?" She spoke his name with a distinct lack of emotion in her voice, and his eyes closed as his head bowed, forehead touching the damp window glass.

"You're awake." He turned, his gaze seeking hers, scanning her wan features. She hadn't eaten enough in the past two days to keep her alive. He'd vowed to himself that today would be the turning point. Today he'd sit beside her until she finished breakfast, or at least made a good attempt.

There wasn't enough flesh on her bones to draw from. Either she began to gain back some strength or he would fear for her health.

"Are you hungry? We've got eggs up the gump stump, honey. I thought we could scramble up a panful for breakfast."

Erin watched him, her mouth pinched as if she held back words that bore a tart taste in her mouth. And then she smiled, a wan little grimace, but better than the solemn look he'd dealt with for two long days. "I'll try, Quinn. I don't want you to worry about me. Except..."

He stirred, reaching for his heavy shirt, and buttoned it as he walked toward the bed. "Except what, Erin? What's wrong?"

She flushed, the pink tinge of her skin changing the look of her, and her gaze dropped from his face to where her fingers tangled in her lap. "I think there's something wrong with me," she said finally. "My chest..." Her hands rose to spread across the fullness of her breasts and she hesitated, biting at her lip.

"Do you feel congested, like a bad cold or pneumonia, maybe?" Quinn asked harshly. God above knew he wasn't ready for this fragile woman to fall sick on him.

She shook her head. "No, I don't mean inside my chest, Quinn. I mean here." She touched her breasts and winced as she pressed gently against her gown. "I feel swollen and hot. I don't know what's wrong."

He wanted to unbutton the front of that sedate flannel gown. He ached with the urge to lay his hands on the fevered flesh beneath it, and his heartbeat increased as he considered that thought.

It was not a good idea. Even for a valid reason such as this, Erin's bosom was out-of-bounds for him. Even though her body had been exposed to his eyes, this was a different kettle of fish.

"Quinn? I wonder if... Do you think maybe it's because I had the baby, and now I'm filling up with milk?"

Of course! Why hadn't he thought of that? The most natural thing in the world. He'd seen newborn calves and colts nurse and thought nothing of it. It only made sense that a woman would have the same function, the same milk forming in her body as any other creature.

He'd just never had access to a nursing mother, or any other mother, for that matter.

"I'd say you hit the nail on the head," he told her. "The problem is, I'm not sure what to do about it."

She shrugged. "Maybe if we just wait, it'll be all right. Maybe, since I'm not..." Her hands reached out in mute appeal. "You know what I mean. I don't have a baby to nurse, so maybe it will go away."

She sounded so hopeful, he could scarcely bear it. He shook his head slowly. "I don't think there's much chance of that, Erin. But I have to admit I don't know what to do about it. Maybe..." His mind searched for an answer.

"How about putting cold cloths on you, maybe make you feel better?" It was a very poor solution, to his way of thinking, but taking care of a new mother was a far cry from his usual line of work.

She looked doubtful. "If you think it will help, I'll do it, Quinn."

"It sure can't hurt anything," he said quickly. "Let me get some snow in here and I'll pack a towel with it."

It was cold, that was for sure, Erin decided a few

minutes later. She held the makeshift compress to her breasts, welcoming the numbing chill against her skin.

At the stove, Quinn broke eggs into her iron skillet and stirred them as they cooked, intent on fixing breakfast. He opened the oven, stabbing the toasted bread with her long fork and dropping it onto a plate. His expertise was not in the kitchen, she decided, her mouth curling in the barest trace of a smile.

For this man she would do most anything right now, Erin thought, straightening in the rocking chair. Even if it meant gulping down eggs and gnawing on a piece of stale bread turned to dry toast. And from the looks of things, that was about all they were going to have for breakfast. She hadn't baked in three days and she doubted Quinn Yarborough was handy with bread dough.

"I've been thinking," he said, casting a quick look at her. "Maybe I should go down to town and talk to the doctor, see if there's something you should be doing to help with your..." His hand waved at her, as if he hesitated to name the cause of her problem.

Again Erin came close to smiling, her eyes catching sight of the faint color that rode his cheekbones. Bless his heart, the man was embarrassed. After all he'd done for her.

"What do you think, honey?" he asked, lifting the skillet to turn a mound of eggs out onto her plate.

"Yes, all right," she answered, agreeable to anything that would relieve the tight throbbing in her breasts.

Quinn carried her plate to where she sat in the rocking chair. "Here, I'll trade you," he said, reaching for her wet towel. "Eat first, then we'll try this some more."

She nodded, willing herself to eat every bit of the food he offered. She'd lost any appetite she'd ever had, but if Quinn was good enough to cook for her, eating was the least she could do.

His gaze was hopeful as he crouched beside her chair. "If you eat every bite I'll feel better about leaving you for the day," he told her. "If I set out now, I stand a good chance of making it back by nightfall."

She placed the fork carefully on her plate. "I hate for you to put yourself in danger for my sake, Quinn. But I know I need to get back on my feet. Maybe if I feel better while you're gone I can set a batch of bread to rise."

His hand covered hers and he squeezed, getting her attention. "Not on your life, girl. I don't want to have visions of you falling against that stove while I'm riding down the mountain. You just rest until the fire gets low. You'll have to put in a chunk of that firewood, but other than that, you park your little carcass on that bed and stay warm. You hear?"

She nodded, a bit reluctantly, aware that he deserved her obedience in this, yet unwilling to give up her independence. "I'll mind, this time," she said with a smile.

"Promise?"

"Yes...promise." Her gaze was held by the determination she read in his face, his eyes dark and piercing as he watched her. Then he nodded, as if to underscore her words.

"I'll be back as soon as I can, honey. I'll build up the fire before I go and get you tucked into bed."

His head tilted and he leaned forward, his mouth finding hers in a quick kiss. His lips were warm against hers, his breath fresh, and she inhaled his scent as he drew back. A prayer of thanksgiving arose within her, that this man should have come to her, that his greater strength had been hers to draw on. It would be so easy to...

"Come on." He held out his hand and she accepted it, rising, making her way to the bed. She took comfort in his touch, allowing him to tuck the quilt around her, grasping his hand in hers as he stood beside her. And then she faced the truth of the matter.

Whether it was gratitude or passion, something about Quinn Yarborough made her heartbeat quicken, made her breath catch in her throat. Her fingers tightened on his and she lifted her head, pressing her lips against the back of his hand.

"God go with you, Quinn Yarborough. God keep you safe."

Chapter Five

"If this ain't a stroke of luck, I don't know what is."
The jovial storekeeper slapped the counter with the flat
of his hand and grinned widely. "That baby's been the
worry of half the women in town for four days now.
They can't make him eat no matter what. They tried
sugar tits and milk in a bottle and he just claps his mouth
tight shut and bawls some more."

His hand waved in the air and he wagged his head as
if delighted with the events he related. "And now..."
He drew out the word. "Now you come in here and tell
me that nice Mrs. Peterson of yours is needin' a baby
real bad."

Quinn felt as if a miracle had just been dropped in his
lap. Of all the colossal pieces of good luck, this had to
be at the top of the list.

First things first, he decided, glancing around the
store, hoping for a glimpse of one of those women the
man behind the counter spoke of. Someone who might
steer him in the right direction. Probably everybody in
town knew where the babe was, he'd be willing to bet,
and the sooner he drew a bead on the location, the better.

Better yet...

"Where's the doctor at?" he asked abruptly, his hopes soaring as he thought of the bereaved woman he'd left in the mountain cabin. This could be the saving of her.

"Who'd you say you were, mister?" the man asked, peering at Quinn over his glasses. "Weren't you in here the day of the fire?"

Quinn nodded. "You were running to help out. The sheriff said a young man was dead already and his wife was safe. He didn't say she was in the family way." He stuck out his hand. "My name's Quinn Yarborough."

"Andy Wescott," the merchant offered, clasping and shaking Quinn's hand with vigor. "Who'd have thought that poor soul wouldn't make it through the birthing? She just got plumb wore out. Mrs. Tobin said she took a deep breath and was gone. Didn't even hold the little tyke."

"Where's the baby? Where's the doctor?" he repeated. Quinn's heart was pumping with anticipation as his mind worked rapidly. Maybe, just maybe, if no one else was able to feed the child...maybe Erin could. Even if it was just for a while, till the woman's family was located and the baby was claimed.

"Doc's housekeeper is watchin' him." Andy Wescott pulled his watch from his pocket and glanced at it. "Doc might be home for dinner about now. Just take a ride past the saloon and beyond the barbershop. There's a tall white house off to the left. Got a fancy picket fence across the front of the yard. That'll be where Doc Fisher lives."

Quinn nodded. "I'll ride by there. If you'll bundle up what I need, I'll be back by to pick it up."

The storekeeper nodded. "Glad to, Mr. Yarborough."

He shook his head, grinning widely. "Who'd have thought it? Yessir! Old Doc'll be happy to see you."

Old Doc had been happy, speaking above the wails of a hungry baby. From the looks of him, the child was healthy and well formed, Quinn observed. The milk from Jeremy Tobin's cow down at the livery stable just wasn't agreeing with the boy, Doc said, shaking his head. Finding a wet nurse was a real stroke of luck. Yessir!

Quinn set off a half hour later, the sun tilting toward the west as he rode out of town. His pack balanced behind him and tied in place, he rode with the well-wrapped bundle tucked inside his heavy coat. Whether the movement of Quinn's horse or the soft whistling of a tuneless ditty accomplished the deed, the tiny package Quinn carried settled down and slept away the first part of the journey.

Erin lit the lamp before dark, dreading the moment when the twilight faded to nightfall and the wind moaned through the tall pine trees at the edge of the clearing. Each night since the small grave had come to be, she'd dreaded the sound whispering in her ears, almost as if it were the cries of her child carried on the wind.

Throughout the day she'd taken the towel to the door, placing it in the snow, then folding it up to hold the chill before she hugged it to her bare breasts. It seemed to help a little, but her flesh was hard and aching, warm to the touch, once the towel was removed.

She'd added big chunks of wood to the stove twice during the day, then, contrary to Quinn's instructions, she had put on a pot of stew to cook. She'd decided against making bread, aware of her own limitations, but cutting up an onion and washing potatoes and carrots and setting them aside had not been beyond her strength.

Outside the door, Quinn had hung a haunch of venison on a pole. She'd wrapped up warmly before she stepped outdoors to cut a good piece from the meat, then ended up chopping at it with her hatchet.

Quinn would probably have a fit, Erin thought, but for some reason, the cold air was refreshing and she found herself feeling stronger, for all that she'd barely been able to string the venison back up the pole once she was done.

Her kettle was half-full by the time the meat was tender and the vegetables were done. The smell was tempting, she was pleased to note, and for the first time in three days Erin was anxious for the meal to be ready. She'd only just lifted the lid to stir the stew a final time when she heard a horse, its whinny a welcome sound in the clearing.

''Quinn!'' With a blend of relief and anticipation, Erin faced the door. He might put the horse away first, she thought, then shook her head. No, he'd probably bring in supplies, then take care of his animal.

She wrapped her arms across her breasts as they throbbed anew. Maybe the doctor had sent some medicine or salve or something that would help.

And then, from outside the door, the wail of a baby reached her ears. Hands trembling, she reached for the latch. Heart thumping at an unmerciful rate, she tugged at the heavy door. It opened, ushering in a blast of cold air, accompanied by Quinn Yarborough, his face half-covered by a woolen scarf, snow frosting his eyebrows and glistening in the lantern glow.

His arms supported a bundle beneath his coat, and his eyes sought the woman within the snug cabin. With a gloved hand he tugged at the scarf covering his mouth, revealing a grin of immense proportions. Then white teeth bit at the fingertips of the leather glove, and he flung it to the floor.

"We have us a problem, Erin, my girl!" His grip was cautious, his hands careful as he undid his coat, then lifted the wrapped, wiggling bundle and placed it on the table. One large palm held it in place as he unfolded the blanket, and his eyes were intent on the contents as he swept the outer covering from its place.

"This is just what the doctor ordered," he announced, scooping the wide-eyed occupant into his hands. The slate blue eyes blinked in the glow of the lantern, and the tiny mouth opened to let forth another howl. "Did you ever hear such a pair of lungs in your life?" Quinn asked, as proudly as if he had had some share in producing such a miracle.

"Oh, my! Oh, my!" Erin's heart fluttered within her breast as her arms reached for the infant. "Where...what... Oh, my!" Her fingers trembled as she touched the rosy cheek.

"Let me tell you, this is one hungry little boy," Quinn said with a chuckle. "He's turned down everything the ladies of Upper Pine Creek had to offer. He doesn't like the milk from Jeremy Tobin's cow, kept tossing it back up, barely holding enough down to keep him going. And sugar tits don't interest him a bit."

He looked his fill at the woman before him. "Do you suppose you could take a turn at trying to make the little fella happy, Erin?"

Her breasts filled again with painful urgency as Erin's hands finally grasped the bundle, turning it so the downy, dark head snuggled into the bend of her left elbow. She felt Quinn's hand on her arm as he guided her to the rocking chair, sensed his touch as he lowered her to the seat.

And then she was lost. Lost in the lusty yells of a hungry babe. Lost in the unfocused gaze of squinted blue eyes that managed to peer into her soul. Lost in the wonder of a mite of humanity that filled her arms, even as it filled the empty space in her heart.

Her fingers moved rapidly, undoing the buttons that closed her robe, then the gown beneath. From her breasts flowed a steady drip of milk.

With shaking hands she guided the tiny mouth to her breast. With teeth pressing into her lower lip, she anticipated the feel of those miniature lips surrounding her nipple. And with a joy beyond all belief, she knew the touch of a baby's tongue, lapping at the abundance of nourishment she offered it.

He latched on to her flesh, sucked twice and released his hold, choking as the milk rushed down his throat. He coughed, nuzzling her; then, finding the swollen nipple, he sought once more to suckle from it.

It overflowed his mouth and his eyes opened, widening with his efforts as he swallowed the bounty she offered.

Quinn thought he had never seen anything so beautiful in his life. Not just the firm, curving loveliness of a woman's breast—although that sight more than brought pleasure to his gaze—but the purity of woman and child, bonded in a moment of giving and taking. A moment so keenly felt, so deeply engraved on his sight, he thought he might never recover from the joy of it.

"He was hungry." Probably the understatement of the year, he thought, grinning as Erin's head tilted back, allowing their eyes to mesh in an instant of pleasure.

"Tell me, Quinn. Where did you find him?" Her

words were whispered, soft as moonlight, as if she were so filled with awe, she could scarcely speak aloud.

"His mama died, Erin. Remember the fire in town, as we were leaving the other day? His daddy didn't live through the fire, and his mama just didn't make it when he was born."

Erin's eyes filled with tears, as if she grieved for the woman whose child she held. "There was no one to care for him?"

Quinn shook his head. "He didn't want what they had to offer. Doc Fisher's housekeeper was trying to feed him when I got there, and when I told her about you, she just snatched up a couple of blankets and wrapped him like a length of sausage and handed him to me."

Erin laughed softly, and then as if the vision he etched pleased her enormously, she giggled, dipping her head to drop a kiss on the wispy dark hair that crowned the baby in her arms.

"Did he cry all the way here?" Her toe touched the floor, and she rocked in time with the patting of her palm against the blanketed form.

"No. Slept the first part of the way, in fact. Poor little mite has been barely getting enough nourishment to keep him going, I guess." He bent to peer at the tightly closed eyes and the cheeks that suctioned milk from Erin's breast.

"You're crying." His hand reached to brush at tears that trickled down her cheek and he squatted beside the rocker, his gaze focusing on her face. Her teeth were gnawing on her lip and she shook her head, as if to deny his claim.

"It's all right, but it hurts, Quinn. I think I'm just so full and the skin is stretched so tight and he's sucking so hard…'' She bit at her lip again, rocking harder, as if the movement would alleviate the pain.

''What can I do?''

She looked at him, shaking her head. ''I'm fine. Really I am. I think it'll be better, after the swelling has gone down.''

''I almost forgot!'' Quinn rose quickly, reaching into the pockets of his coat, fishing out a small bottle between his fingers. ''Doc sent some camphorated oil. Said it would take out the soreness. But you'll want to be careful not to get it in the baby's mouth.''

She nodded. ''I'll use it after he's done.'' As if in reply to her words, the babe released his hold and Quinn watched as a trickle of milk flowed from the corner of the tiny mouth.

Blue eyes opened, and a soft release of air from the infant brought laughter into being. ''He burped! All by himself.'' She lifted the baby, easing her gown into place, holding the child against her shoulder.

The small mouth pursed, the brow furrowed and the downy head turned from one side to the other, as if he sought the warmth he'd been deprived of.

''Do you think he's still hungry?'' Quinn asked, reaching to touch the soft, dark hair.

''Maybe so.'' Erin nodded, turning the infant to her other arm, arranging her clothing and nudging the tiny mouth against her breast.

He was not nearly so greedy now, his hunger pangs numbed by the milk he'd gulped down. But the overflowing supply he was offered was tempting and he began suckling with enthusiasm. His splayed fingers were the size of matchsticks against Erin's breast and he snuffled and snorted as he nursed.

Quinn took off his coat, hanging it by the door, and

headed for the stove. The baby had taken his attention for several hours. Now his hunger demanded relief, and the scent of food cooking reached his nostrils.

"Will you eat with me?" he asked, lifting the lid to peer within the kettle. His sigh of appreciation was heartfelt. He settled the lid into place, heading to the washbasin quickly to make ready for supper.

"Yes." Her appetite was back, her stomach ready for nourishment, as if she must be fed in order to satisfy the child she held. The child she'd been sent by the Fates that decreed such things.

"Will there be someone coming up here looking for him?" she asked. "Does he have any family anywhere?"

Quinn looked up, his hands busy with dishing up the stew into two crockery bowls. "Doc said they were trying to locate family, but most everything got burned up in the fire. I guess they don't know where to look."

Erin's arms tightened protectively. "I'll keep him." Her words were taut with emotion. "He's not my own, but I can't help but think that he's like an answer to my prayers. I wouldn't have wished for his mama to die, Quinn." Her gaze was frightened as she looked at him. "You know better than that. It's just that…he needs me, and God knows I need him."

Quinn nodded. "I wouldn't think that, honey. I know you well enough, even in just the short time I've been here. I'd never think that of you, that you'd wish suffering on another. I'd like to think his mama knows somehow that her child is being cared for." He grinned, a mere lifting of one side of his mouth. "Sound kinda sappy, don't I?"

Erin shook her head. And then stiffened as a whinny from outside sounded loudly.

"I forgot my horse!" Quinn's movements were hasty as he dumped the stew back into the kettle. He snatched up his coat and pulled his hat on. "I'll only be a few minutes, honey. I'll milk after we eat. There's a whole satchel of stuff Doc's housekeeper sent for the baby. I'll bring it in with me."

He was gone, the door latching behind him. Erin leaned her head against the back of the chair and closed her eyes.

That such a miracle could come to be was beyond her wildest imaginings. That such a gift as this could be hers was more than she'd ever hoped. That the tiny mite buried beneath the trees across the clearing was still alive in her heart was a certainty, but the welcome weight of a child in her arms was easing the crushing hurt she'd borne.

For all of that, and for the man who even now was making his way to the shed, and from there back into her presence, she was filled with gratitude. Her mouth whispered the words and her heart echoed the syllables with each measured beat within her breast.

"Thank you, God. Thank you."

"You're crying again." Exasperation lined his words as Quinn tilted Erin's chin up, his mouth set in a straight line. "Didn't the camphorated oil help?" Male frustration made his voice harsh and he watched as twin trickles made their way down her face, the tears dampening the front of her gown.

"I'm fine, Quinn, really." Erin blinked, as if attempting to halt the tears that overflowed, but to no avail. That single fingertip beneath her chin was unrelenting, and she lifted her hand to clasp his fingers. "Don't look at me like that—like you'd like to shake the stuffing out of me!''

His grunt of aggravation was softened by her words. ''I've done everything I can think of, girl. Tell me what's wrong, so I can fix it.''

She shook her head, releasing her grip on his hand. ''No one can fix what's already happened. That poor woman in town is dead, Quinn, and this baby will never know his mama.''

''That poor baby's been given the best shot any child could ask for, Erin. We don't have a lot of choices when it comes to life and death. But we can make the best of what comes along, and that's what you're doing.'' He sat on the edge of the bed, one big hand reaching to curve against the nape of her neck. His fingers slid beneath the heavy fall of hair, seeking the warmth of her skin, relishing the intimacy she allowed.

They were strangers who had been thrust into the roles generally assumed by husband and wife. Indeed, he'd played a part in her life that most husbands were never allowed, a role he'd taken on with reluctance. Tending her, delivering her child and sharing her grief had been the most intimate of all his experiences with the female sex.

In only a few short days they'd formed a marriage of sorts, a blending of lives that allowed him an access to her he might have taken months to gain in other circumstances.

The simple pleasure of touching the nape of her neck, the sensation of silken tresses against the back of his hand, the pulse beating beneath her ear radiating to his fingertips…all blended to form an arousal that had nothing to do with the act of love. For now, it was enough to watch, to touch, to inhale the sweet scent of mother and newborn child.

He bent to press his lips against her brow and she squeezed his fingers within her own, offering a smile that trembled on her mouth.

He returned it, his eyes moving from the tenderness of her smile to the small bundle she cradled in her arm. "You know, if that woman knew where her baby was right now, she'd be tickled pink, knowing he's warm and his belly's full to overflowing."

"Maybe she does know," Erin whispered.

"You really believe in heaven, don't you?" he asked, knowing already the answer she would give.

And then was surprised at her brittle laugh as she glanced at him quickly.

"Living in hell gives a woman reason to hope for some sort of heaven," she said quietly. "My mother used to say we make our own heaven or hell, here on earth. She was right."

"Maybe someone else made it for you, Erin." If she spoke of her life with Damian Wentworth, he needed to hear it all, Quinn decided. "Was your marriage so bad?"

"I had everything a woman could want," she told him. "Beautiful gowns, jewelry, a lovely home... everything but..."

"But what?"

She shook her head, as if dismissing old memories, and her hand moved against the baby she held. "I can only tell you that I'm happier here, with all that's happened to me, than I was in New York City."

He'd pushed her enough, Quinn decided, and he rose from the bed, strangely unsettled by the words she spoke.

"We need to decide where to put the baby to sleep,"

he said decisively, hoping to rouse her from the memories he'd brought to her mind.

"I thought I'd put him at the back of the bed, for now, anyway."

He nodded. "I'll see if there's enough loose wood in the shed to put together a bed of sorts for him tomorrow."

She brightened. "Yes, and I'll need that big pan the grain is kept in," Erin told him. "And a rope to string across behind the stove to hang wet things on."

"Is he wet again?" Diapers had become important items in the past few hours, and it seemed the care of a baby involved a tremendous amount of wrapping and unwrapping, pinning and unpinning.

Erin laughed, a welcome sound to Quinn's ears. "I don't think so. I just changed him a while ago. But I'll need to wash out his things in the morning."

"I thought Doc Fisher sent along enough stuff to keep him going for a while," Quinn said.

"He did, but I don't have much room to hang wet things."

Quinn shook his head in mock dismay. "I sure enough didn't know what I was getting into, did I? My hauling that baby back up this mountain is making a whole lot of work for you." As if she cared, he thought, watching as a smile tilted her mouth at the corners.

"I don't mind." Erin bent her head, her gaze resting on the sleeping child she held. "I don't mind at all."

Chapter Six

The tiny bed was constructed of a mishmash of wood scavenged from the shed and the rafters of the cabin. It was enough to bring tears to the eyes of any self-respecting carpenter, Quinn decided, pounding a final nail into it. It had taken him long enough to get to the project, first one thing, then another taking his time.

Yet, so far, Erin had found no fault with his handiwork. She felt better with the baby in the bed beside her at night. There was plenty of time to settle him in his own bed.

Now she sat in the rocking chair, her lap full of soft flannel, sewing a fine line of stitches in the doubled-over fabric she held. He'd felt her gaze on him as he worked, heard the soft rustle of her clothing as she fed the baby, then placed him on pillows next to where she sat.

Humming beneath her breath, her fingers plying the needle, she glanced up, and he was warmed by her gaze, yet wary of the smile that curved her lips. Perhaps she was amused by his efforts at carpentry, and he watched her closely, ready to defend his poor showing should she do less than admire his accomplishment.

A faint tilting of her head met his look and her hands

stilled. "I doubt the finest baby bed to be found in New York City was made with such care," she said in a low voice.

"Probably with a hell of a lot more skill, though, and some decent wood, I'd venture to say." He leaned back to view his project. "Wish I had some paint to slap on it."

"It'll be just fine. Better than I could have provided him with. And once I put the mattress in, you won't be able to see the wood anyway." She smiled again, and he was lost for a moment in the depths of summer blue eyes.

The winter sunlight from the window was pale within the room, and as Erin bent her head once more to her sewing, her face was cast in shadow. Her lashes dropped to rest against the curve of her cheek, and she flexed her fingers, her hands slender and well formed. She put him in mind of the Madonna in his mother's Bible, the picture a copy of some famous artist's work.

Such purity was not to be believed. Not from a woman who had borne a child, who had come more than a thousand miles by herself, who had holed up in a miner's shack and faced the elements alone. Surely she must bear the scars of her past. Certainly her soul must be shriveled by the sadness she'd endured in her marriage.

And what of the men who had looked upon her as she traveled? Could she have ignored their advances and blunt appeals for her favors? How had she survived hauling her meager possessions up the mountain to this place, and then set about making a home for herself?

She was an enigma, a puzzle Quinn was determined to solve. Even more than that, she was under his defenses already, her fresh appeal and the beauty of her face and form bringing him to startling arousal more often than he wanted to admit. And yet, beneath that masculine need was a protective instinct that kept her safe from the urgent demands of his body.

"Where did you get the down for this mattress?" she asked, her fingers once more weaving her needle through the flannel.

"I gathered some up from the chicken's nests," he told her.

"All this?" Erin held up the bag that held sweet hay and several handfuls of pale down. It fluffed nicely, he thought.

"No. I plucked a little from their undersides," he admitted. "Thought the baby needed it worse than they did."

Her laughter was indulgent, first a chuckle, then a full-blown giggle, and Quinn reveled in it. He'd tickled her funny bone, and that fact gave him a sense of accomplishment.

Her merriment trailed off as she watched him, her fingers slowing their pace, and then on an indrawn breath she glanced toward the window. "Are we in for another snowstorm?" she asked idly, as though the thought lent little concern to her well-being.

He shook his head. "I doubt it. Not for a day or so at least. The sky looks pretty clear for now. But then, you never know what's coming over the mountains next."

He sat the small crib upright and cocked his head. "Guess I need to trim off one leg. It looks a little tipsy, doesn't it?"

"It looks wonderful." Erin's words of reassurance were quick as she leaned forward in the rocking chair. Lifting the makeshift mattress to her mouth, she bit firmly at the thread, severing it neatly behind her final stitch. "Let's see if it fits."

She fluffed the flannel, shifting the hay and feathers within to suit her, and then placed it with careful touches inside the bed he'd put together. A tiny quilt provided covering and she tucked it in place, her fingers deft and quick.

"There!" With satisfaction aglow on her face, she smiled at him, and Quinn felt a warmth deep inside that threatened to melt what little resistance he had left. So easily he'd put aside all responsibility to the man who had hired him for this job. So swiftly he had forgotten the life he'd forged from his own talents and abilities back in New York City. All for the chance to be a part of Erin Wentworth's life.

She'd bewitched him, this small, silken-haired woman whose eyes drew him like a beacon in the night. He'd already set aside his obligation to Ted Wentworth in favor of Erin's needs. His conscience was pierced by fangs of guilt. He'd bargained to do a job, and then in a few short days had turned his back on it.

Instead he'd become downright enamored with the woman he'd come here to retrieve. Her strength as she faced the perils of childbirth, and the bits and pieces of her past she'd revealed to him, had given him a new perception of the woman he'd pursued.

Now, after only two weeks or so of watching Erin with the child, he'd formed a new attachment. The babe he'd carried up the mountain in his arms had imbued him with a need to protect and cherish that was utterly foreign to him. Almost as if in the bringing of the boy to this place, he had accepted what must follow, whatever path opened before him.

"You're so solemn." Erin's words stole into his thoughts and he lifted his head to meet her gaze.

"Just thinking. I've never been this close to a child before, let alone a baby. They kinda take over your life, don't they?"

Her eyes sought his face, as if she would read his mind. "Are you regretting bringing him here?"

"No." Quinn's word of denial was quick. "He deserved a chance to live, and from what they told me in town, he wasn't going to get it there." He rose in a lithe movement and stepped to the window. "It feels as if we're in a world of our own, doesn't it, Erin? As if New York City is so far removed it no longer influences our lives."

"You're thinking of the Wentworths, aren't you? You're thinking you should have taken me back there instead of settling in here." Her words held no trace of censure, only quiet acceptance.

He shook his head. "That wasn't a choice for me. I couldn't have taken you anywhere, not in the shape you were in when I got here. Certainly not since you've had the baby. You're barely on your feet, honey."

"You took money from Ted Wentworth to find me, didn't you?"

Quinn nodded, his uplifted hand dismissing the fact. "Yeah, he paid me, and I put the money in the bank. But there was never any guarantee, Erin. There never is. A bounty hunter usually doesn't get his reward until after the fact. I was hired to search you out. Ted paid me for my time. There's no price on your head."

"I'm not going back," she said quietly. "There's nothing there for me."

"Not even to lay to rest some ghosts?"

"No. There's only one ghost in my life, and I refuse

to feel any guilt for his death. Ted and Estelle didn't have any love to waste on me. They wanted their grandchild, and that's out of the question now. I have no reason to return to New York.''

"So be it.'' A movement beyond the edge of the clearing caught his eye, then a pair of dark forms took shape and Quinn saw a flash of color between the bare tree branches.

He turned back to face her. "Right now we've got something else to think about. There's a couple of horses coming up the trail, and I have an idea they're on their way here. Can't imagine anywhere else they'd be going, can you?''

Erin's hands clenched tightly in her lap, and her startled gaze flew to the sleeping form on the pillow beside her. "The baby! Is someone coming for the baby, Quinn?''

"Doesn't seem likely to me.'' He turned from the window and took his heavy coat from a nail next to the door, donning it quickly. Then he eased his hat into place, tilting it over his brow.

"Where are you going?'' Her voice was fearful and she moved from the chair to pick up the sleeping baby. Holding him closely to her breasts, she cast an anxious look at the door.

"Take it easy, honey. There's no place to hide, and probably no need anyway,'' Quinn told her, his hand on the latch. "I'm going out on the porch to see what they want. Just stay over by the bed.''

The door opened and closed quickly, Quinn moving through the gap like a dark shadow. The sun hovered just past the treetops to the west, casting its glow on the two men who were making their way across the clearing.

One lifted his hand in greeting, and Quinn's breath escaped in an audible sigh of relief.

"Doc! What are you doing here?" he asked, stepping down from the low porch. Two quick strides found him facing the visitors, and he tilted back the brim of his hat with one finger, looking up at their friendly grins, his glance then traveling to the bulky canvas bundles each horse carried behind its saddle.

"Came up to check on the baby. He doin' all right?" Doc Fisher leaned over the saddle horn and cast a glance at the cabin.

"Fine as frog hairs," Quinn said with a grin.

"This here's the preacher from town, comin' to talk to the young lady," Doc Fisher said, waving a gloved hand at the man beside him. "We brought some hay and a couple bags of oats along. Thought you could use a fresh supply."

Quinn nodded in appreciation, eyeing the bulging, tightly packed feed. He'd been feeding sparely for the past couple of days, stretching out the hay. His gaze moved to the second visitor.

Garbed in a dark coat, the slender man looked as if he would like to be anywhere else but perched atop a horse on a mountainside. His eyes moved longingly to the cabin as he offered his greeting.

"Don't suppose you might have a pot of coffee on the stove in there?" His voice was so out-and-out hopeful, Quinn could barely suppress the smile he felt tugging at his lips.

"I think we could rustle up a cup for you, preacher."

Doc Fisher swung a long leg over his saddle and slid to the ground. "Now, that sounds like a mighty nice gesture. The reverend and me got kinda chilled on the trail."

With more haste than grace, the young minister reached the ground and rubbed his hands together. "Where can we tie the horses, sir?"

"My name's Quinn Yarborough, Reverend. I'll just loop your reins over the railing here."

"I'm known as Brother Stephen to my parishioners, Mr. Yarborough." As if his legs were stiff from the long ride, the younger man walked with a stilted gait, and Quinn reached for his reins, leading the placid horse to the porch.

"We've come to have a chat with the young woman," Brother Stephen confided, stuffing his hands into his pockets. "There's been an interesting development."

Quinn's first inclination was to send both men back down the mountain without delay, but his better instincts took over and he lifted his head, tilting his brow in silent query. There was no way on God's green earth he would allow this man to upset Erin.

"That little boy's settled in real good here with Erin," Quinn told the visitors as he opened the cabin door. The warmth within issued its own welcome, and Brother Stephen headed for the stove with outstretched hands to seize the glowing heat it offered.

His head tilted in greeting as Erin rose from the bed. "Ma'am? You're looking well."

"I'm just fine, thank you." Her voice was thin, her face pale, and Quinn walked to her side.

One big hand gripped her elbow and he led her to the rocking chair, glancing with warning at the doctor.

"We're just here to see that things are going well for the boy, ma'am," Doc Fisher announced, stepping inside and closing the door.

"He's growing, I think," Erin said, hugging the small

bundle to her breasts. She rocked slowly, her apprehensive gaze darting from one visitor to the other.

Brother Stephen rocked on his heels, his face beaming. "We've found a family for him. Mr. and Mrs. Bates have three of their own, but they're willing to take in an orphan. They have a little place the other side of town. They're right anxious to see the boy."

Erin's arms tightened and the chair rocked harder. "He's doing well with my milk. I'd think this was a good place for him."

"This is a chance for him to have a real family, ma'am."

Although softly spoken, the preacher's words contained a degree of censure. Erin flinched, dropping her eyes to the warmly wrapped bundle she held.

How could another woman ever feel the bond that had been formed? Spun from the depths of her despair and the fount of love she'd held in abeyance since the death of her child, a veritable avalanche of emotion had overwhelmed her during the past days.

Now this preacher man wanted to take the child who had, with his very presence, begun to mend her broken heart. Her arms tightened and the babe squirmed within her embrace. She bent her head and shushed him with soft words, holding him against her breasts.

"He's doing fine right here," she said after a moment.

"I can see that," Brother Stephen agreed. "But the opportunity to have a real family must be seized, don't you agree?"

"We're pretty near a real family already," Quinn interjected from his place by the window. And that idea was looking better all the time, he decided. His gaze was warm as it rested on her, and Erin smiled as if reassured by his approval.

"We're taking good care of him," she said, her voice stronger with the knowledge of Quinn's backing.

Doc Fisher cleared his throat. "Brother Stephen isn't tryin' to shed any doubt on that, ma'am. He just feels it would be better for the boy to be taken by folks who could be his parents for the long haul."

"The long haul?" Erin repeated the words as if testing their meaning.

"Married folks, ma'am," Doc Fisher said, his face flushing as he glanced back and forth from Erin to the man near the window.

"He thinks we're living in sin, Erin." Quinn's words were hard-edged, his hands rising to rest against his hips. The soft gaze he'd favored her with became a look of chilled anger, and Erin winced as the meaning of his words penetrated.

Her pale cheeks were flooded with color as she bit at her lip. "I've only just borne a child. Surely you don't think…"

As though she could not speak the words, her voice faltered and she cast a pleading look at Quinn.

Brother Stephen's cheeks bore a crimson stain of their own. His mouth pursed as he cleared his throat. "No one is accusing you of improper behavior, ma'am. It's just that, as time goes by, things change. Pretty soon, folks will be wondering about your situation here."

"A single woman is always open to gossip, ma'am," the doctor added quietly. "That's the way of the world, like it or not."

Erin's gaze swept over the three men who watched her. Quinn's hip rested against the window ledge, his arms crossed over the expanse of his chest. He glanced at the preacher and Doc Fisher, both of whom looked decidedly uncomfortable. Lifting one brow in silent query, he watched Erin, as if he asked her permission for his action, and then, at her nod, he stood erect, drawing all eyes in his direction.

"I think we can solve the problem to everyone's satisfaction, Doc." His easy drawl set a new mood, and the two men turned to him anxiously, as if ready to dump the load of concern on his broad shoulders.

"I'm pretty open to suggestion, Mr. Yarborough." Brother Stephen's tone was eager.

"Let's have it." Doc Fisher's face relaxed.

Quinn shot another glance at Erin, his dark eyes scanning her quickly, holding her gaze as he spoke. This was the moment of truth. He'd weighed his feelings, considered his choices, and for the first time in his life he felt a sense of rightness, a sense of belonging, fill him with satisfaction that knew no bounds.

"I'm thinking we've got the solution right in front of us, Doc. The preacher's here already, almost like Providence had a hand in it, sending him up the mountain today. Erin's looking like a new mother needing a husband to tend to her and her child, and I'm a likely candidate for the job."

Erin opened her mouth, whether to protest or not she never knew. Quinn's quick, almost imperceptible movement of his head kept her silent, and his mouth curved in a faint smile of approval. Her thoughts spun rapidly, a tangled mass of confusion. She was a widow, not really a single woman, yet the child she held was not her own. Quinn was offering to marry her, allowing her to keep the baby she cradled.

Within her arms, he was a warm, compact bundle, and her hold on him tightened. He squirmed, protesting her grip, and she glanced down. Piercing blue eyes met her gaze and a small bubble formed between his rosy lips.

A single sound, a cooing whisper of satisfaction, burst the moisture as his mouth opened. Erin bent low, consumed by a spasm of emotion almost painful in its intensity.

This child needed her. Already he'd become her own, easing the pain of her loss, filling her arms with his blessed presence.

She needed him, this small gift from heaven. And more than that, she needed the man who had brought him to her. In order to appease the restraints placed on a woman alone by the society she lived in, she needed Quinn Yarborough.

"Ma'am?" It was the preacher's eager query that gained her attention.

Erin lifted her head, facing the three men who had the ability to decide her destiny, and her mouth quivered as she opened it to speak. As if he'd spotted the telltale, trembling movement, Quinn stepped to her side, then crouched with one knee on the floor beside the rocking chair.

His hand covered hers, fingers spreading wide to encompass her grip on the baby's rounded form. He squeezed gently, bending forward to hide her from the other two men.

"Trust me." The words were soft, whispered against her cheek, his mouth brushing her skin in a movement that might have been a caress. Whatever its intent, his gesture took her breath, and she turned instinctively, her face against his broad chest.

"Yes..." Her acquiescence breathed against his shirtfront and he tightened his grip on her hand.

She inhaled sharply, then repeated the single word as she lifted her head from the haven he'd offered.

"Yes."

"Yes?" The preacher prodded her, his voice eager as he tilted his head, as if to better hear her reply.

Erin met his gaze over Quinn's shoulder. "Yes, I'll marry Mr. Yarborough."

The doctor's chuckle was rich, relief blending with his obvious pleasure in her decision. "Well, that certainly solves things nicely, I'd say. You're a lucky man, and that's a fact, Mr. Yarborough. Not every day a man gets a prize like this young woman handed to him."

Erin didn't hear Quinn's reply, nor did she hear the hum of conversation that rushed to fill the silence, for her ears throbbed as she listened to the beating of her own heart, its pace rapid against her breastbone.

Then she blinked, watching as Doc Fisher and Quinn shook hands and discussed the legalities of the situation. Near the table Brother Stephen fished through his pockets, finding a veritable treasure trove therein, including a small Bible and another book. His satisfaction was apparent as he held both volumes within long, slender fingers.

"We don't have a ring." Erin murmured the words in a small voice. Her announcement silenced the room, as if uttered with the sound of trumpets.

Quinn straightened, his quick gaze slanting in her direction. With only a moment's hesitation, his hand slid into his pocket and he brought forth a slim leather purse. Two long fingers slid inside, withdrawing a narrow gold band that glittered in the rays of pale sunlight coming through the window.

"It was my mother's." It circled the tip of his index finger and he held it in Erin's direction. "Will this do?"

She nodded. "Oh, yes." Swiftly her eyes met his, and she felt them fill with unwanted tears. "Would she mind, do you think?"

Whether it was the evidence of emotion that drew him or only the urge to offer the symbol into her keeping he didn't know. He simply stepped to her side, drawing her from the chair with a hand beneath her elbow.

"Let's see if it fits," Quinn murmured, taking the baby from her arms to hand him to the doctor.

Erin gave up possession with only a moment's hesitation, her gaze fastened on the movement of Quinn's hands as he slipped the narrow band into place. It was almost a perfect fit, needing only a tiny nudge to ease it over her knuckle. She bit at her lip as she blinked back the tears that begged to fall.

"What do you think?" he asked, his voice rough, as if her emotion had spilled in his direction.

"I'd be proud to wear it, as long as you're sure."

Quinn cleared his throat. "I'm sure." He turned his head to where the doctor watched and waited. "You want to hold the baby while we do this?"

"Guess I can handle this little fella for a few minutes." Doc's big hands cradled the small bundle in one arm, and he nodded at the preacher.

"Well, I don't see any reason why we can't make this a legal situation," Brother Stephen announced, his wide smile laced with relief. His fingers slid between the pages as he ruffled through the book he held, then halted as he smoothed it open to the place he sought. He stepped to the window to catch the available light.

"It was handy that I brought along my book of sacraments," he said, eyeing Erin with smug delight.

He planned this, she thought, amazed that no censure marred her judgment, only a certainty of what was right and fitting.

"Let's use the long version of the ceremony," the young clergyman said quietly. "I believe presiding at weddings is about the most important thing I do as a minister, Miss Erin. God willing, this will be a union for life, and it merits taking the time to do it right. It doesn't matter that there's only a few of us here, so long as God is invited to join in the proceedings.''

A rush of gratitude filled Erin's heart, and she nodded her agreement, unwilling to trust her voice. Quinn's hand tightened on her arm and she cast a glance upward, gaining strength from the curve of his mouth and the approval of his gaze.

They stood before the young preacher and heard his words, Erin answering in soft murmurs, Quinn in firm tones that left no doubt as to his intentions.

And then it was over. In less than an hour her life had changed. The door closed behind the three men, Quinn following them outside into the afternoon light.

''You'll need to hustle to get back down to town before dark,'' Quinn said warningly.

''I've been riding these mountains for years,'' Doc Fisher told him with a satisfied grin. ''We'll be just fine.''

The two men mounted their horses, and Quinn watched as they turned to ride away.

''Take good care of that young'un,'' Doc called back, his hand lifting in a wave.

The preacher's mouth was set, as if he faced taking a dose of bitter medicine, hunching his shoulders against the cold.

''Yeah.'' Quinn's single word of response was uttered quietly as he watched them go.

He looked upward at the sky, noting the gathering clouds. It looked like snow by morning, probably a good storm. He'd better feed the stock well tonight and wait till late to milk the cow, just in case he had to dig out in the morning.

The hay and sacks of oats bundled by the porch awaited his care and he lifted their heavy weight, making two trips to the shed to stow them within. And then, with nothing else to keep him from her, he turned to the cabin to join his wife.

Chapter Seven

In the lantern light the gold ring set off sparks that caught Erin's eye, and she turned from the stove, the better to examine the twisted design of the ring Quinn had placed on her finger. It looked to be made of two separate pieces of metal, bound together to make an intricate pattern, with delicate carvings and small bits of glistening stone forming a part.

This was no simple, everyday wedding band, of that she was certain. Whether Quinn's mother had worn it or not, its original acquisition had not been haphazard, but rather a planned, perhaps custom-designed purchase.

Another puzzling part of the man she had agreed to marry. Was it only moments ago she had spoken with such certainty? Yes. One word, her promise given. And now she was legally bound to Quinn Yarborough.

Suddenly he loomed large in her mind. Muscular, strong, his hands capable of both healing and harm. She'd been the recipient of his soothing touch, the focus of his knowledgeable skills. And she knew with a certainty she had no way of proving that those same hands could deal out harsh punishment should the occasion arise.

His shoulders were wide, his chest deep with the power of a mature man, his body well formed. No lightweight piker was Quinn Yarborough. Somewhere he'd worked long and hard to earn the muscular frame he carried.

And then there was the part of him that remained hidden to the casual observer. The tenderness within, the gentleness of his touch, the easy acceptance of chores that would be anathema to another man. Even now he was probably milking her cow, or perhaps gathering up the eggs that had been ignored for the past day or so.

She turned from the lantern glow and reached for the kettle she kept on a shelf. It was time to stop daydreaming and put together something for supper. The slab of bacon she'd hung in one corner caught her eye and she climbed atop a low stool, the better to reach it, her arms upstretched to grasp it from the hook suspending it.

"I'll get it for you." From the doorway, Quinn's voice caught her unaware, and she looked back over her shoulder. Somehow he'd opened the door and come inside without her hearing him. Probably because she'd been...

His hands were on her waist, lifting her to the floor. Caught off guard, she gasped. His grip tightened and her skin felt the chill of his cold fingers through the layers of cotton she wore.

"You don't need to be reaching like that," he scolded, setting her aside, then extending his arm with an easy movement to swing the bacon slab to the table.

She looked up at him, doubly aware of the man she faced, her mind still awash with the multitude of thoughts she'd had. This was her *husband*, she reminded herself. This tall, rugged, whiskery man who watched her every move, who knew her more intimately than any other human being, who had been privy to the depths of her despair.

This man who had married her so that her child would not be taken from her.

"I owe you my life." Without thought she uttered the words, her chin rising, her eyes meeting his.

He grimaced, shaking his head. "Don't say that."

"I do," she insisted. "You didn't have to marry me. You gave me your name and this ring." She held up her hand, watching as the carving caught the light and shone richly against her slender finger. "You've tied yourself to me, Quinn Yarborough, and I can't thank you enough."

"I don't do anything without thinking it over pretty well." His gaze was somber, his eyes shadowed as he looked down at her. He lifted his hand and touched the gold band with his index finger, then curled that same finger around her knuckle and drew her hand to his mouth. His lips caressed her flesh, cool against her skin, and then his mouth opened and the tip of his tongue flicked against the metal, turning it warm, touching her with the heat of his inner fire.

She inhaled sharply, gripping his hand in a reflexive movement. Her eyes were captured by his gaze, those dark brows lowering as he watched her. His lips were closed now, brushing against her fingers, the back of her hand, his eyes darkening, narrowing, glowing, as if he peered within her soul.

Her denial was breathless, her words a whisper. "You didn't have time to think it over, Quinn. You made up your mind, and mine, too, in the space of a few minutes."

"Some things don't take as much consideration as others," he told her, his mouth lifting at one corner, as if a smile lurked there. "When the opportunity arose, I snatched it."

"You don't feel...trapped?"

He shook his head. "Do you?"

Erin considered the thought. Her hand was well and truly captured, held prisoner within his grasp. She was alone in a mountain cabin with a man she'd known for less than a month, a man with only his word to recommend him. She had just promised to honor and obey him.

And love, her conscience prodded.

"Am I? Trapped?" She clenched her teeth. If he wanted to, he could claim his rights. If he felt so inclined, he could make her his wife in fact, as well as on paper.

A paper that resided in Quinn Yarborough's pocket even now.

He released her hand, his fingers slow to relax their hold, as if reluctant to relinquish his possession. Stepping back, he offered a half salute, his mouth twisted with a cynical expression. "You're as free as a bird, Miss Erin. I don't trap innocent prey, only those wild things that know their way in the world."

Her eyes widened. "Innocent?"

He nodded. "You're wise in all the ways that count, but underneath you're..." He hesitated. "I think the word is pure." His words were a whisper as he bent closer. "And that sort of allure is the most dangerous kind, Miss Erin."

Beneath his watchful gaze she'd cooked, folded small squares of flannel and tended the baby all afternoon. The everyday chores had become a part of her life in the past weeks, all things that kept her mind from the small grave beneath the pine trees. Yesterday she hadn't thought of the still, silent form of her child until bedtime.

Now, with supper behind them, she patted the baby's back, pacing with him, waiting impatiently until Quinn headed for the shed, his mumbled words speaking of chores. Not until the air warmed once more, after the stove threw out a measure of heat behind the draft from the outdoors, did she prepare herself for nursing the child.

Her sigh of contentment was audible as she settled in the rocking chair. For this she willingly scrubbed out small dabs of flannel, gladly cleaned and cooked the meals. For these precious moments every few hours, when she could find joy beyond measure in the cradling of an infant in her arms, she willingly tended to the mundane chores that demanded her attention.

She unbuttoned her dress and opened her shift, chuckling aloud as the tiny mouth nuzzled at the front of her bodice, nudging her fingers. With eager cries the baby caught the scent of her milk, and his mouth opened wide as he searched with hasty movements for his prize.

Erin laughed aloud, her pleasure spilling over as she settled back in the rocker, lifting the baby closer to the breast that nurtured him.

After ten or fifteen minutes he released his hold, and his head rolled back against her arm. She shifted him to her shoulder and he grunted his displeasure, only to open his mouth after a moment, allowing a burp to escape.

His mouth was still eager as she offered her other breast and leaned her head back to relax. He'd barely latched on when the door opened, and Erin lifted startled eyes to see Quinn entering the cabin.

His gaze traveled with unerring aim to where she sat, his eyes blinking to rid his lashes of snowflakes. ''It's coming down like blue blazes out there,'' he announced, stamping his feet as he latched the door. His coat was hung quickly, his boots removed and placed close to the stove.

And still he watched her. From the corner of his eye, from beneath lowered brows, from the doorway to the stove and back, he kept her in sight.

Erin felt a flush creep from her chest to her throat and then to her face. His appearance had surprised her, and then confused her mightily. Her left hand tugged the blanket closer, covering the rise of her breast until only the smallest portion of the baby's dark hair was exposed to view.

Quinn was watching her, and that fact should not have caused this sudden rush of heat that enveloped her. He'd been watching her for weeks, his gaze ever concerned, always kind. Now those same dark eyes held a new message, and its portent was confusing. Gone was the patient, caring man who'd done for her what no other person ever had.

In his place was a quiet, somber, watchful man whose gaze filled her with a sense of discomfort, whose eyes were intense with an emotion she could only guess at. She only knew that his mouth against her wedding ring had set off alarms within her that would not be silenced.

Everything was changed. Everything was different. In the space of a few minutes their lives together had been altered beyond belief. In moments, the ease in which they had conducted themselves was gone. The camaraderie was shattered, leaving only a strange, fragile thread to bind them together. No longer did she feel free to nurse the baby, exposing her bare skin to Quinn's eyes, to that dark, shuttered gaze.

''Will he be warm enough in his bed? Or do we need

another blanket for him?'' Quinn approached, and Erin tilted her head back.

''He'll be fine with me in bed, Quinn. I'd rather keep him close by.''

Quinn shook his head. ''You aren't listening to me, honey. I think it's time for him to be tucked into his own bed. We can put it closer to the fire if you like, but either way, he'll do just fine.''

She felt the warmth in her cheeks increase as she shook her head. ''I'd feel better having him...''

Erin's words faltered as Quinn shook his head again. ''I've slept my last night on the floor, Erin.''

Her mouth was dry at the implication of his words. ''You're planning on sleeping in my bed?''

''It's the only one in the place. Reckon that's the one I meant.''

''I don't think it's proper.''

He rocked back on his heels. ''We're married, Erin. Sleeping in the same bed is what married people do.'' His lips thinned as if he suppressed words that begged to be spoken.

Erin slipped her hand beneath the blanket and loosed the baby's mouth from her flesh, tugging her dress into place quickly. A murmured protest was quickly hushed as she lifted the child to her shoulder and cuddled him.

''I've only just had a child, Quinn.'' The words were spoken quietly, yet an unspoken plea echoed within them.

''Aw, hell!'' His voice was rasping as he frowned at her. Then in two short steps he was kneeling by her side, pressing one hand against her shoulder, stilling the rocking of her chair. ''I'm not going to make any demands on you, Erin. You ought to know better than that.''

She fought the tears that were close to being shed. ''I

only know you're planning to sleep with me tonight, and if I know anything at all about men, that won't be the end of it.''

His fingers tightened their grip and his eyes glittered, narrowing in the glow of lamplight. "I think you're tarring me with the wrong brush, Erin. Have I lied to you yet?''

Her eyes swept over his face, the firm line of his jaw, the unsmiling lips and the dark gaze that held a trace of pain. "No, you haven't, not once," she admitted. Her heart slowed and she was aware it had been thumping wildly at the base of her throat. "No," she repeated. "You've never lied to me, Quinn.''

"Then don't doubt me now, honey. I didn't turn into an ogre when I promised to spend my life with you.''

Shame brushed its heat over her cheeks once more and she turned her head, resting her forehead against his arm. "I'm sorry, Quinn. Truly sorry.''

"He gave you a bad time, didn't he?''

She didn't pretend not to understand. She nodded her head. Speaking the words that would admit her unhappiness was too painful a task.

"I'm not Damian Wentworth, Erin. I've never been a man to force myself on a woman, no matter the circumstances, and I can't imagine being a husband who would visit attention on his wife if it wasn't wanted.''

Quinn spelled it out clearly, Erin realized. He would not demand his marriage rights, at least not now. At least not tonight.

Full dark fell early; and once the baby was settled, clean and dry within his small bed, Erin found herself with nothing more to do. The dishes were put away, the coffeepot was ready for a hot fire in the morning and a kettle of water was set to warm atop the stove.

She'd pulled down the quilts and sat on the edge of the bed to take off her shoes. As if he attended the small signal, Quinn had excused himself, murmuring about the cow and taking a last look around outdoors. She'd taken the chance to slide into her gown, burrowing beneath the covers in the bed only moments before he came back inside.

They'd gone from friends of a sort to husband and wife. Too quickly, she thought. With reasons that had nothing to do with love, honor and all the rest of the vows she'd taken with barely a sense of misgiving. Stunned by the suddenness of the proceedings, she'd blithely assumed that it would be a marriage of convenience.

She shivered beneath the quilt as her foot moved from the small cocoon of warmth she inhabited. A bubble of nervous laughter pushed at her lips as she wondered at her own naiveté. Quinn Yarborough would never be content with a pale imitation of marriage.

He was male, through and through. Even the energy that drove the man was masculine in its intensity. His steps were firm, his stride arrogant. His body spoke of muscular strength, of a man's powerful need to be in control.

She should have known, should have recognized the need of a man for a woman that gleamed from the depths of his dark, hooded gaze.

And yet, she'd never met a man like Quinn Yarborough before. Never been treated as Quinn Yarborough had treated her. Never known the kindness and understanding of a man who was strong enough to be gentle.

Her eyes half-closed, she watched him from the bed.

He sat before the stove, his big body shading her from the lamplight, his hands busy with the ritual of cleaning his gun.

When would he come to bed, crawling into the side next to the wall, sharing her quilts, easing his presence onto the mattress beside her? Maybe he was waiting for her to go to sleep, so as not to embarrass her.

Beside the bed the baby stirred, and she rose to lean over the crib. His mouth was pursed and he sucked, frowning just a bit, and her laughter was captured once more within her throat.

"You awake?" Quinn's voice was low, rumbling in his chest as he turned his head to look at her. His hair was rumpled, his shirt pulled from his trousers. His beard was dark against the paler skin of his jaw.

She nodded and then settled herself against the pillow. From beneath the shadow of her lashes she watched as he placed his gun across the table and tidied up around himself. A metal box held his gun-cleaning equipment. Her eyes followed his movements as he replaced the soft cloth he had just used to wipe down the barrel and polish the wooden stock.

He moved deliberately, with a flow of energy about him that intrigued her. He knew how to do so many things that she was ignorant of, things she should have been aware of before she set out to live alone in the wilds of Colorado.

He stood, moving to the wall where a shelf held an assortment of his belongings, stowing his box there. "Need anything?" he asked, removing his shirt and hanging it over the back of a chair, then hesitating before he bent to blow out the lamp.

"No." The word was a whisper, but he heard it, inclining his head in silent reply. With an audible breath he brought darkness to the room, and she blinked against the inky blackness that enveloped her.

His trousers rustled and Erin heard the sound of foot-steps, then felt the sudden draft as he drew back the covers of her bed. The ropes gave with his weight, and she was hard put to stay where she was, his greater weight tugging at her.

"Is the baby warm enough, do you think?" he asked as he shifted beside her.

"I wrapped him good and then covered him with my shawl."

Quinn's scent filled her nostrils, the smell of wood-smoke and fresh air, underlaid by a musky aroma that spoke of all things sensual and forbidden.

But it wasn't, her inner self reminded her. Not forbid-den between a husband and wife. Yet the soft touches, the gentle caressing, always evolved into something more, something not nearly so appealing. At least, not to a woman. What had always followed was obviously for a man's benefit, certainly not for the object of his—

She closed her eyes tightly, counting in her mind. She breathed deeply. One…she would not remember! She inhaled again. Two…tomorrow might find the sun shin-ing through the windows. The breath escaped between her parted lips. Three…soon the baby would wake. She relaxed her hands and drew in another shaky breath.

Four—a foot brushed against hers and she bolted up-right.

"What?" She choked on the word, coughed and looked about frantically. Her eyes were used to the dark now, and beside her Quinn sat up, reaching to press against her shoulder.

"It's all right, Erin. I just shifted around a little. I didn't mean to startle you."

She settled against the pillow and watched as his shoulders took up the space between her own and the edge of the bed. "I was going to sleep," she muttered.

He chuckled. "You were breathing like a locomotive, honey. What on earth were you thinking about?"

"Nothing special." Not for the world would he ever find out that her thoughts had been in the wide bed she'd shared with Damian Wentworth. And "nothing special" about covered the events that had taken place there, she thought grimly. Not unless you were interested in pain and humiliation and the taunts of a man who derided your womanhood.

"Better get to sleep. I'll warrant that baby's gonna be looking for something to eat before too long."

She nodded, turning to look in his direction. His face was a pale blur, but she thought he smiled. "Yes, all right."

"It's going to be just fine, Erin. I promise you."

He moved closer to her and she felt the heat of his body radiating beneath the quilts. She shivered, resisting the urge to scoot closer, and he chuckled.

"Want me to get your back warm?" he offered, the words silky with promise.

Maybe with Quinn it would be different. But probably not. Somehow, she had the feeling that when it came to the physical part of marriage, men were probably all alike.

She shook her head. "No, I'll be fine."

Then she bit at her tongue, lest she be tempted to accept his offer.

Chapter Eight

New York City

"Where is he? Has he found her?" Estelle Wentworth spoke sharply, turning from the fire that burned with a subdued flame to face her husband. Never had a fire blazed out of control in this room. Seldom was a word spoken in less than a well-modulated voice. Rarely was an emotion allowed to escape that might suggest lack of discipline.

Until now.

Ted Wentworth faced his wife, lifting his hands in a gesture that spoke defeat. "Joel Guinan said he heard from him well over a month ago. Quinn was in Denver then, and thought he had a good lead."

"And you believe him?" Her voice had lost some of the rasping urgency, but the tone was doubtful.

Ted approached the fireplace and his wife, who stood near the hearth. "We have no choice, Estelle. Joel is Quinn's partner. He'd have no reason to lie to me. He knows Quinn is working for us."

"You know as well as I do that you can't trust the

Irish.'' Her face contorted with distaste. ''We probably should have gone somewhere else to begin with. Quinn Yarborough may have a good address, but you can't get away from his beginnings.''

''He's an honest man, Estelle. If anyone can find Erin, he can.''

Her mouth pinched as she stepped back from the fireplace. ''She's a decent-looking woman, and Quinn always had an eye for the ladies.''

Ted shot her a look of rebuke. ''He won't be taken in by a pretty face. My money is in his pocket, and when he finds her, we'll hear about it.''

''Well, I think we should locate someone in Denver to follow up on him. It's been too long without any word. She may have already had the baby. Our only chance was to find her when she was—''

''That's enough! I've gone along with you on this from the start, and managed to scare the girl away with the pressure we put on her. I'll give Quinn another couple of weeks, and then we'll follow up on it. Besides, I don't believe the child was to be born for another month or so.''

Estelle sniffed, stalking toward the window that overlooked Central Park. Her pale, slender hand rested against velvet draperies and her back was stiff and ungiving. ''I want my grandchild. I don't care what else comes or goes, I want Damian's child. If I have to find Erin myself, I will.''

Ted leaned one hand on the mantel and gazed into the fire. ''We'll give it two weeks, Estelle, like I said. If we haven't heard anything by then, we'll change our course of action.''

* * *

Colorado

The little pine standing in the corner bore no resemblance to any Christmas tree Erin had ever decorated before. In the place of fragile, blown-glass angels and bells hung pinecones with white-tipped edges. She'd mixed a bit of flour and water together, then dabbed it on each cone, adding small red berries for color.

Instead of garlands of tinsel, she'd managed to paste strips of brown paper into circles, paper she'd colored with a set of paints brought from New York. For some reason, she'd had it in mind to once more take up her love of painting, and she smiled in self-derision now as she considered that idea. She'd be hard-pressed to find the time to do any drawing, let alone put brush to canvas or paper.

It had never occurred to her that life would be so full, that she would be so intent on the art of survival. Indeed, keeping her body warm and nourished had become the order of the day over the past months. There had barely been time to feed her soul. Now she brushed color onto the pieces of paper she'd cut, smiling at the primitive decorations she'd devised.

Quinn had carried the tree in the door this morning with a jaunty step. He'd announced that Christmas was only a day away according to his calculations and they needed a tree in order to celebrate properly.

She'd almost forgotten, which was proof that survival wiped all but dire necessities from thought. Quinn was obviously not concerned about survival. His confidence in his ability to handle their situation was beginning to carry her along with the tide. Else she could not now be

pasting colored rings of paper together, feeling the ela-
tion of a holiday as she readied her home for Christmas.

The scent of her cookies baking filled the room, and
she stood quickly to check their progress. She'd formed
the dough by hand, delighted when she could identify
the shapes of angels and stars on the pan as she slid it
into the oven. There would be no icing, no decorations,
but Quinn would appreciate the addition to the holiday
he'd insisted they celebrate.

Her hand slid into her pocket, fishing for the wrapped
package there. Her fingers caressed the length of it, iden-
tifying the penknife that had so recently been hidden in
the corner of her purse. It had been her father's, years
ago, long before his business had prospered, when she
was but a child. She'd watched him peel apples, long
curls of red dangling from the silver blade, as he carefully prepared the fruit for their mutual enjoyment.

In later years, when he could have purchased much
more expensive pocketknives, he'd clung to the me-
mento of his early years.

It had been a part of his legacy to her, a gift her
mother had pressed into her hand after the funeral. It had
meant more than the house and its elegant furnishings,
more than the library of books and the velvet-lined box
of jewelry that had finally been hers after her mother's
death several years later.

Now the knife would be Quinn's, and she could only
hope that he would grasp the value of it, would sense
the respect she paid him in the giving of her cherished
keepsake into his possession.

The cookies looked even better now, she decided as
she slid them from the pan to a plate. The edges were
ragged, the forms blurred, but anybody with half a brain

could make out the form of angels in those sugared delights.

"What's that?" Quinn stood behind her and she whirled to face him. In the midst of her clanging the oven door and bustling around the table, she'd missed his entrance. Now he faced her, smiling, his cheeks and ears red from the cold.

"What?" Confused, she turned back to the table where his gloved finger was aimed at her cookies.

"Those are sure enough cookies. I figured that out right off." He bent closer. "They're all lumpy lookin', honey."

She drew herself up and cast him a scornful glance. "Anyone who can't recognize angels and stars when they see them certainly doesn't deserve to have his share."

"Angels, huh?" He took off his gloves, grinning delightedly. "Maybe I can see a little wing here."

"That's the head," Erin told him, tilting her chin as she pushed at him. "You don't have to eat any cookies. I can manage to eat every one of them, Mr. Yarborough."

"Aw, I was just teasin' you a little, ma'am," he drawled, bending to rub his nose against hers. "I knew right off those were angels and Christmas trees."

"Stars. Angels and stars," she retorted, scooping up the plate from beneath his nose.

"Stars. Right, that's what I meant." He followed her across the room to the shelf where she placed the plate. "You don't want to leave them there, honey. They're too far from the supper table."

"They're for Christmas."

"That's tomorrow, but doggoned if it doesn't feel like Christmas tonight," he told her, sliding from his coat.

"Stars are bright as fireworks, and that big one over to the east is shining like a house afire. You suppose that's the one the wise men followed?"

"Do you believe the Christmas story, Quinn?" she asked, returning to her paper chains.

"Sure, doesn't everybody?" he asked. "I heard it from my mama when I was just a little tad. I thought it was wonderful, kind of like magic, the way the angels sang to the shepherds. Didn't you hear the story every year on Christmas Eve?"

"I imagine so, when I was small. And then I guess I lost track of it for a lot of years, when it seemed that all the promise of Christmas was wasted on fancy gifts and noisy parties."

"Well, I'd say you've come full circle. This is about as humble as it gets, Erin," Quinn said softly. "A man, a woman and a child. We've got a shed full of animals and all the stars anybody'd ever need, just shining away up there. All we need is a choir of angels."

She laughed aloud. "You've made Christmas happen for me, Quinn Yarborough. And we really don't need a choir of angels to do the trick. That one on the bed over there is all the angel I need."

He rested his hands on her waist and bent his head to look into her eyes. "My angel is right in front of me, Mrs. Yarborough. Merry Christmas." He touched her lips with care, his mouth forming to press tenderly against hers. And then he whispered the phrase again, their lips brushing as the words breathed against her mouth.

She felt her breathing accelerate, her heart thumping rapidly, and she leaned against him, lifting her arms to circle his neck. "Merry Christmas, Quinn." Her head tilted back and she pursed her mouth. "I guess after all those nice words, I ought to let you have a cookie."

"Yes, ma'am, that'd be mighty nice of you," he agreed solemnly, one hand leaving her waist to reach for the plate.

"After supper," she amended, frowning.

"Before and after," he told her, biting off an appendage. "See there, now it looks better," he said, showing her the transformed shape.

Erin shook her head. "If you only knew how hard I worked on those."

"And I certainly do appreciate your efforts," he said. "Let me show you how much." The cookie disappeared quickly as Quinn stepped to the far side of the cabin where his saddlebags were stacked.

Sifting through his belongings, he withdrew a small package and brought it back to where Erin stood near the stove. She watched, her curiosity piqued by his smile and the gift he carried. It was wrapped in silver paper, tied with a bit of red ribbon, somewhat tattered but festive nonetheless.

"I've carried this around for a long time," he told her, offering the gift on his outstretched hand. "It was my mother's. She'd want you to have it."

Erin's fingers circled the flat package. It was round, and through the paper she felt a raised carving on the edge. "May I open it?"

He shrugged. "It's close enough to Christmas, I think."

Her fingers trembled as she undid the ribbon and tucked it into her pocket. The paper held its shape well, and she worked at it, finally revealing a compact, with a clever opening.

"It's still got her face powder in it. Probably no good anymore. We can buy you some to replace it someday."

"Oh, Quinn!" Erin felt a lump rise in her throat. "I'll cherish it always." She looked into the mirror, dusty with a powdery residue, discovering a wistful, youthful expression upon her own face.

"You're prettier than she was," Quinn said quietly.

"Thank you." Erin blinked back tears, then dug into her pocket. "I have something for you, too." She offered the wrapped knife on the palm of her hand and watched as Quinn's long fingers took it from her.

He unwrapped it slowly, his eyes alight with an anticipation he made no attempt to conceal. The smooth silver knife slipped into the palm of his hand and he opened it carefully, testing the blade with his thumb.

"Your father's?" he asked, lifting his gaze to meet hers.

She nodded. "My mother gave it to me. He always kept it in his pocket. He used to peel apples for me with it."

Quinn nodded and grinned. "I can do that. I've never had a knife quite so nice, but I'll get used to it in my pocket real quick. I'll put a good edge on it tonight." He lifted her chin, curving his palm beneath it to circle her throat. Then with gentle care he kissed her, a soft, tender caress.

"Thank you. I'll take good care of it."

"I know you will," she answered. "Merry Christmas, Quinn Yarborough. Merry Christmas."

The Christmas tree held a new assortment of decorations now, propped in a snowbank in the yard. Quinn had hung Erin's suet balls on it, peppered with bits of seed and acorns he'd cracked open, hoping the birds would enjoy them. That a horde of squirrels had made away with much of the bounty was immaterial, Erin decided. The fun of watching Quinn prepare the treats had been enjoyment enough.

She'd never shared so much of herself with another human being, Erin decided. Something about Quinn, something about the sharing of a bed, perhaps even the knowledge that she was totally dependent upon his word of honor, had managed to draw from her all but the most intimate secrets of her life.

And those few, chosen memories were what he was after. She knew it. Knew that he would not be satisfied until he had uncovered the truth about her marriage to Damian Wentworth.

Each night, beneath the covers of her bed, the friendship they had formed in the darkness had drawn them further into a relationship that was without a doubt rare and unexplainable.

She had giggled against the palm of her hand, lest she waken the baby, when he'd related childhood tales of behavior better suited to rascals and scallywags.

She'd gasped in dismay when he'd told her of close escapes, of gun battles and the perils of running down men who fled the crimes they had committed. Then, when his talk turned to his childhood, the early years when he'd lived on the farm with his parents, she'd sensed the wealth of love and generosity of spirit that had formed the man who lay beside her.

She'd not been so generous with her own memories, but he'd managed to pry one after another from her, coaxing and cajoling her until she related the doubts and fears of a young woman, pressured to conform to what society expected of her.

Damian was out-of-bounds. There she had drawn the

line. Whether she felt disloyal to a husband's memory, or whether she was loath to destroy whatever good thoughts Quinn Yarborough still held for his childhood friend, she did not know.

No matter. Either way, she had boxed that part of her life into a tightly wrapped package, and the thought of exploring it, let alone opening it to another's view, was not to her liking.

"Are you awake?" Quinn's voice came from the darkness beside her, and Erin felt the slow thumping of her heart increase. That the sound of his rough inquiry could so affect her was a puzzle she had yet to solve. Rather, she allowed herself to enjoy the moments with him, aware of the arousal of her senses, admitting to herself that she became more enamored of his presence every day and night.

"Hmm..." It was an answer of sorts, but apparently it satisfied him, for he turned in the bed to face her.

"I've been thinking."

Her smile was teasing and its tone was repeated in her voice. "No! Surely not!"

He grunted, as if her words had scored. "You're pretty flip for a little girl all alone with a man on the side of a mountain," he whispered, his words rasping just inches from her ear.

She reveled in the mood he'd set. "Someone showed me how to use a gun, sir. I can defend myself."

"You missed the can five times in a row," he reminded her.

"Ah, but at close range, I'd be a real danger."

"Well," he drawled, "right now the gun's hanging on the wall."

"Then I'll just have to depend on my wits, won't I?"

He was silent for a moment. "No, actually you're

counting on my promise to stay where I belong.'' He shifted again beside her and his hand reached for hers, skimming the quilt until he touched her shoulder, then tracing the length of her arm to clasp her fingers.

She stilled at his touch, her hand warming beneath his, pressed against the quilt. What if she'd been covered to her neck? Would he have searched beneath the covers for her?

''I think you're an honorable man, Quinn,'' she managed to say after a moment. ''I've found no reason yet to doubt your word.''

''I may not always be so agreeable, Miss Erin.'' His voice had become gruff, as if he fought a battle with his male needs.

She turned her hand within his and placed her fingers against the longer, more callused ones that held her. ''I can only put myself at your mercy, sir.''

''You're there already, honey.'' The gruff voice had become rasping as he lifted their joined fingers to his mouth and rested his lips against her knuckles for a moment. Then as if he rued his action, he cleared his throat and moved her hand to his chest. ''I think we need to talk about something else.''

''All right,'' she whispered, already missing the heat of his mouth on her skin. ''What did you want to talk about?''

''You did well with the gun, Erin. Not being afraid to pull the trigger is the main thing. Knowing that you can do it is enough to give you the strength if the need should arise.''

''I don't know if I could ever aim to kill another human being,'' she said after a moment.

''If someone threatened the baby?''

Her nostrils flared at the thought, her fingers tensing,

tightening about his. "Yes. Yes, then I could do it." It was a considered decision, one she was certain of. Should her baby be in peril, she would do whatever was necessary to protect him.

"You know that we've never named him, don't you?"

If he'd changed the subject to calm her, he'd done an admirable job, she decided, relaxing her grip on his fingers. The issue had been foremost in her mind for weeks. And yet to her, the tiny boy was "the baby," needing no other designation.

"Maybe we should," she ventured.

"He's not going to die, Erin. Naming him won't put a curse on him."

"I know that!" Her answer was quick, as if she must deny such a possibility.

Quinn was silent for a moment, and then he squeezed her hand. "Naming him should be sort of a ceremony, don't you think?"

"You mean like…"

"No." His answer was swift, knowing what she was about to say. "Not like naming John, Erin. We baptized him because it seemed the right thing to do. This little fella will be taken into church for that occasion. And that's one thing I've been thinking about."

"It's a long way to town just to take the baby to church," she said doubtfully.

"Maybe it would be a good idea to move to town during the bad weather. I'll warrant we could find a place to rent."

"Are you making plans, Quinn?" Her voice was strained, her body tense beside him, and he renewed his grip on her hand.

"No, just thinking about it. In the meantime, we ought

to consider calling him something besides the baby, don't you think? And since we've waited this long, it deserves some thought. This is going to be just for us, Erin, his family. A happy time, kind of a celebration, not like when you named John. We just need to come up with something suitable.''

Her heart lurched as he spoke the name she'd given to the tiny mite she'd borne. "I always thought I'd name my first son after my father. But there can only be one child to bear that name.''

"Surely your father had a middle name," Quinn suggested.

She thought for a moment. "That might work. I like the sound of Robert. What do you think?"

"Robert." He rolled it on his tongue, giving it an inflection, rolling the first letter deliberately. Then he laughed softly. "My mother would have spoken it that way.''

"We don't know the baby's last name, do we?"

"It will be Yarborough, honey. As soon as we get a chance to make it legal, we'll file with the court for adoption. In the meantime, I doubt anyone will be banging on the door to take him away from us.''

"I'll cook a special meal tomorrow and we can do it after supper. There are a few potatoes left and a good piece of venison. I'll make you some rice pudding." Her voice was eager as she planned her celebration, her fingers squeezing his as their hands rested against the breadth of his chest.

He leaned forward the few inches it took to touch her brow with his own. "You're sure easy enough to please, Miss Erin. Give you a pea-pickin' reason and you're all set for a party.''

"It's a baby-naming party, not some pea-pickin' rea-

son,'' she retorted smartly, tilting her head back from
his. He followed her movement, his mouth brushing hers
as he leaned against her.

It hadn't been a good idea, tasting the fresh sweetness
of her lips, he thought, with the warmth of her breasts
only an inch from his hand. He caught his breath, in-
advertently inhaling the scent of her body. The milky
flavor he'd tasted on the baby's skin had an aroma of
its own, and he found it here, rising from her breasts. It
blended with the woman scent of her, bringing him to
sudden arousal, a state he'd struggled to keep under control.

Quinn inhaled again, deeply, yearning to touch the
source of that mingled aroma she bore, his fingers tightening on hers as if he would beg her to hold him from
his goal. His mouth brushed against her face, recogniz-
ing the line of her cheek, the straight, small blade of her
nose and then rising to the smooth sweep of her forehead.

Erin stirred, moving her head slowly, and his mouth
pressed kisses on her brow. A whimper escaped her lips,
and then she whispered his name.

''Quinn?'' She murmured again, and her voice qua-
vered, her fingers trembling as they drew from his clasp.

His hand left hers, moving across her shoulder and
down, his fingers spreading wide across her back. Only
the flannel of her gown kept him from the warmth of
her body. She shivered beneath his palm and he drew
her closer, lowering his head so that his mouth touched
the delicate pulse that beat at her temple.

His nose was buried in her hair, that silken length of
magic that made his fingers itch to tangle themselves in
its depths. She'd drawn it back and braided it before
bedtime, and his eyes had followed each movement of

her agile fingers. Such beauty should not be confined, he'd thought, and now that notion filled his mind once more.

His hand moved to the nape of her neck to find the heavy plait, tracing it to its end, where a piece of yarn secured it. At a twitch of his fingers, the yarn was gone. With little urging, the braid was released, his hand working its way through the strands, unraveling the three sections.

"What are you doing?" Her whisper was uncertain as she turned her head, straining to peer over her shoulder.

"I want to touch your hair." It wasn't all he wanted to hold within his grasp, but it would do for a start.

"Why?" She sounded truly puzzled as she turned toward him again. In the darkness her face was a pale oval, barely visible, but Quinn Yarborough had never found visibility to be a barrier before.

He lowered his mouth to hers, covering her lips in a gentle taking. She was pliant beneath his touch, inhaling swiftly as if he had caught her unaware. And indeed he probably had. But after weeks in this bed, coaxing her and taming her skittish responses to his will, he found he could no longer ignore the needs of his body.

That a kiss was all he might be given was a possibility. That his errant hands might be forbidden the possession of her soft curves was probably a given. But at this point, he'd take what he could get—and like it.

The reward for his patience was within reach, and the sweet taste of Erin's mouth was worth every minute of misery he'd endured, holding his desire in check as he spent his nights at her side.

His lips softened as he enclosed the supple flesh of her mouth, holding her captive for only a moment before he released her. Then he touched her mouth with his tongue. She inhaled audibly, jerking away in an automatic response.

"Shh...I only want to taste you, sweetheart."

She stilled, then whispered one word, her mouth brushing against his as she spoke. "Why?"

Her breath was flavored with the syrup she'd eaten on her bread at supper, and he had a terrible urge to find its flavor within her mouth. "Open your mouth for me, Erin."

She shook her head, a small but definite movement.

"Haven't you ever..." He hesitated. Surely Damian had done more than press surface kisses upon his wife.

"Yes."

She sounded frightened. In that one softly whispered word he heard a warning, a sadness he could not understand.

"You didn't like it?" He pressed her for an answer, waiting as she lay motionless beside him.

"No. It was disgusting. I felt like I'd suffocate before he let me loose. It made me gag, and then—" She shuddered, an involuntary movement, and Quinn closed his eyes in remorse.

"I'm sorry, honey. Sometimes men get carried away, I suspect."

Erin's eyes closed as she recalled the big bed in New York City, the man who'd held her beneath him and pushed his tongue against the back of her throat, her mouth wide beneath the pressure of his. It was beyond bearing, the humiliation and pain of being used with such cruelty.

"I'd never hurt you, Erin." He waited for her response, but it was long in coming. "Don't you trust me?"

"I've lived with a man before, Quinn. I know what men do when they get carried away, and I vowed I'd never let a man do that to me again."

"You trusted me enough to let me in your bed, honey," he reminded her.

"I didn't have much choice, as I recall."

His silence acknowledged her words.

"I'm sorry, Quinn. That's not true. I allowed it, and I could have been the one to sleep on the floor."

Not likely, he thought. Some way, he'd have kept her within reach. "You slept in Damian's bed."

"Again, I had no choice."

"What did he do to you, honey? Did he hurt you?" For the first time, he was touching the surface of her memories, and he held his breath as he waited.

"He hurt me. Oh, yes! He hurt me. And called it lovemaking." The words were whispered, but bitter with remembrance, and he closed his eyes against the barrier she set in place.

"It doesn't have to hurt. It shouldn't hurt."

Her strained laughter called him a liar, even as she smothered the sound against his shoulder. "I'll never believe that."

"I won't try to persuade you tonight."

Her body shivered, then relaxed as she considered his words. "Isn't that what you've been doing?"

"Maybe. Let's make a deal here. Just let me kiss you, Erin. Let me show you how a man kisses the woman he cares for."

She was quiet, and he could only hope that in some way she was tempted to allow him what he asked. She'd enjoyed his touch. He'd known enough women to recognize her acceptance of his hands against her.

"Erin?" He found her chin and tilted her face upward,

lowering his mouth to touch gently against her face. It was damp, and he tasted the salty flavor of her tears. A groan escaped him, a frustrated moan of thwarted desire, and he acknowledged defeat. He would push no further.

"Are you afraid of me?" If she should nod or whisper a response filled with fear, he would leave her beneath the quilts and seek the dubious comfort of the floor before the stove.

Her hesitation had him rising from the bed, and only the quick touch of her hand against his back as he rose halted his progress. "Please...don't leave, Quinn. Please!"

He sank back on the side of the bed, his feet already cold from the wooden floor. "I don't want to frighten you, Erin."

"I like your kisses," she whispered. "I'm just fearful of what comes after."

He turned his head, seeking her face in the darkness. Her hand fell away from his back and he missed the small presence, the warmth it had engendered against him. "Nothing will come afterward, Erin. Nothing that causes you fear or pain."

Her laughter was strained. "I'm trying so hard to trust you, Quinn. I want to."

He moved cautiously, edging beneath the covers once more and then drawing her into his embrace. She was stiff, unbending in his arms, and her breath came in rasping sobs. Quinn enclosed her in his arms, careful to hold her without undue pressure, allowing her a distance between their bodies.

"If he were still alive, I'd hunt Damian Wentworth down and thrash him within an inch of his life," he muttered against her hair.

Erin shivered in his arms. "It was as much my fault

as his, Quinn. I'm just not the kind of woman he needed.''

''And what kind was that?''

Her shoulders moved in a shrug. ''Someone who enjoyed lovemaking, I suppose. He liked women with…full figures.''

Quinn closed his eyes, his memory finding no fault with the slender form of the woman in his arms. ''You're more than enough woman for me, Erin. You're shapely in all the right places.''

''I am?'' As if she sought reassurance, her words were mournful, and he smothered a chuckle.

''One of these days you're going to let me show you how much of a woman you are, honey.'' At that pronouncement, he shifted away from her, his arousal becoming more apparent.

She rolled to her back. ''If you want to, Quinn…I won't turn you away. I know you have needs and you have the right to…''

''It's not going to be that way, Erin.'' His teeth gritting, he took a deep breath, damning his own forbearance. ''I'm willing to wait.'' His eyes closed as he uttered the lie. He was far from willing, hovering on the edge of desire, but not for the world would he take on the guise of the husband she had feared.

Beside the bed the baby stirred, whimpered once, then was silent again. ''He'll be waking up soon,'' Quinn predicted. ''You need to get some sleep.''

Erin turned from him to peer over the side of the bed. ''I think he's sucking his thumb. Can you believe that?'' Her whisper was filled with humor as she settled down against her pillow once more.

Beneath his breath Quinn grunted words that eluded

her ear and she turned her head in his direction. "Quinn?"

His hand reached to pat her shoulder. "Go to sleep," he muttered.

She hesitated for only a moment, then turned her back to him and tugged the blanket over her shoulder. "Good night."

His mouth twisted wryly. Not likely. Not damn likely.

Chapter Nine

"It's going to be nice out this morning," Quinn announced.

"Really?" Erin stepped to his side, peering out the window at the fragile winter sunlight. "You don't think it'll snow today?"

"Sure doesn't look like it to me. I'd say we're going to have a break in the weather." Quinn sat to pull on his boots, then shrugged his heavy coat into place. "I'll do the chores and see if I can scrape some of the snow aside so the horses can graze. They need to get out of the barn."

"Will you tether them?" Erin asked, wishing for a moment she could join in the proceedings. The snow glittered, an unbroken expanse in the small meadow, reminding her of girlhood memories.

"Want to help?" Quinn asked, his hand on the latch, his gaze watchful, as if he had ascertained her yearning.

She shook her head. "I can't leave the baby."

"Sure you can. You just fed him a while ago and he's sound asleep."

"Do you need help?" Even to her own ears Erin sounded hopeful.

"Tell you what," Quinn bargained with a grin. "You come out and give me a hand and I'll do my share of cooking breakfast when we come back inside."

She nodded, already heading for the corner where her clothing was stashed. "Go on ahead. I'll pull on my britches first." On her knees, she dug for the pants she'd not worn for weeks. Quinn was gone when she looked up. In moments Erin was ready, a flannel shirt tucked into the denim trousers, her belt pulled tightly around her waist to hold them up.

The sun, fully over the slope of the mountain, greeted her as she closed the door behind her. She'd left the coffeepot filled with water on the stove to brew. They'd be more than ready for a cup after tending to the stock.

Erin's legs stretched to full length as she attempted to follow in Quinn's footsteps, and she laughed aloud, teetering on one foot. Then, up to her knees in fresh snow, she made her own path, slogging along contentedly.

Standing in the doorway of the shed, Quinn watched her, the horses close behind him, nosing his back. She waved as he stepped out, leading the animals behind him toward the edge of the meadow. "Sure hope the frost isn't too deep, so I won't have trouble driving these spikes into the ground," he called to her, halting to pound with firm, ringing blows on the first tether. He looked up with a grin as he stood erect. "No trouble with that one."

Standing stock-still, Erin watched him, absorbed with the picture he presented, invigorated by the fresh air and the warmth of the wintry sun. She would still have been beating on that iron stake, she thought as he moved thirty feet or so farther with the other horses. There was something to be said about having a man in residence.

He straightened, flashing her a wide grin, and she responded, aware of a quivering in her depths. So easily he could bring forth a response. Those dark eyes and his warm smile penetrated her defenses with hardly any effort on his part.

He's my husband. The thought burst from her and she gave it voice. "He's my husband." It whispered in the still air, and she watched him continue his task. His wide shoulders flexed as he hefted the heavy hammer the final time, and she noted the taut line of his coat across his muscled back.

He was strong, capable and kind. With a grateful heart she lifted her gaze beyond the treetops, where surely God dwelt. Her lips barely moving, Erin spoke words of thanksgiving.

It had been months since her feet had crossed the threshold of a church. Even her marriage vows had been spoken without the benefit of an altar or any of the ceremony usually associated with such a sacrament. But now, for the naming of her child...for this event, she needed the comfort of tradition.

"Robert. She tasted the word, allowing it to roll over her tongue, as Quinn had done. It was right for the boy. That they name him within the walls of their home was just cause for celebration. She agreed with Quinn on that point. But sometime soon they would take the child to town, place him in the hands of the young minister and observe the ancient ritual of the church.

"You're deep in thought." Quinn stood before her and she blinked, looking up at him, the sun a halo around his head. He'd snatched the wide-brimmed hat from its place, and his dark hair molded his scalp, etching the strong lines of his face into sharp detail. His eyes were bold, assessing her openly, scanning the length of her body, then coming to rest on her uplifted face.

"You're lovely, Mrs. Yarborough. You look good in the sunshine. Makes your hair shimmer like moonbeams are caught up in it, just glistening beneath the surface."

Erin felt the blush rise from her throat and looked away from his dark gaze. "You sound like a poet," she said. "I'm sure I resemble nothing more than a walking ragbag." She looked down at her baggy trousers, the oversize boots, and then, clutching the front of her bulky coat, she held it together across her breasts.

"I know what I see." His words were a gentle rebuke, and one big hand lifted to touch a lock of hair that curled against the side of her face.

She flinched, just for a second caught off guard by the movement of his hand. His fingers tangled in the soft skein and his breath caught for a moment, then he released it in an audible sigh.

"You thought I was going to…"

"No!" She shook her head. "You startled me, that's all."

"You'll learn," he said quietly. "You'll find that my hands will never bring you pain, Erin."

The sun lost its brilliance for a moment as a cloud scudded across its face, and Erin felt the loss of its warmth. So quickly, the memories of Damian returned, dampening the pleasure she'd found in this moment. She lifted her chin defiantly. She'd not allow it. Remnants of the past could not be given space in such a glorious day.

"I trust you, Quinn," she told him, meeting his gaze, her mouth trembling only a bit as she smiled. Her hand rose to touch the side of his face, her fingers smoothing the beard he'd allowed to cover his jaw.

He turned his head, his mouth brushing her palm quickly. "Do you?"

Her gaze faltered and she relinquished the comfort of his touch, plunging her hands into the depths of her pockets. "I'll take care of the chickens. I'm sure there are eggs to be gathered."

"I brought the milk pail out and left it in the shed," he told her. "If you want to tend to the cow, I'll shovel a path for us and get some of the snow off the roof."

Another chore she'd never have been able to take care of on her own, she admitted silently. That the snow should be scraped from the roof was a certainty. Alone, she'd never have thought of the necessity of such a task. She'd been more than foolish to think she could survive here in the dead of winter on her own.

The hens were happy to see her, their greedy squawking noisy in the shed as she spread feed on the ground for them. Quickly she gathered the eggs, setting them aside to take to the house, then broke the layer of ice on the watering dish so the noisy hens could drink their fill.

The cow was next, and Erin welcomed the warmth of the Jersey's udder against her hands. The pail sang with twin sprays of milk, and she watched as the level rose, foaming and frothing.

The chickens pecked and drank, tossing their heads back to swallow, lifting their feet high as they picked and chose what they would eat from the bounty she had provided them. It was a homely task, one she'd performed often, but not of late. She spoke to her animals, becoming acquainted with them anew.

"I could be starving to death, and you'd still be out here talkin' to a bunch of hens," Quinn said accusingly from the half-open door. His grin belied his words, and she answered it in kind.

"It pays to be nice to the cow. Look at all the milk she gave," Erin said, lifting the pail.

Quinn took it from her hand, his leather glove brushing against her fingers. It was cold and wet from the snow and she brushed her damp fingers against her coat. "I could have carried it," she told him, following him out, the basket of eggs swinging from one hand.

He shut the door with his free hand and cast her a glance of approval. "I know that. You can do about anything you set your mind to. But while I'm around, you don't have to be lifting or carrying the heavy stuff."

He was doing his best to make her comfortable with him. Erin recognized his method, and smiled as she followed him to the cabin, stepping easily on the narrow path he'd shoveled. Quinn Yarborough took his duties as husband seriously, and if she was half as smart as she thought she was, she'd do well to allow him full sway.

Quinn held the cabin door open and nodded his head, motioning her to step inside. It was warm, the scent of coffee filling her nostrils. The sound of the baby nuzzling and snuffling caught her attention. She stripped from boots and coat rapidly, then rubbed her hands together to warm them before she touched the tightly wrapped bundle that awaited her attention.

Blue eyes blinked, lids squeezing together, then focused on her face, and she felt a thrill that brought tears to her eyes as she gathered him to her breast. His small noises spoke to a part of her she hadn't known existed, and she whispered nonsense words in return as she carried him to where Quinn was taking the coffeepot from the stove.

"I think he knows my voice," she said softly, never taking her eyes from the miniature face.

"I wouldn't be a bit surprised," Quinn agreed, his own gaze focused on the cups he'd snatched from the shelf and was filling with the hot brew. He glanced up at Erin as he replaced the pot and his gaze softened, taken with the sheer wonder of her.

She glowed with the inner beauty of a mother, he decided. To have those blue eyes aim that much love in his direction would be something to strive toward. A week ago he'd have been satisfied with her passion.

Now he sought more, and it was a selfish seeking. That his own heart was ripe for the taking was not a certainty in his mind. He'd never loved a woman, not in the purest sense of the word. But he thought that this woman claiming his affections and causing him to pledge an undying promise of eternal love was beginning to be a possibility.

"Why don't I hold him while you cook breakfast?" Quinn asked, extending his arms. "He's just lookin' for a little attention, don't you think?"

Erin's eyes crinkled at the corners as she relinquished the baby. "You're just lookin' to get out of cooking," she said with a laugh, then watched as the wide palms curved to hold the small bundle. Quinn settled into the rocker and held the child upright before him so that they could look eye-to-eye. His mouth pursed as he tilted his head to one side and made soft clicking sounds with his tongue, then murmured softly as the tiny forehead creased and the blue-eyed boy peered at the man who held him.

"Can we arrange with the preacher to baptize him?" Erin asked. She placed the bacon neatly in her skillet as she spoke, and Quinn glanced her way.

"I've been thinking I need to go to town. Maybe I can kill two birds with one stone. I need to let my partner know where I am. It's been over three months since I wired him. He'll be thinking I've disappeared from the face of the earth."

"Haven't you?" Erin lifted a brow as she set the iron frying pan at the front of the stove, then began breaking eggs into a bowl. "You're about as far from civilization as can be. Where were you when you contacted him last?"

"Denver." He leaned forward to plant a soft kiss on the baby's cheek, and the small head bobbled forward. "Watch it there, boy!" Quinn leaned him back a bit, resting the wobbly neck against his palm.

"Won't Ted and Estelle be wondering where you are?" Erin asked, studiously minding the stirring of her eggs.

Quinn shot a glance at her. "Could be. Guinan will tell them what they need to know."

"Guinan?"

"My partner," he said.

"Will you tell him you're married?"

Quinn shook his head. "He doesn't need to know that right now. I'll wire him that I've located you, and that weather conditions prevent traveling."

Erin bit at her lip. "When are you going?"

"Not today, that's for sure. This is the day we name the baby and eat that big dinner you promised me. If the weather stays clear tonight, I'll get up early and head down the mountain in the morning."

"Can you send a wire from Pine Creek?"

"Don't know why not. I'll only be gone a day, Erin," he said, finally noticing her hesitant manner. "Are you afraid to be left alone?" The rocking chair came to a halt, and he turned the baby to rest in the crook of his elbow.

"No, of course not." She tossed her head and lifted a loaf of bread from the shelf. Her knife slashed quickly, felling slices to rest on the table. The bacon was sizzling nicely and she turned it with deft movements of her fork, then lifted her coffee cup to drink.

"Erin? Are you sure?"

She nodded, still not looking at him, her attention focused on the bowl of eggs she stirred.

"I won't leave if there's something bothering you." He rose from the chair, carrying the baby to his small crib and placing him carefully within.

"I just feel uneasy," she admitted slowly. "And I don't know why. I've been here alone before." She turned the bacon again and lifted it out to drain on a piece of brown paper. She poured the grease from the pan into an empty tin, then dumped the eggs into the skillet, stirring them as they began to cook.

"I think I'm just being foolish." If her smile was meant to be reassuring, it missed the mark as far as Quinn was concerned. He took the butter from the shelf and placed it on the table, then carried the plates to where she stood at the stove.

"Here, dish those eggs up before you stir them to death," he told her.

She complied and added bacon to both plates. Coffeepot in hand, she turned toward the table, filled both cups and sat down in her chair. "I'll fix dinner early tonight," she told him, buttering a piece of bread. "You'll want to get the chores done and get to bed early if you're going to get up before dawn."

"You're not a foolish woman, Erin." Quinn took a bite of egg and broke a piece of bacon in half. "If you have any hesitation about me leaving you, I won't go."

She smiled, this time a bit more convincingly. "I'll be all right, truly I will. I'll clean the cabin and do up the wash. You won't have to dodge the diapers hanging on the line for a change."

He nodded, already thinking of the supplies he would carry back up the mountain. Already thinking of the wire he would send to Joel Guinan.

"It was beautiful, Quinn. The way you named him and held him between us, so we could both hold him." Erin sighed deeply, thinking of the small ceremony Quinn had devised for the giving of Robert's name. The middle name had been an inspiration on her part, and Quinn had been pleased with his inclusion. Robert Quinn Yarborough.

"Quite a handle for a little fella." His low chuckle was followed by a moment's silence as he blew out the lamp over the table and made his way to the bed.

"He'll grow into it." Erin lay flat on her back and watched as Quinn drew back the covers and found his place beside her.

"He's getting bigger every day," Quinn agreed.

"The sky is clear. The moonlight is so bright, it's like a lamp in the window." Erin breathed a sigh. "You'll be going early on, won't you?" And then as if she would encourage him, she planned for the morning departure. "I think you should just leave as soon as you eat something, and I'll tend to the stock later, after the sun comes up."

He disagreed and turned toward her. "The earlier I milk and feed, the earlier you can take care of the animals tomorrow night. I don't want you outside after dark."

"You'll be home about dark, won't you?" She moved toward the edge of the bed, anchoring the quilt across her breasts, leaving a space between them.

"Where are you going, Erin? I thought we had this all sorted out. You don't have to hug the edge of the bed that way.'' Quinn's long arm reached out and hauled her closer to where he lay. ''I'm going to put my arm around you and you're going to lie there and keep warm. All right?''

She nodded. ''All right.'' He'd pulled her beside him, and the weight of his forearm was across her stomach, leaving her no place to put her own hands. She slid them beneath the covers, tugging the sheet to cover her shoulders.

''I'm going to kiss you good-night.''

Erin turned her head, watching as he lifted himself, his hand sliding to the bed, holding himself above her. He lowered his head, his lips seeking and finding hers. She felt his warm breath against her, the pressure of his mouth making itself known. His tongue was circumspect tonight, she noted, remaining inside his lips.

''Can you kiss me back?'' As if gravel lined his throat, he rasped the words, their lips almost touching.

She drew in a breath, then nodded. ''Yes...'' The single word was whispered between dry lips, and she slid one hand from beneath the covers to press it against his face. Her fingers traced the whiskers that covered the firm line of his jaw, then moved to bury themselves in his hair. She pressed firmly against his scalp and he accepted her invitation.

It was a gentle meeting of mouths, and she sensed a withholding on his part again, as if he would not seek a greater intimacy. His lips were warm, his breath faintly scented with the peppermint candy he'd eaten after supper. She pressed her mouth once, then again, to his, and relaxed back against her pillow, feeling less than pleased by the process.

''Best you can do?'' he teased in that rasping whisper.

''I don't know any other way to kiss you.'' Except

for what had passed for loving during her marriage, and that she'd rather never experience again. Damian's mouth had all but eaten hers, teeth and tongue leaving her bruised and nauseated more often than not.

"Can I show you another way?" He waited, hovering over her as if the night were endless and he had nowhere to go in the morning. "I promise not to...do the other, the part that frightened you."

"Yes, if you like." She could not refuse him, could not turn down the gentle approach of this stranger she'd married.

If she'd thought that kissing was a task to be performed for her husband's sake, Quinn's touch gave lie to that theory. If her memories had prepared her for a painful invasion, she was soon relieved of that threat. She had never known such tender touches could come from a man's mouth, that such pleasure could be found in the meshing of lips.

"Was that better than last night?" he asked, resting on his forearms over her.

She nodded, aware of tingling lips and a damp spot beneath her ear where his mouth had claimed the flesh.

"When I go to town tomorrow, will you think of me?"

Her heart sped at his words. She'd almost forgotten, caught up in the mystery of his tenderness. "I'll think of you. Of course." It felt like a vow, the words a promise she would have no trouble keeping.

Quinn had left at dawn, just before the sky turned pink at the edges. With an uplifted hand, he'd ridden into the trees, the packhorse behind him, his coat collar pulled high to warm his neck. His hat sat at an arrogant angle and his dark eyes gleamed with a fire that made her body shiver and her mouth soften.

The baby took her attention, and Erin fed him, then washed him before the stove, drying his round little body and dropping a multitude of kisses across the top of his head.

She sang as she rocked him, an assortment of old hymns she remembered from childhood, humming when the words eluded her. And then when the water on the stove sent steam rising, she placed him reluctantly on her bed, pillows on either side to hold the heat next to his sleeping form.

Before long she had a line zigzagging across the cabin, from behind the stove to the doorway and back, leaving her ducking and weaving as she hung the small diapers and simple gowns the baby wore.

"I need to begin calling you Robert," she sang out, her eyes on the wrapped infant as he slept upon her bed. Humming, and concentrating on washing one of Quinn's shirts at the scrub board, Erin almost missed the sound of a horse nickering in the clearing. Coming to attention, she let her hands still as she listened.

The thud of boots across her porch jolted her upright and the sound of a fist against her door drained every bit of blood from her head. Erin swayed where she stood, swallowing great gulps of air. Someone—more than one someone, from the sounds of it—was intent on entering the cabin.

"Open the door, ma'am. We know you're in there." The voice was harsh, an overlying humor lending it hor-ror.

"What do you want?" She was amazed at the strident sound of her words, and new strength pumped into her arms as she stepped quickly to the wall, lifting the gun from its place.

"Just a bit of breakfast, ma'am. We saw your man on the trail—thought you might be lonely."

"It's long past breakfast time," she called, her fingers frantic as she checked to be sure that both barrels were loaded. Quinn had prepared it for use and she calmed as she thought of his words.

Knowing you can do it is enough to give you the strength, if the need should arise....

Her breathing slowed as she remembered his words. Quinn had faith in her. In her hands the wooden stock was cool, and she hefted it, liking the balance. Then, with deliberation, her finger curled over the triggers.

"Go away, there's nothing for you here."

Whispers caught her ear, then a raucous laugh as if the men considered a private joke. Probably at her expense, she thought, a spurt of anger lending her courage.

The footsteps left the porch and Erin moved to the window, watching as two men ambled toward her shed. They came out after only a moment, one leading her cow, the other her riding horse, her white socks flashing as she jerked against the stranger holding her halter.

"Ma'am?" The bigger of the two men grinned widely, his pistol held in one hand, its barrel aimed at the middle of her cow's broad forehead. "How would you like me to fetch you a nice beefsteak for dinner?"

His intent was clear, and Erin pushed the curtain back to watch as his gun threatened her milk supply. The cow lifted her head and uttered her own opinion.

"She's beggin' for her life, ma'am," the shorter, stockier man called, his laughter an obscene cackle.

"And then we got this here other animal of yours. Be too bad if you couldn't get to town anymore, wouldn't it, with no horse to ride.'' The pistol shifted its aim, and as if she sensed the danger, her horse sidestepped, jerking the rope, causing the smaller man to stumble awkwardly.

''Damn, don't make me mad at you, horse!'' His collection of curse words flowed in a river of filth over the animal, and Erin strode to the doorway.

She opened the door and stood beneath the portal, shotgun cocked and cradled in her arms. ''Put my animals away and I'll put bread and meat on the porch for you.''

''Now, that don't sound too neighborly to me.'' The shorter, scruffier intruder grinned widely. ''What do you think, Russell?''

''I think the lady needs some manners, that's what I think,'' Russell answered.

''That's my best offer,'' Erin shouted, stepping just outside the door, the gun still at her side. Somehow she must keep these men away from the baby, out of the cabin. She stiffened her spine and aimed the shotgun. ''Come any closer and I'll shoot.''

''Damned if the lady don't look right purty, now, don't she?'' Ignoring her warning, Russell dropped the rope he'd tied to the cow's halter, and headed in her direction. His gun hung loosely at his side, as if he mocked the weapon she carried.

From behind her the baby whimpered, then gathered a breath, announcing his displeasure with a wail that reached beyond the cabin door. Erin's heart skipped a beat as she allowed a quick glance toward the bed behind her.

''Hush, sweetie,'' she whispered, even as the cries escalated into an angry squall.

"Sounds like a young'un in there!" shouted the man near the shed.

"I declare, it surely does," Russell agreed. "I'll warrant you wouldn't want anything to happen to that baby, now, would you, ma'am?" He paused, close enough to the cabin that Erin was sure she could smell the stench of his grimy clothing.

His grin was a mockery. "How about it, honey? Got some breakfast for a hungry man?"

"I won't let you in here." Erin ground out the words.

He spat into the snow, then grinned at her again, broken, discolored teeth visible beneath his ragged mustache. "Be a shame if something happened to you, and that brat was left here all alone, wouldn't it?"

"I'll shoot if you come any closer," Erin warned.

"Aw, I don't think so, ma'am. I think you're gonna behave and do just what I tell you, lessen that baby gets hurt."

"Go on, Russell," the other man yelled. "I'll shoot the horse if she gives you a fuss."

With a disgusted look over his shoulder, Russell took another step, and Erin felt her heartbeat slow, even as she tightened her grip on the trigger. His glance at her weapon was scathing, and he laughed again. "Guess I'll have to take you up on your hospitality, ma'am. I'll just leave Toby there to look after your stock while I come in and keep you company for a while."

A quick glance at the second man allowed Erin a glimpse into eyes that burned with evil, and she found herself faced with little choice.

No choice, in fact. Animals be damned.

"I warned you," she whispered harshly. With a swift clenching of her muscles, the gun was fired. From twenty feet away the spread was narrow, and he caught the full force of her first shell in his chest.

She glanced toward Toby as she backed into the cabin's doorway, only too aware of the limitations of her weapon at such a distance. He cursed loudly, dropping the lead rope he held, his hands scrabbling at the holster hanging at his side.

"I wouldn't do that. I have another shell with your name on it," she called, her voice wintry.

"You'd never hit me from this far away," he taunted.

"Try me."

Hesitating, he shook his head. "Naw, I ain't that much of a fool!" His movement was abrupt as he shoved his barely drawn gun back into the holster. "Hell, old Russell ain't worth it," he announced. "And you ain't either, lady." With a last glance at his companion, Toby headed for his mount, even as Erin stepped back into the cabin.

In front of her the snow was stained with copious amounts of blood. The big man's hands clenched and opened in a repeated movement that told her he was still alive, and she swallowed the bile that threatened to spill from her throat.

Another backward step took her inside and she slammed the door shut, lowering the bar and stepping to the window. Toby had scrambled to the side of the shed where two horses waited, and with a final look at the body of his friend, he hoisted himself atop his saddle and rode off, leading the other horse behind.

Erin drew in a deep breath, lowering the barrel of her gun, easing her finger from the second trigger. Beyond the mutilated body in her yard, her animals stood, the horse moving restlessly, pawing with one hoof at the snow. The cow, lifting her head to sound her distress once more, turned and made her way back into the shed.

Erin shivered, aware that the baby had stilled his crying, leaving only the sound of her heart beating in her ears to break the enormous silence. A trembling such as she had never known seized her body, and she bent to place the shotgun on the floor, uncertain if she had enough strength to hang it back on the wall.

"I have to take care of the horse," she whispered. "I can't let her run off."

Her coat was heavy in her hands and she slipped into it woodenly, quickly glancing at the silent baby before she opened the door. There was a risk to be taken, walking across the open yard. But her sensible mind told her that Toby was long gone, his bravado having vanished with the death of his partner.

The sight of the man sprawled just a few feet away drained her courage, and she hesitated. Moving any closer to that still form made her stomach churn, but the thought of her horse making her way down the mountain was an incentive she could not ignore.

Erin sidestepped the outstretched hand, its fingers spread wide, limp and lifeless now. Near the shed, her horse watched her, tossing her head at Erin's approach. Erin tugged on her rope and the mare obligingly turned back to the warmth of her stall. There she quickly tied the cow in place, then closed the door behind her, making her way back to the cabin.

Leaning against the barred door, she drew a deep breath, faced with the prosaic lines of laundry crisscrossing the room. Quinn's shirt lay across the scrub board where she'd left it only minutes before, and on the bed the baby moved within his cocoon of blankets. As if nothing had happened, her world inside this building awaited her return.

As if nothing had happened.

Chapter Ten

It was done. He'd backed out of the deal, wired Joel Guinan with explicit instructions for handling Ted Wentworth. His business was safe in Guinan's hands for now. And Ted and Estelle had no hold on him, once the retainer was returned.

On top of that, Erin was waiting for him. He smiled and urged his horse ahead.

The cabin was dark, as he approached, only a wisp of smoke coming from the chimney. Just in front of the porch a body lay, dark against the white snow beneath it. With a muffled exclamation, Quinn swung from his horse, dropping his reins to the ground. Heart pounding at an unmerciful rate, he bent beside the still form, knowing even as he did that it was not Erin, but a man.

Quickly his gaze swept the clearing, taking in the hoofprints, dark in the moonlight. Then, swiveling, he headed for the porch. The door was latched and he listened, holding his breath as he pressed his ear to the rough wood.

"Erin!" It was hushed, more than a whisper, yet contained. "Erin!" He spoke again, listening lest he miss any sound from within.

A tiny whimper caught his ear and his heart leapt. "Open the door, sweetheart. Let me in. I don't want to break it down."

"Quinn!" It was a pleading sound, his name spoken as he'd never heard it uttered, and his heart clenched within his chest.

"Open the door, Erin." It was an order now, as if he sensed he must gain her attention in this way. From inside, he heard the creak of the rocking chair, then the soft shuffle of footsteps across the floor. Finally the door moved beneath his hand as she lifted the latch, and he pushed it open.

She was there, a slender figure in the dark, visible only because her dress was washed in the moonlight from behind him. Quinn brushed past her, his relief alive in his throat. First he had to light the lamp. Then he could look at her, assess the damage.

As he lit a match, the bundle she held in her arms stirred, and the whimper of a waking baby relieved one of his worries. He raised the lamp's wick, lighting it quickly before he replaced the globe. From the corner of his eye he saw Erin lift the child and pat his back, the lamp glow etching her in its halo of light.

"Are you all right?" He walked back to close the door and then stripped off his coat. His hands felt like blocks of ice, and he hesitated, not wanting to touch her with cold fingers, yet feeling an urgent need to hold her against himself.

She took the choice from him, her stumbling steps gaining her his embrace as she flung herself into his arms. With the baby between them, Quinn held Erin, his hands running up and down her back, around to her sides. Then he cradled her head in his big palms.

"You're all right?" He knew she was safe, unhurt, yet the assurance must come from her lips.

She nodded, her head pressed against his chest. "Yes."

From outside, his horse neighed, a protest against being left alone in the clearing. And close behind, another nicker added its complaint.

"I must put the horses in the shed," he told her, even as his arms slid to hold her closely. "I'll be right back. Do you hear me? I'll only be a couple of minutes."

"I haven't milked," she whispered. "The cow will be in misery by morning."

Quinn nodded. "I'll take care of it. Will you be all right for a little while?"

"Yes." She stepped back, relinquishing the warmth of his body, and stumbled to the rocking chair. "I'll feed the baby." She looked up at him and her eyes were wide. "I called him Robert today."

Quinn shivered at her tone and her mannerisms. As if she were oblivious to the carnage in the yard, she settled herself to nurse the child. He pulled his coat back on, with a last glance assuring himself of her physical well-being.

She was still in the chair when he came back in, a bucket of milk in his hand, a heavy bundle across his back. "I brought in some of the supplies, Erin. The rest can wait till morning."

She rocked, humming beneath her breath, and he hurried with his task, placing the milk pail on the sinkboard and leaving the supplies near the door. The fire burned down, and he loaded the stove with four chunks of wood before he hung his coat and removed his boots.

Still she rocked, and Quinn rubbed his hands together

as he neared the chair. "Let me take the boy, Erin. He's asleep."

She handed him the warm bundle and Quinn's hands enclosed the child, lifting the baby to his face to press his mouth against the fair skin at the fragile temple. Robert smelled clean and milky and his eyes squinted tightly closed. With a shushing sound, Quinn placed him in his crib and drew Erin's shawl over him.

She'd risen from the chair and watched him from empty eyes. "I shot a man, Quinn. You told me I could if I had to."

His mouth opened, then closed. There was no comfort to be offered, no pat phrases to be spoken. She'd taken a life, and the pain of it was eating away at her.

"He would have hurt me, and maybe the baby, too. I couldn't let him, could I?"

"No, you couldn't let him, honey. You did the right thing." Quinn held out his arms and she came to him. Enclosed in his embrace, she shuddered, her body trembling against him.

"Will God forgive me, do you think?"

Anger at the loss of her innocence swept through him. Never should a woman need to defend herself in such a way. The taking up of a weapon was man's business, had been since the beginning of time. A woman should be kept safe, secure within the walls of her home.

And today he had left her to fend for herself, had taken the trip down the mountain, leaving her a prize for the taking. Only the courage contained within that slim body had kept her and the babe from harm. Guilt tightened his grip, and he bent over her as if his body could shield her from her own pain.

"You did what you had to, Erin. Defending yourself

is never wrong. You committed no sin against man or God.''

"I pulled the trigger, Quinn. He wasn't even aiming his gun at me. I didn't give him a chance. I just lifted the shotgun and pulled the trigger.''

"He took his chances when he came here looking for trouble.'' His mind swept back to the flurry of tracks by the shed. "Was he alone?''

She shook her head. "No, a man named Toby was with him. They were going to shoot the cow and my horse if I didn't let them in the house. He said they wanted something to eat.'' Erin lifted her head and her eyes were disbelieving. "I knew he was lying. I knew what he wanted.''

"He didn't touch you, did he?'' He didn't believe so, but something in him needed to hear her assurance.

"No, I shot him as he was coming up to the porch. The other one was getting ready to come at me, and I told him to come ahead, that I still had one shell left in the gun. But he must have thought better of it. He rode off. And then I had to go out and put the horse away and tie the cow in her stall.''

Quinn's hand patted at her back in an awkward fashion and he closed his eyes, shaking his head at her despair. "I'll take care of the body, Erin. He must have come from over the mountain. My guess is that they were a pair of miners from Big Bertha, just lookin' for trouble.''

"Don't leave me now. Stay with me, please.'' Her grip on him tightened and he dropped his head to bury his face in her hair.

"I'll only be outside for a few minutes, honey. Then I'll get a bite to eat before we talk.''

She shivered and levered herself away from him. "I'll find you something."

With precise movements she unloaded the supplies, dragging out the process while Quinn headed out the door. She wielded her big knife carefully, slicing bread and cutting chunks from a piece of cheese the grocer had wrapped in cloth. It was crumbly and rich smelling, and she ate a piece that fell from the knife. For the first time in hours, she felt hungry.

Quinn was true to his word, back within five minutes. "Eat something, Erin," he told her, washing his hands at the sink, splashing water over his face and smoothing his hair back with damp fingers.

"I will. I can't take a chance on losing my milk." She poured hot water from a pan into her cup and added a small sifting of tea leaves. "The cook always used to say that tea makes milk." She looked up at Quinn with a startled glance. "Isn't it strange that I should remember that now? It's been so many years..." Her voice faltered and trailed off into silence as she stirred the cup, then left it to steep.

He placed cheese on his bread and took a mouthful. It was good, the bread still fresh, the cheese strong and ripe-flavored. He watched as Erin tore her bread into bites, chewing slowly, waiting for her tea to be strong enough to drink.

She sipped the tea while he put the food away, his gaze ever watchful as she pushed at bread crumbs on the table, hovering over her as she drained the last of the tea.

Then Quinn took her arm and led her to the bed. His big hands felt clumsy as he undid the buttons on her dress. His fingers brushed it from her shoulders, and she watched as it slid down the length of her arms. Beneath it, her petticoat and chemise tempted him, and Quinn bit at his lip as he undid the small buttons and untied the ribbon that held the muslin fabric over her breasts.

"My gown," she whispered, one hand rising to halt him.

He cleared his throat and lifted her pillow, exposing the neatly folded garment. It enveloped her as he drew it over her head. Beneath it she shed the rest of her underwear. In moments she was tucked into bed, Quinn drawing the crib close to her side.

In short order he'd banked the fire, blown out the lamp and made his way to where she waited. He undressed slowly, almost reluctantly. She tempted him in a mighty way, his body more aware of her tonight than ever. But if she wanted comfort, he was ready to give it without measure.

The smooth rise of her breasts above the chemise had brought him to arousal, and he fought now against the urge that rode him. He closed his eyes, her presence in the bed an enticement he fought to resist. She was warm and softly scented, all that was womanly, tempting his hungry heart.

Yet if she should be overwrought still by the events of the day, she might well shun his touch. The thought that she would be fearful of his man's body was a possibility, and he held himself separate from her beneath the quilt. If ever he must fight the fierce need that held him in its grip, that time was now.

Erin felt the bed move, heard the ropes groan their protest as Quinn settled against the mattress. Her heart was slow, heavy within her breast, empty and bereft, with a need she could not explain abiding in the depths of her soul.

"Quinn?" She spoke his name with diffidence. "Quinn...I..."

He hesitated for only a moment, then rolled to face her, reaching out to brush the hair from her face as if it were a temptation he could not resist. Beneath his hand her flesh warmed. She embraced that heat, leaning to his touch. His face was in shadow, the moon sulking behind wispy clouds and refusing to lend its light, yet she felt the piercing scrutiny of his gaze. Her body eased closer to his.

"What is it, honey?" Once more, his voice offered comfort.

A comfort that beckoned, one she could not deny. She reached for him blindly, driven by an urgency she could only obey. His arms enclosed her and his hands spread to cover her back, brushing against her gown as he enclosed her in his embrace.

The horror of death rose before her and she winced from it, choking on the words that fell from her lips. "Please, Quinn. Help me. When I close my eyes...I see him." Her flesh was chilled, her body trembling, and she welcomed the soothing strength of his hands.

"I've got you, honey. It's all over," he whispered, drawing her nearer, forming her against the length of his body.

But it was not enough. A haze of crimson blurred her vision and she cringed from it, tears finally holding sway as she gasped out her pain. "I saw it...the blood ran down his chest when he fell. The snow...all around him."

Silently Quinn cursed as the pressure of his manhood rose, answering the movement of her body against his, making itself known, its firm length rising against her stomach. Her indrawn breath was a reaction she could not contain, and he jerked back, his big body shifting away from her.

She would not allow it, though, and her hands tightened their hold. She whimpered his name, refusing his retreat, her murmur almost smothered against his chest.

It was a plea of anguish, and he gritted his teeth, determined to banish the evidence of his need. He was washed with shame, fighting to overcome the urgency that begged for relief.

In vain he eased from her, for she followed, edging closer than before, her legs twining with his, her feet squeezing between his calves.

"Quinn!" It was a harsh sound, followed by a sob that sounded as if it were wrenched from the very depths of her.

"Shh...hush now," he whispered, giving up the struggle for distance and shifting with her to the middle of the bed. She pressed against him, her sobs shaking her body with cruel strength, and he gave himself over to stroking her back, brushing countless kisses against her forehead and cheek.

Tasting her tears, he silently cursed the men who had caused the turmoil that wrenched her soul. "Hold me closer," she begged, the whispered words adding fuel to the flame he sought to suppress.

He would live with guilt, that was a certainty. He shouldn't have left her alone. That was the crux of the matter. No matter what excuse he used, no matter how urgent the trip to town had seemed, he'd been wrong to leave her, when her senses had told her to be fearful. And he'd ignored his own instincts, that last moment upon leaving when he'd almost turned back.

"Hold me closer, Quinn!" He answered her frantic plea in the only way he knew. Easing her to her back, he spread his body atop her slender frame, holding himself from crushing her as best he could.

"Yes." She whispered the single word, closing her eyes, relishing the weight of him, clinging without restraint to the man who made himself a shield in her behalf. That he gave without care for his own comfort brought a measure of peace to her heart and Erin brushed her face against the skin of his throat, there, where his shirt was open.

Gripping him tightly, burying her pain in the solace of his embrace, she edged her arms beneath his, her fingers spreading over his back and shoulders. Yet, still, within her an emptiness yearned for another comfort, a need that cried out for what this man could give her.

With an innate knowledge that overcame the fears of her past, she recognized the craving of her flesh, and with a gasping cry she parted her legs, enclosing him in an embrace that brought a groan of protest from his lips. She shook her head against his denial.

"Please, Quinn." His manhood surged against her and he bowed his head, his muscles taut as he rose above her, searching in the dim light for her face.

"Erin...no. You don't know—"

"I need you." Her whisper was muffled, a call from her heart. In that moment she allowed the birth of a trust that went beyond the surface, that extended to the inherent need of a woman for her man. Her knees rose, tightening against his hips, and she trembled, her thighs enclosing him in that most intimate embrace.

Quinn was lost, his body almost beyond control as she moved against him. *I need you.* Her words echoed inside his head, a symphony he'd not thought to hear.

His hands slid down her sides, drawing up her gown

on the return trip, then shifting to slide his own clothing
from place.

I need you. The trust implicit in those simple words
humbled him, yet filled him with a pride he could barely
contain. She was the essence of all that was good in his
life, this small, strong woman.

And for tonight, for this moment, she was willing to
accept his strength and make it her own.

She surrounded him, the scent of her body, the touch
of her skin, soft and supple beneath his hands, bringing
him to a new knowledge of her beauty. And beneath the
surging power of his loins, the warm depth of her
woman's flesh was open to his masculine need.

Quinn moved carefully, easing his way lest he cause
a moment's pain, fighting the urge to thrust. Erin whispered her plea once more, moving beneath him, as if she
were made for his taking. He pressed within, his
breathing ragged, his eyes tightly shut, his teeth gritted
against the awesome, wonderful clenching of her flesh
as she claimed him.

It was a taste of paradise, one he'd yearned for. Yet
it was with a sense of foreboding that he took what she
offered, surging against her, in only moments spilling
his seed within her.

"Erin…" He breathed her name, dropping his head
to bury his face in her pillow. "Oh, Erin."

"It's all right," she whispered, holding him with an
urgency he could only be thankful for.

"Did I hurt you, sweetheart?" Torn between the need
for her body and the guilt of his actions, he rocked with
her in the bed, unwilling to ease from her, reluctant to
free her from his touch.

She shook her head, only a trace of the sobs that had
racked her frame just minutes past remaining. "You've

never hurt me, Quinn. You've only brought me comfort.''

If comfort was what she had gained, he could not regret what had passed between them. He could only be grateful that his own urgent need had been given ease. That he had not brought any degree of pleasure to her was a regret he would live with. An issue he would face in its season. A debt he would delight in paying when the time was right.

She moved beneath him, as if she had only just become aware that their bodies were still joined. She shifted, and he groaned, chagrined by the resurgence of his arousal.

He rose above her, gritting his teeth at the renewed desire that stirred him. It had not been enough. He'd been long without the comfort of a woman's flesh, and his desire had been spent too rapidly, leaving him yearning for a longer, slower loving that would assuage his hunger. With reluctance, he withdrew from her, regretting the loss.

She was delicate in his hands, for this moment appearing smaller, more fragile somehow, as he turned to his side, bringing her to rest against his shoulder. Pliant in his hands, Erin melded her body to his, her fingers resting on his chest. Quinn eased the covers over her shoulder and nudged her chin upward with his index finger, watching her as he lowered his head.

His kiss was fierce, his lips opening to capture hers in a taking she allowed, as if she sensed his need to possess her in this way. She was his, his woman, his wife, and he reveled in the pleasure that thought produced. She'd given herself to him, perhaps not with forethought, but with a sweet generosity he had not expected. That her feelings were in upheaval was a certainty, but that did not negate her actions.

A deep sense of satisfaction rose within him. The marriage had been well consummated, no matter the circumstances, and no power on earth would take this woman from him. Whether he was ready for a declaration of love, or only willing to admit a terrible need for her, it mattered little. The end result would be the same.

Chapter Eleven

"What will we do now?"

Quinn swallowed the coffee he'd been sipping at, wincing as it burned the length of his throat. "About what?" he asked, leaning back in his chair.

Erin turned from the stove, her cheeks flushed from the heat, her eyes dark pools of uncertainty. "About the man I killed." It was a stark statement, delivered in a flat tone that told Quinn little about her frame of mind.

Whether she merely accepted the fact that she had been forced to defend herself and the babe, or whether she was holding herself aloof from the shock of her actions, he could not tell. He sipped again at his coffee, watching her, his eyes focused on her unsmiling mouth.

"I'll take care of him, Erin. There's a choice to be made, but either way, I'll tend to it."

"The other man, Toby…I'm sure he's raising all sorts of Cain. I imagine the sheriff will be on his way to put me in jail before long."

Quinn shook his head. "I doubt it. The question will arise as to what they were doing here. I can't imagine the law will dispute your right to defend yourself."

She breathed deeply and carried the skillet to the table,

her skirt brushing against Quinn's trousers as she spooned gravy over his biscuits. He relished the sensation, enjoying the faint scent of soap and the warmth of her body as she leaned closer to serve him.

"What are the choices?" she asked, straightening and looking down at him. Her gaze, as it had been all morning, was aimed at his shoulder.

Quinn's long arm snaked around her waist, holding her in place, not only to keep her where she stood, but because he had an urgent need to touch the woman he'd married. His fingers spread against her, and he stifled the impulse to bring her to his lap. At his touch, she'd lowered the skillet to the table, then looked at him with startled eyes.

"Quinn?" It was a breathless whisper, her mouth forming a small O before her lips pressed together.

"I don't want to leave you here alone, Erin, but I think I need to take the body back to Big Bertha and get things sorted out. Either that, or bury him here and take you and the baby to town to see the sheriff."

She was motionless, as if his touch had fused her in place.

"Which would you rather have me do? I know I said I'd take care of it, but if you're afraid to be alone here, I won't leave you."

Her eyes were grave as she finally turned them to meet his. "I'll be all right alone, if you think delivering him to the mine is the right thing to do. I have baking to do, and I didn't get the clothes folded yesterday."

She'd emptied the lines before breakfast, while he took care of the stock, and the bed was piled with the assortment of laundry.

"Come eat now," Quinn told her, releasing his hold on her. "There's no hurry, either way."

Erin served herself from the skillet, then brought sausage from the stove and sat down across the table. She sawed at her biscuit and forked a bite to her mouth. "Last night...I didn't mean to fall apart the way I..."

Quinn reached to grasp her hand. "Don't. Don't ever apologize for being human, Erin. Don't ever be sorry for turning to me. I'm your husband." He felt a smile that would not be suppressed curve his lips. "I can't tell you how pleased I was by your 'falling apart,' as you put it."

She flashed him a quick glance, drawing her hand from his grasp. "Well, I just wanted to say..." She inhaled as if drawing strength from within. "I guess thank you is sort of inadequate, but those are the only words I can think of. Not just for the comfort you gave me." She shook her head, groping for words.

"Because I didn't hurt you?" His tone was solemn, and Quinn wished fervently that she had more to be thankful for than that meager blessing.

Her eyelids fell and she concentrated on her plate. "That was no small thing, Quinn. You can't know how...different..." Her voice failed her and he waited, watching as she took a bite of food.

She was chewing slowly, and he'd be willing to bet she had no notion of what she had put in her mouth. "Different, Erin? Because I didn't cause you pain?"

At her murmur of assent, his jaw tensed. Damn, Damian Wentworth had a lot to answer for. "I want you to..." How to say it? "Look, I can only promise it will be better another time."

She looked up, startled. "Better?"

Quinn's lips curved once more in the smile he could not restrain. "Yes, much. Not for me, honey. I'm not sure it could have..." He paused, choosing his words carefully, lest he embarrass her into silence. "I want you to need me the way I need you, Erin. One day you will, not just for comfort, but for the pleasure I can give you."

If he didn't put a halt to this conversation, and right soon, he decided, he might not be able to walk away from her this morning. Already the urgency of his arousal was keeping him in place, fearful that he might frighten her with its prominence should he stand.

She nodded slowly, but with a look that clearly told him she did not comprehend his meaning.

"I'd like some more gravy," he said. "I have biscuit left over, it looks like."

"Yes, of course." She rose quickly, served him, then scraped her own plate into a pan in the sink.

"When will you leave?"

"Right away. I don't know how long I'll be, probably not more than four or five hours to head over the mountain and get back. I'll use your packhorse." He made quick work of his second helping and rose. The sooner he left, the sooner he'd be back, and that thought hurried his footsteps.

Erin watched as Quinn readied himself—his scarf covering his throat, his coat in place and his hat tugged over his forehead. He looked somber now, his smile in abeyance, as if the solemn task before him had drained his moment of good humor. Hand outstretched, he beckoned, and she stepped to where he waited by the door. His fingers were warm against hers and she fought the urge to cling to him, the need for reassurance had come to the forefront now that he was on the verge of leaving.

His head dipped, his mouth touching hers with a gentle kiss, and she found herself responding, her lips moving against his. He inhaled, and his hands pressed her shoulders, pulling her against him. Soft kisses turned to a firm possession, and Erin leaned submissively against Quinn's solid length, supported by the masculine strength of his body.

Lifting his head slowly, he opened his eyes, allowing her to see the desire he made no attempt to hide. "Will you be all right?"

She nodded, aware of the flush ridging his cheekbones, the flare of his nostrils and the heat of his appraisal.

"I'll fix dinner while you're gone. You'll be hungry."

His nod was quick, and he put her aside to take his rifle from the corner. With a mighty blast of cold air, the wind made its presence known as he opened the door, and he stepped out at once, closing it behind himself.

Erin moved to the window and watched as Quinn drew on leather gloves, then made his way to the shed. In a few minutes he led the horses out, the packhorse carrying an ominous burden wrapped in a piece of canvas. He mounted quickly, then cast a glance at the house and lifted his hand in a salute. She raised her own, spreading her fingers against the window glass, watching until he disappeared into the trees.

The snow began to drift across the front of the cabin before noon, the wind increasing in volume, whistling beneath the eaves and groaning down the chimney. Erin added wood to the fire, walking from stove to window and back as she tended her kettle of soup. Before long, the cabin was filled with the scent of baking bread, and a custard cooled on the porch.

And still Quinn did not come home.

She brought in the cold custard and settled down to nurse the baby for the third time, keeping track of the hours by the hunger of the infant. "He's been gone a long time, Robert. Over seven hours,'' she crooned, her fingers brushing back the dark hair as blue eyes watched her closely. She'd stopped singing an hour ago, having run through all the music she could remember.

Then she waited, pacing to stir the soup, covering the bread with a towel, then finally slicing a piece when her hunger nudged her to take action. Robert slept against her shoulder, and she was comforted by the warmth of his breath against her neck. But her arms ached from holding him and, with a sigh, she placed him in his bed to sleep.

Quinn would be ready for hot coffee when he came in, and the pot on the stove had been keeping warm all day. Fresh grounds were in order. Erin dumped the thick residue off the porch, clutching her shawl around her shoulders as she searched the edge of the clearing for movement. The cold was bitter and she scurried back inside, pausing only to cut free a skinned rabbit from its moorings.

Quinn had hung three from the edge of the porch roof, handy for her use. It would thaw quickly inside and she could fry it up for supper. Soup would not satisfy a man who'd gone so long without food.

It gave her something to do. She washed the frozen carcass at the sink, then chopped it into pieces with her big knife.

''Erin...'' From the porch she heard her name, a faint voice calling to her, and she paused, knife in the air as she aimed for the leg joint of the rabbit.

''Erin!'' It sounded louder, stronger this time, and she went to the window, leaning to the side to search out the source. Across the step, lifting himself on one knee, arm outstretched toward the upright support, a man struggled to rise. Snow covered his coat, as if he had rolled in it, and his head was bent as he strained to get his feet beneath himself.

He turned his head to face her, and a gasp of horror escaped her lips. Quinn! Even in the twilight of early evening she could see blood staining his cheek and forehead.

"Quinn!" She whispered his name, the knife clattering to the floor as she turned to the door. It had never seemed so heavy in her hand as she pulled it open. Her feet had never moved so slowly as she stumbled across the narrow porch.

"Erin…" His voice was a whisper and he reached for her, his arm a deadweight on her shoulder. She braced herself and gave him her support, staggering as he leaned heavily.

"Cold…so cold," he muttered, and she was hard put to stay erect as she half supported, half dragged him into the cabin. Once they cleared the portal, she eased him to the floor, then shut the heavy wooden door, still shivering although she was surrounded by the warmth of the stove.

Her fingers worked at the buttons on his coat, then flew to his head, tugging his hat from its place, brushing snow as she went, noting the dark bloodstains it bore. He was silent now, his eyes closed, his breathing shallow. His gloves were stiff as she drew them from his hands, and she tossed them to the floor near the stove to thaw.

"Your boots! I have to get your boots off, Quinn. You need to have your feet warmed," she murmured, unsure if she'd seen his eyelids flicker or not. "Let me help you roll over, so I can get your coat off. Please, Quinn! Help me."

She worked quickly, impatient with the snowy boots,

yet tugging at them as gently as she could, lest his legs should be injured and she cause more harm than good. The coat sleeves slid from his arms as she rolled him from side to side, and she unwound the scarf from his neck.

Blood stained his face, and she searched for its source. Then, with a muffled growl of exasperation, she dipped her dish towel into the pan of water she kept on the back of the stove, wringing it out quickly. Back at Quinn's side, she washed the dried blood, working gently at his skin, moving finally to the side of his head, where, several inches above his ear, she found its source.

A shallow groove creased through his hair, its length still oozing a crimson stain, and she washed it with care. It didn't appear to be deep. With a sigh of relief she gathered up two of the baby's diapers. She folded one into a thick pad and tore the other into strips to bind his head, holding the bandage in place.

Quinn had begun to shiver as she worked, and Erin dragged her heaviest quilt from the bed, arranging it nearer the stove. Then she rolled him across the floor, her hands careful to protect his head, until his big body was almost centered on the warm blanket. Trembling from her efforts, she stripped him hastily of the wet trousers he wore and, finally, of his long underwear, grunting from the effort of lifting him. His legs, long and muscled, were strangely pale in the lamplight and she covered them quickly, averting her eyes as she dragged the second quilt past his male parts.

His shivering had become almost violent as she worked, and she brought the third quilt from the bed, tucking it around him, reaching beneath to rub gently at his feet. They were like chunks of ice in her hands, and she found clean stockings in his pile of clothing and pulled them into place. Finally, she wrapped them in her warm shawl before she pulled the quilts over them again.

Still he shivered, his teeth clenched together and chattering. ''Cold, so cold.'' The words reached her as she returned to him again, this time with a pillow in hand. Kneeling by his head, Erin lifted him with one arm beneath his neck, to push the pillow beneath his head. Quinn's eyes fluttered open and he looked at her, blinking as if he did not recognize the face above him.

''Cold...'' The single word reached her ears, and then his eyelids closed again. Erin took off her shoes, then pulled back the quilts she had tucked so neatly around him and slid beneath. With a growl of frustration she recognized that she could warm only one side of him at a time. She murmured a word of assurance, shifting about beneath the quilt, and inched her way atop his form, her head on his chest, her feet reaching almost to his toes. Moving carefully, she tugged the quilts in place, leaving only her head exposed. For a moment she willed herself to relax, to soften, molding her trembling body to his as her flesh absorbed the icy chill that invaded his flesh.

Then she began moving against him, using her arms and legs, her hands rubbing his sides and down the length of his long arms, her feet against the sides of his legs. Quinn stirred a bit beneath her now, his constant trembling turning to shudders that had her clinging to her perch.

He was so cold, so chilled to his very core that Erin trembled within as she finally considered the thought that he might not live through this ordeal. His breathing was shallow, and she found herself listening to the sound of his heart, her ear pressed to his chest. It had become more regular, pounding with a steadier beat; yet still he retained that deathlike chill.

His hands were warming, she decided as she spread her palms over their backs again, rubbing gently at the skin. And then he slid them upward, his movements ungainly, as if his arms could not support the effort. She lifted herself beneath his elbows and he enclosed her in a desperate embrace, using her warmth as a blanket.

"Quinn?" She lifted her head from his chest and edged one hand to his face, her fingers sensing a change in the temperature of his cheek. "Quinn?" She repeated his name and he moved his head. It was a barely felt shifting against the pillow, accompanied by a groan of pain and a murmur that might have been her name.

"Shh." Her whisper was automatic. "I'm here, Quinn."

The whisper came again. "Erin...my head."

She rose over him, just enough to make out the dark slits of his eyes. "I washed the wound, Quinn. It's pretty shallow, I think. There's a bandage on it to help stop the bleeding."

"Took my horse..." His eyelids closed as he groaned the words, and Erin was seized with anger. Someone had taken his horse? In freezing weather had doomed him? Leaving him to the elements with a head wound? An anger she could scarcely contain rose within her, and she clenched her teeth against the rage.

He'd been left to die. The taking of his horse was the ultimate crime in this part of the country. As a child, she'd heard what happened to horse thieves, reading the pulp novels that were passed among the children at her school. Even then, in her early years, she had yearned for the life of adventure depicted in their pages.

Now she was more than immersed in that existence,

struggling to save the life of the man who had married her and had gifted her with the knowledge of the possibilities inherent in such a union. In so doing, Quinn had brought her to this, Erin reflected as she snuggled against him, aware finally of the cessation of his shivering as she warmed his flesh. She felt the flexing of his muscles, the movement of his legs beneath hers. Finally the desperate clasp of his embrace eased and his hands moved against her back.

"Erin." Unutterably weary, his voice brought pain by its very tone, and yet also joy. Joy that he had returned to her. Exultation that pushed her anger into abeyance. Sweet, piercing delight in the sound of his voice, calling her name.

A recognition of her love for this man, love that astounded her with its fierce possession of her soul, that filled Erin to brimming, and overflowed in a soft cascade of tears.

"Yes, Quinn. Hush, now. As soon as you're warm enough, I'll get you into bed." She fought against the sob she feared would alert him, and breathed deeply to allay its sound.

His arms tightened again, a momentary message, and he relaxed beneath her. "Yes..." It was a weary sigh, but she felt the renewed strength of his body beneath her and was satisfied.

Erin closed her eyes, suddenly weary, almost dozing. And then she stiffened. From the crib, came a snuffling, squeaking sound, as Robert began to stir. She'd lost track of time. Perhaps it had been minutes, perhaps hours. She could not be certain how long it had been since Quinn had stumbled and crawled to the porch. But no matter. Robert would not be appeased until she satisfied his needs.

"I think we'll have to move you now, Quinn," she said quietly, and was relieved by his grunt of assent.

She rolled from him, her arms clinging, reluctant to leave the intimacy she'd formed in the time since he'd come back to her. Rising to her knees beside him, she bent to lift his shoulders.

"Help me. Can you lift your head?"

He groaned, and she felt the muscles in his neck and shoulders clench as he attempted to rise. She crept behind him, supporting his back as she levered him to a sitting position. Her arms enclosed him, lest he fall sideways, and she felt the deep, convulsive breaths he took as he struggled to stay erect.

"All right. I'll get up now," he muttered, rolling from her grasp to his hands and knees. His head hung heavily and she bit at her lip, mourning his pain. With slow movements he knelt, finally, and she got to her feet beside him.

"Push the table over here," he told her, and she recognized his objective immediately. In seconds the table was within his reach, and Erin slid beneath his far shoulder as he eased himself up with one hand flat against the tabletop. Quinn swayed, groaning aloud as she turned him toward the bed, and stumbled almost to his knees again as several steps took him to his goal.

He slid from her grasp with a sigh and his body slumped to the mattress, falling full-length across the bed. He lay from corner to corner, and she lifted his feet, bending his knees and urging him to turn a bit.

Her head swam with the effort expended and she gulped deep breaths of air as she hurried to snatch up the quilts, hastening to cover him before he became chilled once more. His legs and bottom were cool, feeling like smooth marble to her touch, and she hesitated, wondering if she should find underwear to cover him. But Robert's impatient cries chased that thought from her mind.

The quilt would have to do for now, she decided, tucking it around him, easing his head to the pillow. She spread the other two quilts over the top to insure his warmth.

The baby was wet through and Erin washed him quickly, changing him from top to bottom before she nursed him. He was indignant at the wait, and only the scent of her milk as it answered his call eased his displeasure. He latched on to her with vigor, and she could not suppress the chuckle that met his hunger.

Love, overwhelming and all-encompassing, filled her as she curled her arms around his warm body.

Her head tilted back and she was struck by the resemblance between this moment and those just past. When she had given of herself to the man she had married. When she had used her body as the remedy for his need, covering him, taking his trembling and making it her own. When her body heat had supplied the fuel that nourished his flesh and warmed his very blood.

When she had, for the first time, felt the overwhelming outpouring of love that marked him as the man she would gladly spend her life with.

Chapter Twelve

In the dark silence of the night Erin curled against Quinn's side. She'd done all she could. Had coaxed him to drink water, urged him to eat soup from a spoon, mostly to no avail. She'd finally pushed the kettle to the back of the stove and left the rabbit to cook overnight in a small pan. It would fall off the bones by morning, a fit addition to the soup kettle.

Her hand caressed Quinn's chest beneath the quilts, and she traced the lines of his body, as if she must reassure herself of his presence beside her. Along the path of his bearded jaw to the strong cords of his neck, her fingers moved gently. His shoulders were wide and strong, his chest full and well muscled above the spare line of his waist. Below that her hands followed the narrow line of hair that ran down to his navel, her fingertips marking its route.

She slid her index finger into the small indentation, enjoying the texture of his skin, discovering the small knot of flesh at its base. He shifted as she explored, his hand moving to cover hers, and he muttered her name again.

"Erin?"

"I'm here, Quinn." With haste she moved her fingers from beneath his hand, and rose on her elbow beside him. "Are you awake? Do you need a drink of water?"

"Umm…yeah, I'm dry," he answered. "Damn, my head hurts!"

Erin rolled from the bed and groped through the dark room to the table, where she'd left the cup of water he'd only sipped at earlier. Returning to his side, she crawled next to him, rousing him again.

"Let me help you to sit up a little, Quinn." Her arm was beneath his neck again and she lifted his head. He drank, long swallows that told her of his thirst, and she wiped at the dampness that overflowed either side of his mouth. She leaned to place the cup on the floor beside the bed and then pulled up the quilts again.

"Thanks," he murmured, settling back down on the pillow with a muffled groan. "Got bushwhacked…damn miner took my horse and left me for dead."

"I was so worried," Erin whispered as she hovered over him. His face was barely discernible in the darkness, and she peered at him, trying to make out his features. Her hand formed to the curve of his cheek and she bit at her lip, moving her palm to touch his forehead.

"I think you may have a fever," she said. "You're warmer than you were earlier."

"Wouldn't take much," he grumbled. "I was half-frozen when I finally saw the lighted windows in the clearing."

"Does your head feel any better?"

"Hurts when I move it. Aches like a son of a pup."

She felt for the bandage, adjusting it where it had slipped high above his ear. Her fingers moved across the padding and she was relieved to feel no sign of bleeding, the torn, folded diaper dry to her touch.

"I'll wash your wound out better in the morning," she told him. Relaxing, she rested against his chest, her ear once more echoing with the resonance of his heartbeat. It was a bit more rapid than before, but strong and regular, and she breathed a sigh.

"Did you take him...Russell...back to the miner's camp?"

"Yeah. Left him there." His voice sounded weary, his words heavy, as if they were too great a burden for his tongue to utter. "Someone followed me. Thought I heard a horse behind..." He paused, catching a deep breath. "Damn head...hurts like—"

"Hush. You can talk about it in the morning," Erin whispered, her eyes filling with tears as she thought of the hours he must have spent stumbling through the forest, searching for the cabin.

One of her arms stretched across to hold him close, the other hand moving to brush against his hair, checking again the position of the bandage. He was here, he was safe, he was going to be all right. She would see to it.

The sound of Robert crying woke him, and Quinn's eyes squinted, the lamplight shattering into prisms as he focused on it. Erin was by the crib, bending low to lift the squalling baby in her arms, murmuring softly to hush his cries.

"Is he all right?" Quinn growled, his voice dark with pain. He closed his eyes against the light and turned away from its glow.

"I'm sorry he woke you," Erin said quietly. "I thought I could catch him before he let loose at full strength."

"Good lungs," Quinn said, each word an effort as he

reached to prod at the bandage on his head. It hurt more than being kicked in the head by his father's mule, back on the farm.

"I'll tend to your head as soon as I feed him." Erin's voice came from the other side of the room, and then he heard the rocking chair creak as she settled down to nurse the baby. The sound of it moving against the floor was loud in his ears, and yet it was a comfort to him as he envisioned the woman and child.

"Is it morning?" If it was, if the sun was ready to come up, he'd need to think about milking the cow. There was only one horse to feed, but even the thought of measuring out a handful of oats and a bit of hay made his head pound. Whether or not he could make it to the shed was a question he'd just as soon not have to consider right now.

"Pretty soon. The sky's kinda gray around the edges." The chair creaked in a steady rhythm, and her voice hummed softly as she crooned to the child in her arms.

Quinn stretched out one foot, aiming toward the edge of the mattress. His other leg edged to join the first, and he shoved the covers from him. Maybe coffee would help.

"You just pull that quilt back up and lay yourself back down in that bed!" The rocker squeaked in protest, and the soft shuffle of Erin's shoes marked her movements. Quinn opened his eyes and watched as she neared the bed. Still holding the baby against her breast, she resembled nothing more than an avenging angel.

Her face was a bit out of focus and he narrowed his eyes, the better to make out her features. Sure enough, she looked like an angel, with that dark, shimmering cloud of hair and the blue eyes that had the ability to look deep within his soul.

"You're not getting up, Quinn, and that's that!" she told him briskly. "If you want anything, I'll get it for you." And then she halted, an indecisive look settling over her features. "Do you have to…you know…"

He shook his head, and an anvil somewhere inside shifted. A groan he could not repress slid past his lips and he slumped back against the pillow. With his feet hanging over the edge of the bed and his body shivering as a chill possessed him, he felt about as helpless as the baby Erin was holding.

"Damn!" As curses went, it was not up to his usual standards, but he was too weak to come up with anything better. His heart was chugging away, double time, and he'd barely reached down to tug the quilt back in place when he felt Erin's hands doing it for him.

"The baby…" he muttered, not wanting her to neglect the child on his behalf.

"He's fine." Her words were soft, whispered against his ear as she tucked the sheet and quilt over his shoulder. Her hands were cool against his face as she managed to touch him, smoothing the coverings against his back, then allowing her hand to brush his hair from his forehead.

Her hand paused, then slid down his face, resting for a moment against his cheek. She leaned over and he caught a whiff of her, that womanly, milky aroma, mixed with the other scent he couldn't put his finger on right now. If he could just persuade her to stay right where she was and hold her hand just so for the rest of the day, he'd feel a heap better.

"Don't go." It wasn't what he'd meant to say. But he couldn't resist that soft, small hand, and he turned his pounding head to press his mouth against it. Her fingers were cool and he snagged one of them between his lips, holding it for a moment.

"I'm not going anywhere," she said, her voice strangely hushed, almost as if she were holding back tears, he thought, frowning as he considered the idea.

"Don't cry."

"I won't," she whispered. She withdrew her finger from his mouth and traced the line of his lip with its tip. "I won't."

The clanging in his head grew louder, almost beyond bearing, and he gritted his teeth against the noise. "I don't think I can milk the cow this morning," he managed to mutter.

She bent low, and he felt her presence even before she pressed her lips against his forehead. "It's all right. It's my turn, anyway. Please don't try to get up, Quinn. I think you're feverish. I'm going to put a cold cloth on your head and I want you to be still and leave it there. Hear me?"

He managed a sound that seemed to satisfy her and she left him for a moment, returning to place a cold towel across his forehead. It felt wonderful, covering his eyes and allowing him to blank out the lamplight.

He heard her movements in the room, heard the door scrape across the floor once, and then again. He drifted, the bed changing form beneath him, cushioning his body like the salt water he'd floated in at Newport one long-ago summer. He could feel the sun on him as the water shifted beneath him, and he moved restlessly beneath the hot rays. He'd have a sunburn at this rate, and his mother would have to mop his skin with vinegar. If only he weren't so tired, he'd turn over and swim toward the shore and escape the sun within the cool walls of...

"Quinn, you must stay covered." His mother's voice was softer today, as if she'd shed that old-world accent and found a newer, gentler form of speech. Even her hands felt different, smaller against his, as she peeled his fingers from the quilts.

Quilts? No wonder he was so hot. Someone had wrapped him like a mummy. Quinn pushed at the suffocating weight that threatened his breathing, and heard a protesting voice. She was scolding him again.

"Please, Quinn. Let me put this towel on your head. I've taken the rest of the covers off, but you must have the sheet over you or you'll take a chill."

The cloth was cool, and he subsided, allowing the hands to capture his in a firm grip, the mouth to press against his lips in a kiss of comfort. Then the towel was lifted and his eyes squinted against the sun. No, that wasn't right. He was in a bed, and the light was from a lamp. And Erin had taken his mother's place.

For a moment Quinn grieved for the absence of the woman who had loved him better than anyone else could have. Who had forgiven all his childhood sins and given him her approval, even when he didn't deserve it.

"Mother?" He heard the word pass his lips and knew even as he breathed aloud that it had been a dream, a delusion.

"It's Erin." Her whisper was accompanied by the return of the cool towel and he tried to nod his understanding, but the pain would not allow it.

"Don't move, Quinn. You've been feverish for the whole morning, but you're cooling down now. You've been dreaming."

He tried to answer, but the effort was too great. Only a muffled sound that might have been a moan left his lips, and she shushed it with a soft whisper and the pressure of her fingertips.

"I'm here. Don't try to talk."

Erin...it was Erin. The cloth was lifted again and Quinn slitted his eyes to watch as she crossed the room, dipping the towel into a bucket by the door. Snow...she'd brought in snow to cool him. The windows were bright with noonday sun, and he closed his eyes against the brilliance.

"Erin." He tasted her name on his tongue, and then repeated it. "Erin."

He was cooler now, she was sure of it. The terrible heat of his fever had eased, and Erin sensed that he was aware of her presence. A cup of water in her hand, she settled on the mattress beside him.

"Quinn, I want you to drink now. You need water, do you hear me?" Her arm behind his head, she lifted him and pressed the cup to his lips. He sipped and swallowed, then breathed deeply as if the effort were too much to bear.

"Again," she told him firmly, offering the fluid his body needed.

He growled, but his mouth accepted the rim of the cup and she tilted it, nodding her approval as he swallowed once, twice, and then held the third mouthful for a moment before he swallowed it. His head shifted, a barely perceptible movement, but she lifted the cup.

"All right. That's enough for now, but we'll try again in a bit. Right now I'm going to change your bandage."

It wasn't what she wanted to do, but necessary, nevertheless. Erin untied the knot she'd formed at the side of his head, undoing the long strip of diaper. The pad was stained with blood, but not as much as she'd expected. She bent to the basin on the floor beside the bed and wrung out a clean cloth.

His wound was shallow but angry looking, the edges puffy. She washed it with soap, cleaning the dark hair that surrounded it, then rinsed it thoroughly and inspected it, leaning close to see if it showed signs of infection. Should he get blood poisoning...the thought made her shiver, and she bit at her lip.

Her meager medical supplies offered little, and she settled on a tin of carbolic salve, smearing a generous amount on the new bandage she'd fashioned. In moments she'd tied it in place and settled his head on the pillow.

"Thank you." Quinn's dry lips barely moved as he breathed the words, and she was touched by the automatic response. The mother he'd called for in his delirium earlier had taught her son well. Quinn Yarborough was a gentleman. He was a man any woman would be lucky to call husband. And by some providential quirk of fate, she'd been given that right.

Erin smoothed back his hair, noting the lack of fever as her fingers touched his forehead. "Do you think you could eat some soup?" she asked. "You need nourishment, Quinn. I cooked up a rabbit and made a big kettle full for you."

"Umm..."

He might not have intended it as assent, but she took it as such and rose quickly. In moments she was back by his side, tucking a clean towel beneath his chin, offering a scant spoonful of broth against his closed mouth. He opened his lips and she tipped the spoon, watching as he swallowed.

"Good." His mouth opened again and she repeated the small ritual, easing tiny bits of vegetable and meat past his teeth, watching as he chewed slowly and swallowed with effort.

''Enough.'' He turned his head, frowning as he moved against the pillow, and she brushed the towel across his mouth.

''You did well.'' He did look a little better, she decided, his color more normal, his cheeks losing the hectic flush they had worn all morning.

He slept then, deeply and quietly, only stirring when the baby squawked his need in the middle of the afternoon.

She watched from the rocking chair as she nursed Robert. Quinn's eyes opened just enough for her to see the dark gleam beneath his lashes.

''Is he all right?'' His voice was husky with sleep, but the words came easily past his lips.

''Yes, he's fine, just hungry again.'' She spread her hand across the top of her breast, aware that Quinn's eyes were intent on her. His dark gaze warmed her flesh from across the room, and she lifted her head to meet it with her own.

''Don't do that. Don't cover yourself from me.''

She felt her eyes widen at his words, was conscious of the flush of color that painted her cheeks, and knew a quickening deep inside her body as she responded to the words he spoke. Her fingers withdrew from the rise of her breast, and she cupped them beneath Robert's round bottom.

She'd never felt this degree of intimacy in her life. Not once during the years of her marriage to Damian, not during the hours when she'd given birth, when Quinn had delivered her child. Not even during the night she'd been warmed by Quinn's loving had she known the heat of his appraisal. That had been a surcease of sorrow, a panacea for her grief, a coming together that had held comfort for her.

This was different, this deliberate baring of herself to his view. As if she were offering herself to him, and he were accepting the gift, his dark eyes drinking in the sight of her.

"Beautiful…" His mouth rose at one corner in a faint smile. And then his eyes closed and he relaxed. She watched as his breathing changed, slowing, deepening as he slept.

The baby released his suction and she tilted him, smiling as a burp escaped his rosy lips. He snuffled against his tiny hand and sighed, a bubble forming in the center of his mouth. Her heart swelled within her as she watched him, then looked again at the man who slept in her bed. Quinn was better for now, it seemed.

And this was no time to dawdle, with butter to churn and diapers to wash out. She rose and put the baby down, moving quickly to do her chores before either of these male creatures needed her again.

It had been two days. Two days and nights of fever alternating with chills. Quinn roused from the tangled dreams and moved his head. The anvil had stopped clanging, but had been replaced by a hammer. No, that wasn't right. It was something outside that thumped loudly.

He moved cautiously beneath the covers, easing to the edge of the mattress. Robert was just inches away, his tiny body swaddled in a blanket and covered by Erin's shawl. Only the small dark head was exposed to view, and Quinn reached one hand to brush his fingers across that precious downy spot.

The thumping from outdoors sounded again, and

Quinn's feet touched the floor. What on earth could she be doing out there? And then he knew. She was chopping wood, the sound vibrating in time with the faint throbbing of his head wound.

She'd be lucky if she didn't cut her foot off. Fool woman ought to know better. He slid from the side of the bed, his knees unsteady, holding to the footboard for balance. His legs were properly covered, at least. He faintly remembered Erin struggling to slide drawers up his legs yesterday. Or was it this morning?

He'd been flat in that bed for three days, maybe, with Erin tending him like an infant, waiting on him hand and foot. And now, to beat all, she was out there swinging an ax. Quinn staggered, reaching for the table to steady himself, and then headed for the window.

Two horses were tied to the shed door, and Erin was sitting on a chunk of log near them. In the middle of the yard two men were busy making a fresh woodpile. One, the biggest of the pair, swung the long ax as if he knew what he was doing. The other, keeping him supplied with chunks of wood to split, was stacking them in a neat pile near the porch.

Quinn watched, leaning against the wall, squinting against sunlight that glittered on the snow, his head swimming. Damned if that didn't look like the sheriff out there, and the other one, with a shiny star pinned on his coat, was almost certain to be the deputy.

"What the hell?" He shook his head, peering through the glass, shoving the curtain to one side, the better to see.

As if his movement had caught her eye, Erin looked up, her gaze meshing with his, and she rose, hurrying to the cabin. "Quinn! What are you doing out of bed?"

She brought a draft of cold air in with her, her face rosy, her hair hanging in a long braid down her back.

"Tryin' to figure out what's goin' on out there," he muttered, easing his way to sit on a chair at the table.

"What does it look like?" Erin unbuttoned her coat and went to the stove. She poured coffee into a mug, then placed it before him.

"Looks like you've turned the sheriff into your chore boy," he told her, picking up the steaming cup and breathing deeply of the steam. "How long since I've had a cup of coffee?"

"Since before you got yourself shot," she answered, her tone brisk as she filled two more cups and headed to the door. "Don't you get up until I come back in, you hear me? I'm going to take these out to the sheriff and young Tater."

"What are they doing here?" Quinn asked, carefully turning his head to follow her as she paraded past him.

"I haven't found out yet," she said. "They saw me scouting up firewood and getting ready to split some big chunks, and Sheriff Mason took the ax from me and set Tater to work."

"Tell him he's done enough. I'll be able to use an ax in a day or so." Quinn knew his tone was beyond grumpy, but watching some other man splitting firewood for his wife was not setting too well.

"Please, Quinn. Get back in bed as soon as you've finished that coffee. I'll make you some dinner right away." Erin scooted outside, her attention on the full cups she carried, then she reached back in to pull the heavy door shut behind her.

Quinn bent over the table, propping his head in his hands, leaning on his elbows. He'd never felt so useless in his life, with legs like wet noodles and his head all in an upheaval. The coffee was strong, and his stomach growled as he swallowed the first of it. Food was what he needed—not the soup he'd been getting lately, but a good piece of roast venison or some fried steak.

The thought of the two men in the yard finding him in his drawers lent him strength, and he headed for the corner where Erin kept his clothes. Clean trousers were the first order of business, and by the time he managed to get them buttoned up and his belt in place, he was about out of breath.

His coffee was cool enough to drink down, and he swallowed it quickly. The bandage on his head had come loose and he snatched it away, impatient with the infirmity that had turned him into a man too weak to tend to his own chores. The pad was smeared with a residue of salve, but he found no trace of pus on it. He lifted a stove lid and tossed it within, just as the door opened again.

"Well, you sure don't look like you're about to take on the world," Sheriff Mason said, heading for the wood box, his arms full of freshly split logs. Depositing his load, he turned to Quinn and tugged off his gloves. He stepped closer to the table and offered his hand.

"I'm Henry Mason, and this here's Tater, my deputy." Erin and the younger man stood just inside the door, and Quinn cast her a quick glance before he shook hands with the lawman. "Your wife tells me you're nursin' a head wound, Mr. Yarborough. Want to fill me in?"

"You here on business, Sheriff?" Quinn asked curtly. "Or just out visiting?" He doubted the latter, and had a strong hunch that the trek up the mountain trail had had a purpose behind it.

"Actually, I came to see your wife, but it sounds like there's more here than what meets the eye."

"What did you come to see Erin about?"

"Had a report that there'd been a shooting up here the other day. Seems your wife was involved."

Quinn nodded. "Just what did you hear, Sheriff?"

"Heard tell she shot a man without provocation."

At his words, Quinn heard Erin draw in a quick breath from close behind him. Within seconds her hand was on his shoulder, fingers pressing against him. He reached up to clasp them in his palm.

"Do you believe that?" Quinn drawled the query, one eyebrow rising as if to signify his own doubt. "Have you asked Mrs. Yarborough what happened?"

Sheriff Mason shook his head. "Haven't had a chance yet, to tell the truth. We saw her rollin' a chunk of wood across the yard, gettin' ready to split it, and me and Tater here just set to and gave her a hand."

"I appreciate your concern, Sheriff." He squeezed Erin's hand. "How about some more coffee for our visitors, Erin?"

"I'll get their cups from the porch," she said quickly, turning to the door. "I have stew cooking. Would you like some?"

"You might not be so friendly once I tell you what I'm here for, ma'am," Sheriff Mason said quietly.

Erin opened the door and snatched the cups from the porch. Her steps were brisk as she walked back inside and across the floor to the sink. "I'll just get these washed up first." Her face was flushed by more than cold air, Quinn thought, watching her work. Her hands trembled as she placed the cups on the table.

"Ma'am, I've got to ask you some questions." The sheriff sat down across from Quinn and watched Erin closely. "I heard tell you had a couple of visitors the other day and when they asked for a bite to eat, you got all uppity and aimed your shotgun at one of them. Shot him without warning."

The coffeepot she held suddenly appeared too heavy for her to handle and it tilted precariously in her grip. Quinn reached across the table and balanced it, scorching his hand on the hot metal.

"Oh, Quinn!" Erin snatched a towel from the sink and dampened it in her pan of water, covering his fingers with the cool cloth.

"It's all right, honey. I doubt if it'll even blister," he said quietly, holding her against his side, one arm around her waist.

"Ma'am? You want to tell me about it?" the sheriff prodded.

"Two men were here, that's the truth. They asked for something to eat, that's the truth, too. I came out on the porch with my shotgun, just like you said. But I doubt you were told that they threatened to kill my cow and horse. And that they said vile things to me. And when they heard the baby cry, they told me if I didn't let them…" Her voice broke, as if she had gone as far as she was able, and Quinn's grip on her tightened.

"I think the sheriff knows what you're trying to say, Erin."

"Did you shoot the man, Mrs. Yarborough?" Sheriff Mason's eyes were kind, but his face wore a somber cast as he asked his question.

Erin nodded. "Yes, I shot him. He had his gun drawn and he was coming up to the porch, and he said it would be terrible if something happened to the baby, but he didn't mean it. And then he said it would be too bad if something happened to me, and the baby was left here all alone.'' She drew in a deep breath, and her voice was stronger as she continued. ''I couldn't let that happen. When he got almost up to the porch and I knew he wasn't going to stop, I just lifted the gun and pulled the trigger.''

''Well now, the miner, Toby Jones, I think his name was, said you just got real mean with them and didn't give them a chance to leave. Said you just shot his partner without cause.''

Erin shook her head, and her denial was a whisper that mirrored the horror of her memories. ''I wouldn't do that. He was going to hurt me or the baby, or maybe both, and I couldn't let him.''

''Did he have his gun aimed at you, ma'am?''

''No, it was in his hand, but pointed at the ground.''

Quinn cleared his throat. ''Don't you suppose he could have aimed it pretty quick, if he'd a mind to?''

The sheriff shrugged. ''Maybe he was defending himself.''

Quinn's voice was incredulous. ''Against a little bit of a woman like my wife?''

''Anybody looks pretty big when they're pointin' a gun in your direction, Mr. Yarborough.''

''You don't believe me, do you?'' Erin asked.

The sheriff levered himself up from his chair. ''I didn't say that. The fact is, I have to get to the bottom of the matter, ma'am. The judge will be comin' to town next week, and we need to let him hear everybody's story, I think. In the meantime, I'm gonna have to take you back to town with me.''

''You're going to put me in jail?'' Her words were bleak and she stiffened, drawing away from Quinn's touch. ''I have a baby to care for, Sheriff.''

''I know that, ma'am. We'll have to take him along,

I reckon. But don't worry, I'm not putting you in jail. We'll find somewhere for you to stay.''

He turned to look at Quinn. ''Now, how about telling me who shot you.''

Chapter Thirteen

He'd never felt so damned helpless in his life. Erin was on her way down the mountain with the baby, escorted by the sheriff, and the man who should have been taking care of her was left behind.

Quinn groaned in frustration, too weary to make his way back to the bed, his head aching too badly to sit at the table.

The door opened and closed, Tater Folsom filling the room with his presence. "Sure is a cold one today, Mr. Yarborough. I shut the shed up good and brought the milk in with me. You want to tell me what I'm s'posed to do with it?"

Quinn lifted his head, glaring at the hapless young man. "You can dump it in the snow for all I care."

Tater had the grace to look abashed. "Looky here, I didn't plan on stayin' up here and gettin' in your way, mister. I'm sure sorry you lost your horse, and I'm sorry as hell you got shot, but the best I can do is stay here for a couple of days till you get on your feet, so's I can milk the cow and keep an eye on you."

"What you can do is help me to the bed. I've been up long enough," Quinn said gruffly. He rose gingerly, aware of the tendency of his legs to tremble beneath his weight. Tater's shoulder was more than enough support, and Quinn was in the bed in moments.

He tugged the quilts over himself and closed his eyes. A vision of Erin assailed him: atop her mare, Robert bound to her bosom with her shawl, her coat covering him from the elements. He gritted his teeth. Damn fool sheriff had no business hauling her away like that.

One way or another, he'd get to her. Somehow, he'd make his way down the mountain to town and find her. If he had to walk, he'd figure out a way to be with Erin, if it was the last thing he ever did.

The trail was well marked with hoofprints. Not only those of the sheriff and Tater it seemed, but others who had managed to plow a path that was easy to follow. Erin clung to the pommel of her saddle and held the reins loosely. Ahead of her the sheriff rode at a steady pace, looking over his shoulder regularly to check on her.

"You doin' all right back there, ma'am? Am I goin' too fast for you?" He twisted to one side and watched her for a moment. "You want me to take that young'un for a while? It'd give you some rest."

Erin's arm tightened under the precious bundle she carried. "No, I've got him. He's fine." How she would fare should Robert awaken and be hungry she hadn't figured out yet, but manage it she would.

Only the thought of Quinn battling the sheriff and his deputy had allowed her to agree to this trip so readily. He would have fought to defend her until he dropped, that was a certainty. She could not allow it to happen. He'd barely begun to recover from his head wound. He needed at least another day or two to regain strength before he ventured far from the bed.

"It won't be long, ma'am. We're on the last leg," Sheriff Mason called back to her. "We're pret'near on level ground now."

Her mare picked up her feet a bit more quickly, as if she scented a barn or a haymow ahead, and Erin shifted in the saddle. The baby had begun to move around, yawning and stretching within his blankets. She could hear him snuffling at his hands, and she feared it would be only minutes until he expressed his displeasure at the close quarters he'd endured for the past hours.

The town loomed before them, twilight settling in quickly. The sheriff led her past the hotel, between the jail and the emporium, to where a cluster of houses lined a second street. Smoke trailed from their chimneys, and the scent of wood burning caught Erin's attention.

Wherever he took her, she surely hoped they were about to serve supper. She was in dire need of a cup of tea, a clean diaper for Robert and the use of an outhouse for herself.

"Here we are, ma'am." Her mare came to a halt and bent her head, blowing and snorting. "Hand me down that baby and I'll give you a hand off your horse," the sheriff said kindly, reaching up with both hands.

Erin shook her head. "I don't want to unwrap him. If you'll just let me lean on your shoulder, I'll make it."

He shrugged. "I can do better than that, I reckon." His big hands gripped her waist and he lifted her, easing her from the saddle and to the ground. She clutched at Robert and held her breath, then staggered as her legs trembled beneath her.

"Thank you." She inhaled deeply and looked around. The largest of the small assortment of homes was in front of her, and Sheriff Mason was opening the gate to usher her up the path.

"My wife will take good care of you and the child," he told Erin. "I'll just get you inside and then put these horses up. They need to be tended to. Tell Alice I'll be in shortly."

"Alice?" Erin plodded up the path, her feet feeling like chunks of ice inside her boots.

"My wife, Alice." He pushed open the door, and the aroma of baking bread assailed Erin's nostrils. "Alice! Come see what I brought you."

His shout was enough to raise the roof, Erin decided. But it certainly got results. A buxom lady with graying hair bustled into the kitchen, her front well covered with a white starched apron, and her hair wrapped around her head in fat braids.

"My, my! What have we got here?" she exclaimed, her face beaming. "Is this the little girl from up the mountain who's been nursing that poor little orphan child?"

Erin heard the door close behind her. "I'm Erin Yarborough." Her arms had begun to tremble with the strain of clasping the baby to her breast, and she looked around for a chair, fearful of remaining erect much longer.

"Let me help you, child! Here, just unbutton that coat of yours and let me give you a hand." Mrs. Mason hauled a chair from the table, and in moments Erin had been divested of her coat and hat, and Robert was squalling to beat the band. Mrs. Mason plopped him on the table, beaming at him, clucking her tongue and, in general, expressing her approval of his beauty.

"Isn't he just the sweetest thing? And hungry as a bear, I'll warrant. I'd say he's needing a good feed."

She stripped him down quickly and turned to Erin. "Where's his diapers, honey?"

Erin looked around helplessly. "I brought a bundle tied to the back of my saddle."

Mrs. Mason laughed heartily. "I'll bet that man of mine hauled it off to the stable with him. Never you mind, we'll just use something else for now." So saying, she snatched a clean towel from the kitchen dresser behind her and folded it with ease. Robert's eyes were screwed shut, and his cries were becoming lustier by the second when the last pin was in place.

"Here you go, mama. Just give this child a little nourishment and see if that don't put a stop to his caterwauling."

Erin reached gladly for her child and opened her dress. She smiled as he searched for nourishment and then settled down to fill his stomach. Before she'd had a chance to toss her shawl over her shoulder to shield herself, a cup of tea was before her, the cream pitcher and sugar bowl within reach.

"Thank you so much," she said gratefully.

"I surely don't hold with you bein' dragged down here to see the judge, I'll tell you that," her benefactress said stoutly. "I told my man he had no business huntin' you down. But as long as he was determined to bring you to town, he could just bring you here and let me take care of you and the babe."

As if she'd been delivered to the mother she barely remembered, Erin smiled at the woman, aware of the tears that slid in a steady fall down her cheeks. "I can't thank you enough for your kindness," she said after a moment. "I didn't want to come and leave Quinn at the cabin, but the sheriff insisted. I told Quinn we really need to get this all cleared up."

"And what did your Quinn say to that?"

Erin blushed as she remembered. "You don't want to know, ma'am. He said some words I can't repeat. Suffice to say, he wasn't too happy with your husband, but with a gunshot wound alongside his head, he wasn't in any shape to argue. The sheriff left Tater up there with him."

Mrs. Mason huffed her way across the room to the big cookstove that took up one end of the kitchen. She tended to the pots that required her attention, lifting their lids, which sent forth a marvelous assortment of aromas. Three loaves of bread sat on top of the warming oven.

Only the need for privacy kept Erin awake in the warmth of the room, and she waited impatiently as she nursed the baby, until the food preparations were under control. Mrs. Mason turned to her guest. "I'll warrant you'd like to get washed up, wouldn't you?"

"I need to use the outhouse." Erin felt a blush suffuse her cheeks once more as she whispered her distress.

"Land sakes, child. Give me that baby and go on upstairs. First room on the right. There's a slop pail and a washstand you can use."

"Yes, ma'am." Erin headed for the stairs, buttoning her dress as she went, even in her distress giving thanks. She could have been stuck in jail, and well she knew it. Instead, she'd been given the welcome of a daughter in this house. Quinn was the one in jail, stewing away in the cabin halfway up the mountain.

"You think he put her in jail?" Quinn growled his query from the depths of the bed, where he'd managed to sleep for several hours. His head had left off throbbing and he lifted it cautiously from the pillow. Sure enough, it had ceased the *thump, thump, thump* that had plagued him for three days.

"There any hot food over there?" he asked Tater.

"Yup. That wife of yours ain't only handy with a shotgun, mister. She's a right good cook, too. And she might be in jail. Either that or Miz Mason's lookin' after her." Tater rose to pour coffee into his cup. "You wanna come to the table? I'll dish you up a bowl of whatever this is in this here pot."

"Probably rabbit stew," Quinn grumbled. "I've been eating it every meal for a week, it seems like."

He made it to the table with barely a wobble, congratulating himself as he slid onto a chair. "Pour me some of that coffee, will you?" he asked, fishing in the spoon jar for a utensil.

"Tastes pretty good, don't it?" Tater asked, watching as Quinn devoured a full bowl of stew.

It might be the same potful, but Erin had added more vegetables to the soup and thickened the gravy. Quinn relished each bite, his mind traveling the trail to town.

He couldn't imagine where she was, and he yearned for the certain knowledge that she was safe and well. If he knew for sure that she was under a warm roof, with food in her stomach and the baby fed and dry, he wouldn't have this anguish to deal with. But he didn't know, and the thought of anything happening to his wife and child was setting up a frenzy in his heart.

He slept all night, rising at dawn when Tater left the cabin to answer nature's call. For the first time in four days his head felt as if it was firmly attached to his neck and he found he could walk with no trace of dizziness.

"I'll find you today, Erin," he whispered, searching out the whereabouts of young Tater's belongings. Success was not long in coming, the cabin holding few hiding places, and his eyes lit with triumph as his search panned out.

"Smells like fresh coffee," Tater said enthusiastically as he came through the doorway a little later.

"Probably not as good as Erin makes," Quinn answered, turning to face the door as he poured himself a cup from the blue speckled pot. He'd added chunks of wood to the stove before he dressed, and heat radiated from the cookstove. Now he exposed his backside to the warmth, nursing the coffee as his hands wrapped around the hot cup.

"I'll take a chance on it," Tater said with a grin. He shed his coat and found a clean cup on the shelf. "Looks like it's gonna be another clear day. Maybe the sheriff will send someone up with a horse for you this morning. You feelin' like takin' a ride yet?" His smile was eager as he watched Quinn over the rim of his cup.

"Yeah, that's kinda what I had in mind, as a matter of fact," Quinn said with an easy grin. "To tell the truth, I was thinking of taking a ride down the mountain and sending someone back for you myself."

Tater looked stunned. For just a moment Quinn was tempted to laugh aloud, and then lost the urge as the young lawman reached for his gun. The effort was futile. His weapon and holster had been placed by his side of the bed during the night, and Quinn had confiscated it while the coffee brewed. He was conscious of it, tucked in the back of his denim trousers, and felt a twinge of pity for the man he'd so purposely betrayed.

Tater's head tilted and his eyes narrowed. "I can't let you do that, Mr. Yarborough. Sheriff Mason left me here to look after you. He'd be mighty upset with me if you ran off." Carefully he placed his cup on the table and strode across the floor to the far side of the bed.

"It's not there," Quinn told him quietly. "I'm afraid I hold the winning hand, Tater. Hope you don't hold grudges. I'd rather not leave you here alone without a horse, but somebody's got to tend to the cow, and I've got a wife and baby I need to be with.''

"You can't do that. You think I'm just gonna stand here and let you ride off and not do nothin' about it? Not on your life, mister!" Tater blustered, his face red, his eyes glaring their wrath.

Quinn shook his head, and then thought better of it as he subdued a wave of dizziness. "Sorry to do this, but I'm going to tie you up till I get your horse saddled and I'm ready to be on my way." He reached behind his waist and drew the gun he'd confiscated. "Just sit yourself down in that chair, Tater, and don't give me a bad time of it. I'm not too long on patience this morning."

She'd spent a restless night, and morning had come none too early for Erin. The baby slept soundly beside her, tucked between two pillows, his cheeks pink, his fragile eyelids shut. Erin leaned on one elbow to watch him in the dim light coming in the window. Winter sunshine was never so bright as that of full summer, she thought. The sky was not nearly so blue, the trees were bare, and over a foot of snow covered the ground. The day matched her mood, barren and chill.

Quinn was miles away, up the mountain, with no one to care for him. No doubt Tater was a fine young man, but he didn't know how Quinn liked his eggs cooked, with the yolks almost hard and the edges crispy.

She bit back the urge to succumb to tears and rose from the bed. That she should miss him so intensely after less than four months in his company didn't seem possible. But the fact was, he'd found a place in her life, not to mention her heart. And that foolish organ felt as if it would burst this morning as she considered what her life would be like should she not be able to spend it in the presence of Quinn Yarborough.

A rap at the door invaded her brooding, and she picked up the borrowed robe she'd spread over the quilt for extra warmth last night, donning it quickly. The wood creaked as the door opened a bit and Alice peeked in.

"You up, honey? I've got breakfast ready downstairs, and Mr. Mason is about ready to go on over to the jailhouse. It's almost time for the morning stage, and he has a prisoner to take to Denver. I think he's wishin' he had Tater here to do the job."

"The sheriff is leaving town?" Erin asked, looking back at the bed as she reached the door.

"He'll be back in the morning," Alice said. She peered toward the sleeping baby. "You might as well bring him along. You won't rest easy with him up here and you down in the kitchen, if I know anything about young mothers."

Erin stepped back to the bed, gathering up the sleeping bundle, pausing only to snatch up clean diapers from the pack she'd deposited on the dresser last night.

The sheriff was wiping his plate with a piece of bread when Erin entered the kitchen. He looked up, his gaze searching her face and then focusing on the baby she carried.

"You about over bein' mad at me, young lady?" he asked with a wry grin. "I felt those blue eyes burnin' holes in me all the way down the mountain yesterday."

"I'm not mad." Her mouth felt puckered, as if she'd sucked on a dill pickle, and she couldn't resist needling the hapless sheriff. "I know you have to keep law an' order, and I'm sure I'm a threat to—"

"I never said you were a threat to anybody, r

I just have to have you here when the judge comes in tomorrow morning. We need to settle this thing and let you get on with your life, one way or the other.''

Erin's breath caught in her throat and she felt a stab of apprehension. "You mean the judge might send me to jail?''

Sheriff Mason shrugged, lifting his brow with a gesture that bespoke his ambivalence. "Can't say that I know for sure how it'll go, ma'am. There's a couple fellas comin' over from Big Bertha in the morning, and you'll all appear before the judge and he'll make the decision on whether or not you go to jail.''

"For land's sake! This girl's not going anywhere, Mr. Mason,'' Alice said, sputtering her protest loudly. "What's this world comin' to when a fine young lady like this has to defend herself against the law when all she was doing was trying her best to—''

"Now, Alice! That's about enough. You weren't there, and neither was I. All we've got to go on is her word against a miner's.'' He shrugged into his heavy coat and slapped his hat on his head. "You just see to it you keep her right here today. No visitors, no leaving the house, no nothing!''

Alice nodded, her lips pressed tightly together, obviously not in agreement with the letter of the law. "I'll do what I have to, mister, but I don't like it. Mark my words, you're wrong as wrong can be this time.''

"Too damn bad when a man has to defend himself to his own wife,'' the sheriff muttered, gritting his teeth as he went out the door.

Alice followed him, pulling the door open as he stalked down the path to the street. "You just keep that scarf over your throat, you hear me? I don't want you down with the quinsy, riding in a drafty stagecoach all the way to Denver and back.''

She closed the door with a subdued bang and turned to her guest. ''Men are the most obstinate creatures God ever created. All he'd have to do is take a gander at you and he'd oughta know you never did a rotten thing in your life. If you shot that rascal from the mining camp, I'll bet my bottom dollar you had a mighty good reason.''

She'd done it—had shot a man and watched him die— and it was no laughing matter. And yet Erin felt a giggle erupt, and to her amazement found herself unable to withhold the mirth that bubbled within her. It burst forth in a chuckle, escalating to a full-blown laugh as she faced her champion. Robert opened his eyes and looked at her, as if stunned that she should awaken him so abruptly. And still she chortled. Until Alice nodded and approached with arms outstretched.

''Let me take that child.''

Erin relinquished her hold, amazed to find that tears were streaming down her cheeks, even as she stifled a fit of giggles. ''I don't know what's wrong with me,'' she managed to gasp. ''It really wasn't funny, was it?''

''You're about wore out, girl. What you need is a good cry. Wash all that heartache right out of you.''

And cry she did, her face pressed against a pillowy bosom while Robert sucked on his fingers and watched. Alice's work-worn hand patted Erin's back, rising to brush her hair back from her face, and then patting again.

The storm subsided after a few minutes, and Robert's suckling began in earnest. ''He's got himself thinking he's hungry, sucking on that hand,'' Alice said, watching as Erin mopped her eyes and nose with a handy diaper.

''Let me take him,'' she said, with one hand unbuttoning the robe and gown she wore as she took the baby in the crook of her other elbow. "I'll settle him down."

She nursed him, watching as Alice loaded the table with an abundance of food.

It was the longest breakfast Erin had ever consumed. They ate slowly, Alice drinking copious amounts of coffee, having made Erin a full pot of tea. The sheriff's wife was a good listener, and Erin found herself divulging the events of the past years with hardly a pause.

"That young man married you to help you keep the baby, didn't he?" Alice asked, nodding her head, as if she answered her own query. "Does he love you?"

Erin swallowed a mouthful of tea and considered that idea. "I don't know," she said finally. "But he takes care of me and Robert. I don't think a man needs to love a woman to marry her, does he?"

Alice grinned. "Sometimes there's something else that convinces him to tie the knot. A lot of times the love comes later on."

"He likes me, I think," Erin offered, her cheeks pink as she remembered the night she'd almost begged for Quinn's possession.

"I'll just bet he does," Alice replied. "And I'd be willing to lay odds that you're more than a little in love with the scallywag."

"He's not..." Erin shook her head. "He's from good people, and he has a thriving business back east."

"Well, whatever you want to say, he got into your house and managed to make you fall in love with him, and all the time he was a bounty hunter sent to bring you in." Alice looked out the window. "Land sakes alive, it's past noontime already and I haven't even set my bread to rise or started anything for supper."

Erin grinned. "I don't think I'm going to be hungry

for a while. We've eaten all morning long, Alice. And if I don't use the outhouse pretty soon, I'll be sloshing with all the tea I've swallowed. This baby surely won't lack for milk today."

The sound of a horse outside caught their attention as the two women rose from the table. Erin looked up expectantly, her heart beating a rapid rat-a-tat against her ribs.

"Who is it?" Her voice was thready as she glanced to where the baby lay in a clothes basket near the stove.

"Don't you fret, Erin," Alice said quickly. "There's nobody going to hurt you here." She bustled to the door and set the latch, then stepped to the window. "Tall son of a gun with a hat cocked like a gambler, walkin' with a little bit of a hitch, with his saddlebags slung over his shoulder. S'pose it's that man of yours, come down the mountain lookin' for you?"

"Quinn?" Erin peered over Alice's shoulder, then ran to the door, lifting the latch and swinging wide the heavy wooden barrier, lest Quinn have to wait outside. "Quinn! What are you doing here?"

She reached for him, tugging at his arm, and he leaned for a moment against the wooden frame. His eyes were shadowed, his mouth pinched as if he fought a weakness too great to combat, a weariness too consuming to ignore.

"I think I need to sit down, honey," he murmured, dropping his load to the floor. Then, with an obvious effort, he stood erect and headed for the kitchen table. Erin insinuated herself beneath his arm and he leaned on her. She relished the weight of him, his hand clutching at her shoulder as he eased into a chair.

"How did you get here?" she asked, snatching his hat and working at the buttons of his coat.

"Rode Tater's horse. I'm probably in a heap of trouble, but…" He cast a glance at Alice and lifted his brow. "Are you Mrs. Mason, ma'am? Sheriff's wife?"

Alice nodded, her eyes glittering as she listened to Quinn's easy drawl. "That's my name, Mr. Yarborough. Just call me Alice, if you will. We don't stand on formality here."

"I hear the sheriff went to Denver this morning. You suspect he'll have a problem with me finding a place for my family and moving my wife while he's gone?"

Alice grinned. "I don't know about him and I don't have any problem, but I'll warrant you could use a soft bed and a full meal before you start worrying about cartin' off this girl and her child. No reason in the world you can't stay right here till my husband gets back."

"Alice was told to keep me here, Quinn," Erin said quietly.

He nodded, bowing his head as he inhaled deeply. "Could I bother you for a cup of coffee, ma'am?" he asked after a moment. He looked up at Erin and his gaze scanned her face. "You all right, honey? Is Robert…"

"He's right over in that basket, Quinn. He's fine," Erin said quickly. "We're both fine." She glanced at Alice's back, as a cup was located and coffee poured into it. "What happened?" she asked in a whisper.

"Got hold of Tater's gun and tied him up while I got my gear together. I loosened the ropes before I left. He probably didn't take more than a minute or so to get loose."

"I'll bet he was madder than a wet hen." She couldn't suppress a chuckle, even as she felt worry surge to the forefront.

"Oh, yeah…he was mad, all right," Quinn agreed. "Cussed up a storm, threatened me with everything short of burning in hell." He scanned her again. "You sure you're all right?"

She shook her head. "You're the one that got shot, Quinn. You need to be in bed, not running around the countryside."

"I'm better. Not even dizzy anymore," he boasted. He looked much healthier, Erin decided, watching as he swallowed half the cup of coffee at one gulp. "I got your money, Erin. Stuck it in that little wooden box of yours. It's in my saddlebag." He pointed to the set of leather bags he'd dumped just inside the door.

"You found it?"

"I watched you lift the floorboard the day we came to town together. I knew it was there."

"You never mentioned it."

He allowed a grin to lift one corner of his mouth. "It wasn't any of my business, honey. I just didn't think it was a good idea to leave it up there."

She nodded. "I'll probably need it. Do you think I should hire a lawyer?" She frowned and looked at Alice. "Is there even a lawyer available in Pine Creek?"

"Sure, we got Mr. Painter. He's got an office in one corner of the bank," Alice answered. "But I doubt you'll need one, Erin. If that judge has a lick of sense, he'll dismiss charges lickety-split."

Chapter Fourteen

Judge Herbert Beal peered through his spectacles at the woman before him. "You ready to speak your piece, young lady?"

Erin nodded, and Quinn sat on the edge of his chair, yearning with every bone in his body to stand by her side. It was not to be, the judge having made it clear that, in his court, tradition must reign.

"Did you shoot and kill the miner known as…" He lowered his head to read the paper before him. "Let's see, now, Russell Hogan's the fella, it says here." His voice drawled the words. "Well, did you fire point-blank at the man?"

Erin's chin rose and her words were firm. "Yes, sir, I did."

"You don't look to me like the kind to run around shooting people." The judge cleared his throat and eyed Erin judiciously. "You want to tell me what happened?"

Erin nodded. "I heard two men outside my cabin. They wanted to come in." She swallowed audibly and licked her lips.

Quinn clutched the arms of his chair, resisting the urge to go to her, lend her his strength. She looked so alone, so forlorn, holding Robert in her arms, standing before the table where the judge had set up court, here in the jailhouse.

"I offered to give them something to eat. I told them I'd put it on the porch for them, but that wasn't what they wanted."

"What did they want?" the judge asked, prodding her.

"They wanted to come inside. They brought my cow and horse from the shed and threatened to shoot them if I didn't let them in the cabin."

The judge lifted his brow. "You killed a man over two animals?"

Erin shook her head. "No, sir. That was only the beginning of it. The smaller man stayed with my animals and the other one, Russell, came toward the house. He already had drawn his gun, and he still had it in his hand. Then when they threatened my baby... Anyway, the man, Russell, said it would be too bad if something happened to Robert. He said he wondered what would happen to the baby if something happened to me and Robert was left all alone. He was going to rape me, Judge."

"Did he put his hands on you or hurt the child?" the judge asked, frowning.

"No. I didn't let him. When he came toward the porch I told him to stop, and he wouldn't. I pointed my shotgun at him and pulled the trigger." Her arms held Robert against her breast and she rocked him to and fro. She was small, fragile appearing, and Quinn's heart thudded within his chest, yearning to hold her safe.

"Was he pointing his gun at you? Did either man shoot at you?" the judge asked soberly.

"We didn't do nuthin'," a voice whined from behind Quinn, and he looked over his shoulder. A whiskered, grimy miner stood by the wall, his gaze focused on Erin's back.

"You're Toby Jones?" the judge asked.

"Yessir, I surely am. This woman's a killer, and she's lyin' through her teeth."

"Come up here, Mr. Jones," the judge ordered. He watched as the miner crossed the room to stand near Erin, who moved a step away, shrinking from contact with her accuser.

"Is this one of the men you say threatened you?" the judge asked her.

Erin nodded, and Quinn saw the shudder that traveled her spine. He leaned forward in his chair, ready to move should she need his protection. "Yes, he was near the shed," she whispered.

"Did he draw his gun against you?"

"No, he was going to, after I shot the first man, but I told him I'd shoot him if he did."

"You were going to shoot him with a shotgun from how far away?"

Erin looked over her shoulder at Quinn, an unspoken query in her eyes. "About a hundred feet, Judge," Quinn said quietly, then smiled at Erin.

"Mr. Jones. You believed she could hit you from that distance?"

Toby Jones shook his head. "Naw, I didn't think any such thing. But I didn't see any sense in givin' her a chance, so I left." He glanced at Erin and glared his hatred, showing teeth that were darkened and sparse. "We were just funnin' you, lady. And you couldn't take a joke."

Quinn growled, coming to his feet. A fury he'd been holding in abeyance powered him, and he stepped to the table, moving between Erin and her accuser.

"You'll have to take your seat, mister," the judge told him. "I haven't even gotten to you yet."

"This man threatened my wife in the worst possible way, Your Honor," Quinn said between gritted teeth. Forgotten was the pain of his head wound. He'd have gladly taken on a whole damn posse for the chance to spend one minute alone with Toby Jones.

"We only have her word against his," Judge Beal said sternly.

"Where are you from, Judge?" Quinn asked in a deceptively calm voice.

"St. Louis, Missouri, if that makes any difference." He glared at Quinn. "Take your seat."

"Anybody threatens a man's property or his family out in this neck of the woods leaves himself open to whatever happens to him," Quinn told him fiercely. "I came here from New York City, and even I know that."

Erin turned to him. "It's all right, Quinn. I'm fine. Here, take the baby and sit down with him."

Quinn reached for the child, scanning Erin's pale features. She was in control once more, her trembling a thing of the past, but her fingers were chilled as she relinquished Robert to his embrace.

He stepped back to his seat, the pain in his head responding to the anger he struggled to control, throbbing in unison with his heartbeat.

"The laws are the same in Missouri, young man. What we need to decide is whether or not these men were only asking for neighborly concern from your wife, or whether they were, in truth, threatening her."

"Doesn't it matter that someone shot Quinn when he took the body back to the mining camp?" Erin asked.

The judge lifted his brow. "Who shot him?"

"He doesn't know. He was shot from ambush, and then left to die, without his horse or packhorse."

Judge Beal looked beyond Erin to where Quinn sat. "That true? You were ambushed? Somebody stole your horses?"

Quinn winced as he nodded. "I've got a crease in my skull to prove it. And I'll warrant if you visited the mining camp, you'd find my horses."

"Well, I sure didn't shoot you!" Toby Jones blustered. "There's no need to be lookin' for your animals at Big Bertha."

"No one's accusing you," the judge said. "But I think it might be beneficial to check out this man's claim, don't you, Sheriff?"

Sheriff Mason cleared his throat. "Probably wouldn't hurt a thing to keep all three of these folks on hand till we find out all the facts."

"You got no reason to send me to jail," Toby whined, turning to face the lawman. "I got a job to tend to, up at Big Bertha."

Sheriff Mason gave him a dismissing glance. "I'll be making charges against Mr. Yarborough here, too, Your Honor. He tied up my deputy and took his horse, then hotfooted it down here after his wife."

The judge inspected Quinn from beneath bushy eyebrows. "You attacked a lawman?"

"No, sir. I just borrowed his horse. My wife needed me, and there was only the one horse."

"Where's your deputy?" the judge asked the sheriff. "Is he in the room?"

Tater Folsom spoke up from near the door. "Yessir, I'm right here. Quinn didn't attack me, sir, and he loosened the ropes so's I could get free right quick." He shot a grin at Quinn. ''I guess I could understand why he did it, sir.''

''I sent a man back up the mountain with an extra horse to get my deputy yesterday morning,'' Sheriff Mason said.

''Well, I think we need to get these folks behind bars till we get to the bottom of this thing,'' the judge said sternly. ''Sheriff, I want you to go to the mining camp and talk to the boss up there. Can you do that?''

Sheriff Mason nodded. ''I reckon I can.''

''In fact, I want you to take Mr. Yarborough with you, so he can identify his animals.''

''You're puttin' me in jail and lettin' him loose?'' Toby whined in a high voice.

''He's not about to run off,'' the judge stated. ''His wife's going to be right here where I can keep an eye on her.''

Quinn surged to his feet. ''I don't want Erin in a jail cell.'' Robert roused from sleep at the abrupt movement and began to cry, a frightened, high-pitched wail. Quinn shifted him easily to his shoulder, patting his back in an automatic motion.

The judge appeared hard put to keep his demeanor official, a smile playing about the corners of his mouth. ''Well, I don't see as how what you want has much to do with it, young man. She'll stay where I say, and you'll go where I tell you.'' He lifted his gavel and rapped sharply at the table. ''Court's dismissed until day after tomorrow.''

Quinn stepped to Erin's side, and she reached for the crying baby. ''I'll be all right, Quinn,'' she whispered. ''Just go with the sheriff and get this thing all straightened out.''

Tater had stepped forward, grasping Toby Jones by

one arm. The miner looked back at Erin, glaring from rheumy eyes. "Yer a damn lyin'…" The pressure of Tater's fingers silenced him, and he winced, turning his attention to the deputy. "I ain't the one killed somebody here. You're puttin' the wrong one in jail."

"Don't you worry." The sheriff spoke up. "Mrs. Yarborough is headin' for her cell right quick."

"You got more than one cell back there, Sheriff?" Quinn asked in an ominous tone.

"Yeah, but we keep women prisoners across the way," he answered, beckoning Erin with his index finger. At the back of the room Alice Mason waited. Once again Erin was given in to her custody. With a motherly arm around Erin's shoulders, Alice led her out the door.

"You fit to ride?" Sheriff Mason asked Quinn. He eyed him, taking his measure. "I'm thinking we might wait till tomorrow morning. It'll save campin' out up there tonight."

Quinn nodded. "The morning might be better." He ached to follow Erin out the door, but his better judgment told him he was only about twenty feet from his bed for the night.

"Mr. Yarborough?" The voice of Tater Folsom called from the other side of the bars, and Quinn rolled to his side, then sat on the edge of the hard cot.

"Yeah, what do you want?" he asked, rubbing at his eyes. It was pitch-black outside the panes of wavy glass over his bed, and he shivered as a draft caught him from the poorly framed window.

"Miz Mason wants to check out your head wound tonight, before you leave in the morning. She told the sheriff you couldn't ride out until she made sure you were fit to travel."

Quinn stifled a groan as he rose to his feet. "Where is she?"

"Over at the house, sir. Better grab your coat." Tater turned the key in the cell door and opened it wide, grinning in the faint light of the lantern in the other room.

"Where you takin' him? You ain't lettin' him go, are you?" Toby Jones sputtered from the other cell.

"Nope, just doin' what I'm told," Tater answered, leading the way from the cell to the outer office. "Come on, Mr. Yarborough."

Erin's gaze met his as Quinn entered the sheriff's house, the blast of warm air from the big cookstove more than welcome. She sat perched on a chair, pouring from a teapot, and the pretty little container hit the table with a clatter as she rose to her feet.

In three steps she was in front of him, her hands reaching to press against his coat. "Are you all right?"

He nodded, scanning her pale features, her shadowed eyes. "How about you, honey? Is the baby—"

"We're fine," she interrupted, shaking her head as if to dismiss his concern. "Sit down and let me look at your head." She led him to the chair she'd abandoned and urged him to the seat.

In seconds her fingers were combing his hair from the scabbed-over wound, exposing it to the lamplight. Her indrawn breath spoke of her distress, and he soothed her instinctively.

"It's about healed up, honey. Don't worry, I'm about good as new." He closed his eyes, enjoying the touch of her fingers against his scalp, inhaling the sweet scent of her body as she stood between his knees. His hands itched with the urge to enclose her waist, his arms yearning to enclose her in his embrace.

"Let me take a look," Alice said, bustling to his side.

expedition could not be measured in money. Bounty had never had such power to charm him.

Sweet bounty. She was prime, this woman he'd married.

"Quinn?" She whispered his name and he bent his head to listen. "Quinn, do you remember the night…" She hesitated, and he grinned in the darkness.

"The night we made love?" he asked, tipping his head to brush a kiss across her cheek.

"Well…whatever you call it…it seemed to me that I was…" She caught her breath. "You know…like I talked you into it."

He muffled his laughter against her hair. "Sweetheart, I was more than ready for you that night. I only hesitated because I was tryin' my best not to take advantage of you."

"Well, what I'm trying to say is, if you wanted to now…you know…well, it would be all right with me."

A sense of supreme well-being surged through Quinn Yarborough. His only wish right now was that the happiness he held within his arms at this moment would last for an eternity. He rolled with her, rising above her to brush his mouth against her face, tasting the faint flavor of her skin.

"Erin." His mouth suckled at her lower lip, and she whimpered. "Sweetheart…" He nibbled at the lobe of her ear and nuzzled against it. She moaned, a soft, desperate sound deep within her throat, and he felt the surging power of his arousal spring into being.

It was no good, he decided morosely. The baby dozed fitfully beside the bed, their hosts slept just beyond a thin wall, and his own needs were going to have to be put in abeyance for now.

"Baby? We can't do this now," he murmured with

regret. "When we make love again, I want to have a long night ahead of us and someplace more private than this. I don't want Sheriff Mason knowin' what I'm doin' with my wife, while I'm doin' it."

She wiggled, her hands rising between their bodies to push against him in a futile gesture. He pressed her into the mattress with his weight, his mouth against her ear.

"Hush, sweetheart!" he whispered. "Don't make the bed jiggle that way."

"Quinn Yarborough!" She made the whisper sound like the voice of doom, and he sighed. "What a way to talk!"

"Don't you go gettin' mad at me." He breathed the words in her ear and she shivered.

"You'd think I was trying to talk you into something," she hissed.

He chuckled, enjoying the movement of her slender form beneath him, even as he bemoaned the discomfort he would live with for the next little while.

"Don't wiggle like that, honey," he pleaded softly.

"Then just get yourself off me," she told him, her voice rising a bit.

"Shh...hush now." The urge to laugh aloud was almost more than he could contain and he rolled to his side, drawing her with him, his arms enclosing her in a grip she had no chance of breaking.

Not that she seemed in a mood to. She settled against him and sighed. "For married folks, we surely haven't done much...you know."

"You may not understand this, Erin, but holding you gives me more pleasure than the thought of makin' love with a passel of women, and that's the truth."

"A passel of women?" She drew out the words in a

taunting fashion, and he cringed as he considered the implication she had drawn.

"Now, I didn't mean it that way. I haven't been with that many...." Somehow he felt he was becoming mired in a mud hole he might never escape, and he began backtracking. "You're my wife, sweetheart. I'll never look at another woman, so help me. What I meant was that I'd rather cuddle up with you, and put up with hurtin' a bit, than anything else in this world. For right now," he amended quickly.

"For right now?"

He nodded. "But just you wait till I have you all to myself, with no one around to hear, and the baby sound asleep."

From the laundry basket beside their bed, Robert snuffled and cried out, subsiding quickly as he found his hand. He suckled against his fingers for a moment, and Erin sighed.

"He's going to want to eat." She rolled from Quinn's embrace and reached over the side of the bed to lift the infant to her side. She undid her gown, preparing herself for nursing, whispering soft, cajoling words to pacify the baby. Then, with a sigh of contentment, she brought him to her breast and inhaled sharply as he drew her nipple into his mouth.

"Does it hurt?" Quinn asked from behind her, rising on one elbow to peer over her shoulder into the darkness.

She giggled, and he buried his face against her shoulder, wishing for just a moment that he were the supplicant, and that Robert were tucked away, dreaming whatever dreams babies enjoy in the middle of the night.

His grumble was halfhearted as he slipped one arm under her head and drew her back against his chest and belly. His legs cradled her thighs and he settled his other hand against Robert's back, holding him in place.

"Quinn?" Her whisper bore a wistful note and he smiled in the darkness.

"Yeah?"

"What will we do? What if the judge finds me guilty? Will you take Robert? Or will they let me take him with me?"

He rocked her in his arms for a moment. "Don't borrow trouble, honey. That judge is just letting old Toby dig himself a hole. Once we find my horses up at the mining camp tomorrow the game will be over, and Toby's gonna be in deep trouble."

"What if they're not there?"

"They'll be there. I have to believe that, Erin. What we need to be thinking about is where we're going from here. If you want to go back up to the cabin for the rest of the winter, we can do that. For myself, I'd rather think about finding a house here in town till the weather breaks. How about it, honey? What do you think?"

She was quiet for a while, so long that he wondered if she had fallen asleep. And then she took a deep breath. "I love the cabin. It's where I began to like myself again, Quinn. But it holds some bad memories, and I guess I'm not permanently attached to it."

"That settles it, then. Once we get this whole thing cleared up, I'll find us a place to live and we can settle in until the snow melts and it warms up. If you want to move back up the mountain then, we'll see about it."

Robert's small body squirmed beneath Quinn's hand and Erin pushed herself erect, sitting up to place the baby on her shoulder to burp him. She listened for the bubble of air and then turned to her other side, offering her other breast.

"What about your business in New York?" she asked Quinn, facing him in the middle of the bed, the baby between them. Quinn's features were a blur in the dim light, but she caught sight of his mouth, his lips tightening in a firm line.

"We've got all the time in the world to talk about that, honey. For right now, Joel Guinan has things under control, and he deposits my share of the profits in the bank every week. Later on, things may change." He eased a little closer to the baby, slipping his long arm into place across Erin's hips.

Her voice was hesitant. "I'm not sure I'll ever want to live in New York City again. I don't think I was cut out for all that hubbub and fuss and bother. And for sure I'm not interested in anything to do with society."

He chuckled softly. "Well, I can't say that afternoon tea holds much interest for me, either. I've gone out of my way to avoid high society. I spent most of my time in other parts of the country anyway."

"You've traveled a lot, haven't you?"

"Not pleasure trips, honey," he said with a dry laugh. "I've chased down crooks and criminals from one end of the country to the other over the years, even before I settled in New York. It's not the easiest way to make a living, but the money's good."

"How much was I worth?" she asked after a moment. Her voice sounded wistful to his ear, and he was struck by a pang of guilt, that she would equate herself with any monetary value. Surely she knew that he had no desire to claim a reward for finding her for Ted Wentworth.

"I won't be making a plugged nickel on you, sweet. My deal with Wentworth went down the drain a long time ago."

"Does he know that?" She moved away from his touch to place the baby back in his makeshift crib, and Quinn's hand clenched against the sheet.

"I haven't communicated with him directly, but Joel Guinan has. I'm going to wire Joel and let him know we're here for the duration. He can notify Ted and Estelle that I won't be in communication with them any longer."

"They're going to be angry." Erin snuggled back down in the warm nest of covers, and Quinn waited for her to move to his side.

"They weren't honest with me, Erin. I started out after you blind. I don't owe them a thing." He felt the warmth of her body only a few inches away, but it wasn't enough. Only the soft curving length of her nestled in his arms would satisfy the urgency of his need tonight. That he could not spend his desire within her was a fact he was willing to live with for now. But he wouldn't settle for less than holding her throughout the long, dark hours that remained, before dawn sent him on his way up the mountain to the mining camp.

He reached for her, the few inches between them disappearing in a second as he molded her to his masculine form. She was pliable in his arms, soft and curving against his lean strength, and he caressed the line of her waist and hip with a firm touch. She was rounded nicely, he decided, her bottom fitting against him, cushioning the proof of his desire.

"Now, just close your eyes for tonight," he whispered against the top of her head. "We'll sort everything out after I ride up to Big Bertha tomorrow with the sheriff."

Chapter Fifteen

"So that's where he is!" The owner of Big Bertha lived up to the image of his mine; he was a big man, and his voice boomed out in anger. Wayne Tucker ran a tight ship, as he had a reputation for saying, and the news that one of his men was residing in jail had put a ruddy hue on his broad face.

"Damn piker barely earns his way as it is. Forever whining and carrying on. I'd say jail's the place for him." His small eyes were narrowed as he considered the sheriff and Quinn. "What'd he do?"

Sheriff Mason glanced around the small community of mining shacks. "You got any extra horses around here you can't account for?"

Wayne Tucker hesitated. "You're telling me Jones brought stolen horseflesh into my camp?" If possible, his face grew even more florid.

"I'm missing a packhorse, a bay with a wide blaze, and a stud, chestnut with a pale mane and tail. Someone took a shot at me the other day and left me for dead. Took my horses."

"Say, ain't you the fella brought Russ Hogan's body

back last week? I caught sight of you when you was riding out.''

Quinn nodded. ''He and Toby Jones threatened my wife, and Hogan got shot for his trouble.''

The mine owner shook his head. ''I thought Jones's story sounded kinda fishy when he came back without Hogan last week. Jones said there was a gunfight, and he couldn't get close enough to tote Hogan back here.''

''Well, Mr. Yarborough here says he thinks Toby Jones was the man that shot him from ambush,'' the sheriff said. ''If those two animals are here, it backs up his story, I'd say.''

The mine boss nodded slowly. ''Poor pickin's these days hereabouts. I'm down to a dozen miners now. Since the mother lode played out, we're just cleanin' up what's left, and a man can't be choosy about what he hires.'' He rose from his chair in the cookhouse, leaving his half-eaten meal behind. ''Let's go out to the shed and take a look. There's a dozen or so horses out there. Most of these men brought their own with 'em, and I've got a couple of mules.''

The door slammed behind them, leaving the cook to his chores, and Quinn followed the sheriff and Wayne Tucker across the small clearing. It was cold this morning, with snow clouds gathering, and he pulled his collar high to keep out the bitter gusts of wind that swirled across the side of the mountain.

The memory of the woman he'd left behind nudged him, and he was warmed by it. Her face flushed in slumber, she'd answered his goodbye kiss with the soft pressure of her lips, opening her eyes in surprise as he knelt by the bed.

''You leaving already?'' she'd asked in that whispery, early-morning voice of hers.

"Yeah, we need to get an early start. You take care of yourself and Robert, hear?" He'd wanted nothing more than to crawl back in that warm bed and... Well, that didn't bear thinking about, he decided, reaching up to jam his hat down tighter over his forehead.

The first thing he wanted to do was find a place to put his family for the next couple of months. A house with furniture in it, namely a nice, comfortable bed, one that would hold two people, without a man's feet sticking out over the end. Quinn's grin was subdued as he assessed that thought. He was a married man, sure enough, thinking about sleeping with the same woman for the rest of his life.

The shed was shabby but weatherproof, and Quinn eyed the line of standing stalls with interest. Most horses looked pretty much alike from the rear end, except for color, but his stallion was seventeen hands. Ought to stick out like a sore thumb in this row of ordinary-looking mounts.

Wide chestnut haunches caught his eye, along with a pale tail that was swishing as the big horse bent to snatch a bit of hay. Quinn stepped up closer. "Hey, there, boy. They feedin' you all right?" His tone was quiet, but the horse turned his head as far as his halter rope would allow. A low nicker answered Quinn's query, and Boss Tucker strode to his side.

"That your animal?" He eyed the stallion. "Can't say I've seen him before. I don't get in here every day, and we haven't turned these horses out since the weather got bad." He walked on down the line of stalls. "Here's another stranger. Come take a look."

The bay was broad backed and stocky, and Quinn sidled into the stall beside him. He grasped the halter, turning the horse's head so that the other two men could see the wide white blaze that almost covered the animal's face.

"This is my wife's packhorse, sure enough." He released the halter and rubbed the wide forehead with his knuckles. "How you doin', boy?"

The relief that flooded him kept Quinn stationary for a moment. He could barely restrain the shout that begged to be let loose on the cold air. Finding these horses was vindication enough for any fool, and Sheriff Mason had a head full of common sense, as far as Quinn could tell. Toby Jones might as well start packing for that Denver prison. Unless Quinn missed his guess, he was headed there in a hurry.

"I'm sure enough sorry I didn't notice I was feedin' a couple of strays, Sheriff," Wayne Tucker said, stuffing his hands in his pockets. "My men are allowed feed for their animals, and they take turns muckin' out the place and feedin', a week at a time."

Sheriff Mason nodded, accepting the mine owner's explanation. "Well, I don't think you'll be seeing much of Toby Jones anymore, Mr. Tucker. You've got yourself a new horse for your trouble, I'm thinking. He won't have much use for it where he's headin'. A man takes another man's mount, he's just about committed murder in these parts. Especially in the middle of winter."

"Especially when he's taken a potshot at the fella," Quinn added.

"Get your horses together, Quinn. It looks like you're pretty near in the clear."

"Pretty near?" Quinn looked back at Sheriff Mason as he untied the packhorse.

"You're still in hot water for leavin' my deputy up there all alone." Sheriff Mason shook his head in a mocking gesture. "Poor old Tater had to lead that cow of your wife's all the way to town the next day. Said he heard catcalls from half the folks in Pine Creek, wonderin' what the cow'd done to get taken into custody thataway.''

Quinn grinned, too relieved at the outcome of this trip to worry about Tater Folsom's feelings. "I'll ride my stud and lead the other two back, Sheriff." He turned to the mine boss. "Where's the tack room, Tucker? I need to find my saddle."

The livery stable had room for extra horses. Jeremy Tobin was always eager for business, the sheriff said, and Jeremy's wide grin was proof of that prediction. He settled on a price with Quinn, then turned the stallion into a box stall at the back of his big barn.

"Nice-lookin' piece of horseflesh," Jeremy said. "Wouldn't be interested in sellin' him, I suppose?" His voice was wistful, an incongruous sound from such a giant of a man, and Quinn smiled, shaking his head in reply.

"No, we've come a long way together." That his stud had ridden a lot of miles in a boxcar over the past couple of years was only the half of it.

"I'll pay you by the week," Quinn told the stable owner. "We may be in town for the rest of the winter."

Sheriff Mason lifted an eyebrow. "You're not headin' back up to the cabin?"

Quinn shook his head. "I'm going to look for a place in town for a while. You know of anything empty that'd work out for us?"

"Matter of fact, I might. Let's take a walk down the street here."

"It's got two bedrooms, Erin. A real house, with a lean-to for doing the wash and a big fireplace in the parlor. There's water in the house, and the outhouse is clean.''

Erin's eyes sparkled as she heard the news. She'd run to Quinn as he came in the kitchen door, her arms winding around his neck as she stood on tiptoe to hug him in welcome, only to flush and duck her head when Alice Mason chortled a teasing remark.

"Did you find the horses?"

Quinn nodded. "Don't know what he thought he was going to do with them. The man who was feeding the stock and cleaning the barn said he thought Toby was planning on selling the packhorse and his own gelding and keeping my stud. But I guess we'll never know for sure now. Doesn't matter, anyway. Where he's going, he won't have need of a horse for a while."

"Horse stealing's a hanging offense," Alice said bluntly.

Quinn laughed. "Damn horses are worth more than my scalp."

"Not to me," Erin retorted, and then looked away, as if she had given voice to a hidden thought.

"You're pretty fond of me, lady. Don't try to deny it," Quinn said with a chuckle, squeezing her tightly. If they were alone, he'd be tempted to trundle her off to the bedroom and see if he couldn't get her to admit more than that. Fond wasn't what he was after from Erin Yarborough. He suspected she was pretty taken with him, but he wouldn't be satisfied until she said the words right up front.

"I'll be more fond of you when you get us moved into that house you've been bragging about," Erin said smartly, pushing at Quinn's chest, freeing herself.

He released Erin reluctantly, good manners prevailing.

It wasn't quite the thing to be hugging in front of the sheriff's wife, even if Alice did have a big grin on her face. "We've got to wait until we go before the judge in the morning, honey. We're still technically prisoners, you know."

Erin's face sobered. "Is there any chance we won't be free tomorrow?"

Quinn shook his head. "I doubt it. In fact, the sheriff said I could plan on staying here. He's over at the jail, giving Toby Jones the bad news now."

"I think we're gonna celebrate tonight," Alice said cheerfully. "Reckon I'll bake us a big cream cake, and put a roast in the oven for supper."

"Ma'am, you may have me for a star boarder, if you keep that up," Quinn teased. Not likely, though, he thought. The idea of privacy was looking better and better.

New York City

"He's giving you back the retainer? What does that mean?" Estelle Wentworth asked icily. She stood in front of the bay window, facing her husband.

"Just what I said," Ted replied. "Joel Guinan came by my office today and gave me a draft for the full amount of Quinn's retainer. Said he was off the case. He's going to send me a full report of what he found."

"Where is he? Did he find her? Has she had the child yet?" Estelle's eyes were narrowed and dark with anger as she fired questions at her husband.

"Guinan didn't say. All he told me was that I'd be getting a report from Quinn in a couple of weeks."

"And you're going to sit around and wait for that crook to…"

"He's not a crook, Estelle." His tone was firm as Ted's temper flared. "What would you like me to do? Chase him down?"

"Are you willing to give up claim to your grandchild that easily, Mr. Wentworth? It's Damian's child that Irish creature was carrying when she left here. Somewhere, she's hiding the last surviving trace of our son. If she isn't living in a shack someplace, I'll eat my hat. And that baby is probably… Well, it makes my heart hurt just to think of Damian's child being raised by that woman."

"*That woman,* as you put it, was married to our son, Estelle. She certainly isn't going to neglect her child."

Estelle's eyes glittered with blind hatred. "You said you thought there might be reason to think Damian's death wasn't an accident, Ted. What if she pushed him down those stairs? Is that the kind of mother our grandchild should have?"

"I'll talk to Guinan again. See if I can find out anything at all." Ted Wentworth's shoulders were bent as he turned from his wife, as if the burden he bore weighed him down.

Colorado

"I find no reason to hold you, Mrs. Yarborough. That jackass Jones has lied about everything else. No reason I should take his word against yours. We'll call it justifiable homicide and close the case." Judge Herbert Beal's gavel struck the table with a resounding crack, and Erin drew a deep breath.

She turned to Quinn, fearful that one sympathetic look from him would set loose a geyser of tears, hoping he would simply take her hand and lead her out of this place. Quinn's eyes were alight with satisfaction, and his smile was wide as he nodded at her.

"Nothing to it, ma'am. That judge knows an honest woman when he sees one." He grasped Erin's outstretched hand and drew her to his side.

"Just a minute, young man," Judge Beal said soberly. "There's a matter of tying up a sheriff's deputy and taking his horse that needs to be settled before I can clear this docket."

"Damn!" Quinn's exclamation was whispered, but heartfelt nonetheless. He released Erin's hand and walked to the table where the judge presided.

"Now, I understand that Mr. Folsom is not wanting to press charges against you, but the law is the law, and you broke it."

Quinn nodded agreement. "I had to get to my wife, sir. I don't have any other defense but that. I didn't harm Tater in any way, and I made sure he could get loose in a matter of minutes. He was left in a warm cabin with food to spare, and I figured the sheriff would send someone up to get him in a day or so."

"That all sounds very nice and thoughtful of you, young man, but the fact remains that you took the man's horse."

Quinn swallowed the impatience that threatened his good sense. "I know I did, sir, but the truth is, I didn't steal it. I brought it right here to town and left it at the livery stable for him."

The judge looked past Quinn to where the sheriff and Tater Folsom stood. "You got anything to say about this, Sheriff?"

"Seems to me this is where those things called extenuating circumstances might come into play, Your Honor," the sheriff said slowly. Tater grinned and nodded his agreement.

"Hmm…" The judge glanced at Quinn again, then turned his attention to Erin, who had moved to stand beside her husband. "Young woman, you got anything to say about this?"

"My husband came to me because he was worried about me being in jail. He rode down that mountain with a bullet wound in his head. Maybe he wasn't thinking clearly."

"Damn, Erin! I knew—"

"That's enough, young man!" the judge said firmly. "I think your wife might have something there." He peered at the sheriff. "This might be that extenuating circumstance you were spouting about a minute ago, Sheriff. Mr. Yarborough obviously was acting irrationally because of his head wound. I reckon we can understand that. And since he already spent two nights in custody, we'll just dismiss those charges, too." With another bang of his gavel and a loud "Case dismissed," he turned to the sheriff once more.

"Now, let's haul that miserable cayuse out of his cell and tend to business."

"May we leave, Your Honor?" Quinn asked, taking Erin's hand and edging toward the door.

"Yeah, might as well. We've got this rascal dead to rights, seeing as how the sheriff is testifying against him. You better take that wife of yours home, young man. Let her look after that head wound of yours." He waved at the door. "Now go on, get out of here."

"I sure hope you like this place, honey," Quinn said, inserting the key into the front door of the small house that sat three doors down from the sheriff's home. He'd opened the white gate with a flourish and led Erin to the porch, pointing out the ice on the steps, lest she slip and fall.

"It's not very big," he warned her, ushering her into the hallway.

"A whole lot bigger than the cabin," Erin told him with a nervous laugh. She felt like a brand new bride, she decided. As if this were her wedding day, almost. For unless she was reading him wrong, Quinn expected to move into this house before the day was over.

She followed him through a wide archway into the parlor, noting the fireplace and the meager furnishings. A sofa, a chair, two tables with lamps in place and a library table in front of the window took only a few seconds to inventory.

"I thought we could make do here for a while. If you want to, we can order some furniture from Andy Wescott over at the general store. He can get it in from Denver for us."

Erin smiled at Quinn's concern. "It's fine just the way it is, Quinn. Let's see the rest of the house." She followed as he left the parlor and showed her the kitchen, complete with a built-in flour sifter in the dresser, and a small pantry with walls of shelves lining the windowless area.

Upstairs, two bedrooms snuggled beneath the eaves, with sloping ceilings and open grates on the floor that would allow the heat to rise from the rooms below when the stove was lit. A double bed, dresser and a wooden chair occupied one bedroom, while the other contained a single bed and a wide chest of drawers.

"Not much to brag about, is it?" Quinn asked, hands

shoved deep in his pockets as he watched Erin's reactions.

Her smile was bittersweet as she turned to face him. "I couldn't help but compare it to the house I lived in in New York."

He'd lay money it was a mansion, Quinn thought, complete with butler and maid. "Quite a comedown, I'll bet, having to live in a place like this," he muttered, turning from her.

"Oh, no!" Her denial was vehement and she wrapped her arms around him, her face against his back. "This will be a happy house, Quinn. I don't care about fancy things like china and crystal and fine rugs on the floor."

But she'd had them, probably all of them purchased by Ted Wentworth, Quinn decided, for their darling only son and his bride. "You had a maid, didn't you?" he asked, aware of her hands pressed against his coat, feeling her warmth even through the heavy fabric.

"Two of them," she admitted with a sigh. "They kept cleaning up behind me, until I was afraid to touch anything, for fear I'd make them more work."

Quinn turned in her embrace and framed her face in his big hands. "This is nothing like the bedroom you slept in there, is it?" His gaze touched the meager furnishings, stopping finally on the double bed.

She shivered, closing her eyes. "No, thank God. I never want to think about my room there again, Quinn. I have nothing but bad memories of that place."

"Even when you were a new bride?" Why he pushed her for information was beyond him. It was as if he must know all the details of her life with Damian Wentworth in New York before he could decide how to continue with the marriage he and Erin had set into being here in Colorado.

She lifted her lashes, shaking her head sadly. "It didn't take long to discover what a dreadful mistake I'd made, Quinn. Damian had a cruel streak. He delighted in keeping me under his thumb. Our honeymoon didn't even last as long as the wedding night." Her cheeks flushed as she made the confession, and Quinn was shamed by her words. He'd pushed her to admitting her unhappiness, making her relive it in her mind. And all for the sake of his selfish satisfaction in knowing she was better off here, with him.

"You didn't even have a wedding night with me," he reminded her with a chuckle, hoping to lighten her mood.

It worked. Her grin was playful as she tilted her head, lifting one hand to touch his mouth. He slid his arms around her, tugging her against him. She relaxed, allowing him to take her weight. He leaned back against the dresser, his feet on either side of hers, his hands smoothing down the length of her back. She shifted against him and he grinned at the awareness in her eyes as she felt his growing arousal.

"We had a wedding night. We just didn't...you know," she whispered, her gaze unwavering as she bit at her lip.

"No matter. It wasn't time, then. And when it happened it was..." There were no words to describe the happiness she'd brought him that night. He could only drink in the fragile beauty of the woman he held and yearn for more of the joy he'd found in her embrace.

As if she sought reassurance, she prodded him. "Was it all right? Did you..."

He nodded. "It was more than all right. I only wish I'd been able to give you the pleasure you deserved. I know you didn't..." This was not the time, he decided abruptly.

Erin's forehead furrowed and she shook her head, her expression puzzled. "I didn't...what?"

She truly didn't know. His bride, for all her years of marriage, was unaware of what she'd missed in the bed she'd shared with Damian Wentworth. Quinn's heart soared with gladness, his mouth twisted in a grin he had no hope of concealing, and his hands drew her even closer.

"Are you laughing at me?" Erin's words were slow, dubious, and she shrank back from his nearness, her cheeks crimson.

Quinn shook his head, rocking back and forth with her. "Not on your life, lady. I'm just pleased as punch that you're in for a surprise, and I'm the one who's gonna give it to you."

"Quinn?" She looked confused and he took pity, bending to touch her lips with his own. It was a mere kiss of promise, for he knew that to loose his pent-up passion on her now would be a mistake.

"We need to get back to the sheriff's place, Erin," he said, his mouth still brushing against hers. "We'll pack up our things and bring them over here. I wonder if Alice would lend us some sheets and pillows until we can go to the emporium and pick up some supplies."

Her eyes widened at his words. "I never thought of all that. We have bedding at the cabin, and my quilts and..." Her words halted as if she were overwhelmed by the chore of moving into a different house.

"We'll take care of all that in the next few days," Quinn promised her. "For now, let's just locate a lamp and some candles and get the baby's things together."

Erin's glance shot to the bed once more. "We're going to sleep here tonight?"

"If you don't mind making do for a day or so," he told her, his smile urging her to comply.

"As long as it's warm enough for Robert, and we've got water, I'll be fine."

"I'll check out the wood supply, but I think we're all right there. Sheriff said the woodshed out back was in good shape. We'll have to prime the pump, and I'm afraid everything in the kitchen needs a good scrubbing."

"After the cabin, this is like a palace, Quinn," she told him with a laugh. "You should have seen the mess there. It took me three days to make it fit to live in."

"I still can't figure why you—"

"I was desperate. I thought no one would ever look for me there." Her laughter had evaporated, and sadness touched her eyes. "I wasn't even thinking straight, Quinn. I just knew I had to hide, and when I heard that there was an empty cabin and that the old miner wanted almost nothing for the deed, I bought it."

"It was a lucky day when I heard about the woman whose hair was darker than midnight, living halfway up the mountain from Pine Creek."

"Darker than midnight?" Erin's brow rose in disbelief.

Quinn nodded. "That's what the man said. It cost me a five-dollar gold piece to hear those words."

"How did he know?"

"He was passing through on his way to Denver. He'd left Big Bertha and was heading east. I asked about you in the hotel, and he was waiting to get a room."

"Then it was just chance that you found me, wasn't it?"

"I had a man in Denver working on it before I got there," Quinn said slowly, strangely reluctant to reveal the details of his search. "That miner just saved me a couple of days."

"And I thought I'd covered my tracks so well," she whispered, shaking her head.

"This is what I do for a living, honey," he told her. "A woman who looks like you pretty much stands out in a crowd, you know. I'd have found you, one way or another."

Her gaze meshed with his. "I'm glad you did. With all that's happened, I couldn't have made it on my own." Her eyes shone with tears, and she lifted a hand to touch his face, her fingers brushing at the dark beard that covered his jaw.

"Don't cry, sweetheart," he said quickly, turning his head to press his lips against her palm. Her hand was cold and he frowned. "Let's get downstairs, so I can build a fire. I want this house warmed up before we bring Robert from Alice's."

She nodded, drawing her hand from his grasp to delve within her pocket for a hankie. Her tears were dried in a moment and she followed him down the stairs.

"I can't ask Alice to give up her laundry basket, Quinn. Can we get one from the store for Robert to sleep in?"

"He can bed down in a dresser drawer for tonight. We'll figure out something else tomorrow," he told her. "You go on back and get our things together while I tend to the fire and make sure we have water."

He pulled her collar up and buttoned the top button on her coat. "Where's your hat?"

"I'll use my scarf," she said, lifting it to cover her hair, then tossing the long ends over her shoulder.

His hands lingered on her, touching her face, his fingers brushing at her cheek. "I'll only be a few minutes here. Be sure to ask Alice if we can borrow a lamp for tonight, all right?"

"And candles," she added, as if she mentally made a list.

He nodded. "And candles."

Chapter Sixteen

She'd expected Quinn to be waiting for her in the bedroom at the top of the stairs. What she hadn't anticipated was the setting he'd arranged for her benefit. Candles glowed softly from the dresser, a pair of them, reflecting her vision in the wavy glass of the mirror. Another taper on a small table next to the bed illuminated the quilt she'd borrowed from Alice, beneath which Quinn waited.

Erin hesitated in the doorway, Robert in her arms, her heart expanding in her chest, its rapid beat sending the blood rushing to her throat. The warmth spread throughout her body, except where her feet touched the bare wooden floor. There her toes curled, and she watched in silence as his hooded gaze touched that small, involuntary gesture.

"You're cold," he said. For a moment she felt vulnerable, her flannel gown no defense against the look he offered her—his nostrils flaring, a ruddy hue invading the dark skin that covered his cheekbones. She was a woman full grown, almost twenty-four years old. She was married to Quinn Yarborough, but he had touched her with a husband's hands only once, and then in comfort. That he had found release in her body was a fact, and she had gloried in his possession.

Now he watched her from the bed, his narrowed eyes gleaming beneath dark brows. His hair was black against the pristine pillowcase, and her fingers yearned to twine themselves in that silky length. Erin shivered, as if her body craved the heat of his flesh against hers, and she thought, for just a moment, that the air held an aroma that was uniquely his.

Quinn was past thirty years old, experienced, perhaps cynical at times when it came to the women who had found a place in his bed. Not that there had been a countless number parading through his life. He'd chosen to live circumspectly, as if he awaited that one female who would strike a spark within him. And, it had seemed, he'd waited in vain.

Then he'd found her, there on the side of a mountain, this faerie creature who had allowed him a glimpse of her soul. Who had shared her memories, her grief and her capacity for love with him in a hideaway where nothing was concealed between them. Where two people, for a time, took refuge together.

In his memory those days still wore a patina of perfection he could not explain, given the events they had survived. They had battled pain and injury, and fought the horror of death. Only to come together in a blending of body and spirit that bore no resemblance to anything he'd ever experienced in his life.

It had been a time of bonding, days and weeks of living closer to a woman than he'd ever imagined. She had taken his strength and made it her own, taken his infirmities and spent her energy on his wounded body.

And now she stood before him, carrying against her

breast the child they had claimed. Her slender form was bathed in the glow of the candles he had set in place, one on a small table by the bed, two on the dresser.

Flowing over her shoulders to her waist, her hair was a sable cloak glistening in the light of the flickering tapers. Her gown was nondescript, a pale covering that hid from him the tender flesh beneath, and there, below its hem, her toes curled against the wooden floor.

"You're cold," he said again, lifting the covers to sweep them aside. He'd propped the pillows behind his bare back, wondering if he expected too much of the woman he'd married. Would she hesitate at the sight of his body so exposed to her view? Perhaps he should have retained the covering of his smallclothes, or waited for her fully dressed.

It was too late to question his actions now. Erin watched him from the doorway, Robert in her arms. Her eyes shone in the candle glow, her face radiant, luminous with a pale light of its own. And then she moved toward the bed, to where he'd arranged a sleeping place for the child.

A pillow provided the mattress, and she laid the babe within the dresser drawer, tucking her shawl over his blanket-wrapped form. He nuzzled his fist and sighed, a drop of milk showing evidence of his recent feeding.

"I should have worn my house shoes," Erin whispered, her fingers lingering on Robert's soft, dark hair. She glanced up, her gaze warm as it rested on Quinn's face. "Will you get me warm?"

It was far from what he had expected her to say. It was an offer he had not dared hope for. An overture he could only accept with open arms, his body already forming a welcome of its own. His hand met hers as she lifted one knee to the mattress, guiding, balancing her as she moved to where he waited.

And then he held her, enfolding her warm, willing body against himself, breathing in the sweet scent of her flesh, his mouth seeking the tender skin of her throat. She curled in his lap, his thighs cushioning the curve of her bottom. Her legs drew up beneath her gown, and he felt the chill presence of her feet against the side of his thigh.

Quinn laughed softly, possessed suddenly with a happiness he had thought never to attain. He'd bargained to warm her, and the anticipation of what that might involve brought him to a state of readiness.

Warm her he would. But the knowledge that her woman's flesh was not prepared, that she knew little of the pleasures to be found in the marriage bed, was a deterrent he could not ignore.

Cradling her in his embrace, he reached one hand down to caress the small feet that were beginning to take on the heat of his body. "Feeling better?" he asked, his words rasping against her ear.

Erin nodded, her voice hushed as if in deference to the sleeping baby. "You radiate heat like the woodstove downstairs." Her hand slid up his arm, fingers tensing against the firm muscle. An almost silent sigh signaled her contentment as those wandering fingertips continued across his shoulder until they laced through his hair.

The pressure of her touch turned his head, and Quinn allowed it, willing her to do as she pleased, watching through slitted eyes as she tilted her chin and shuttered her gaze from his view. Her mouth touched his, her lips soft, her breath warm as he inhaled its sweetness. His name was a hushed sound that barely reached his ears, and she repeated it, her lips moving as the single syllable issued forth.

His hunger could not be denied. His body tensed and hardened beneath her fragile weight, and he cradled her closely as he turned in the bed, levering her beneath him. The fabric of her gown twisted around her body and he groaned his frustration, even as he grasped folds of material and eased it from her.

She lifted her arms as the flannel sleeves were pulled over her hands, and she caught her breath, a quick blush turning her ivory flesh to a rosy hue. The fullness of her breasts drew him, and he laced her fingers with his, holding her hands to either side of her shoulders. Warm lips met cool skin and the dark crests puckered at his touch.

Erin smothered a gasp, her body surging upward in reaction, and Quinn was hard put to cover his delight as her hands escaped his grip to clasp behind his head. He smiled, aware of each fingertip that clutched his scalp. His mouth pressed the underside of her breast, feeling the tender bit of flesh against his cheek, even as a drop of liquid traced a path across his skin.

He lifted his head, his tongue touching the pale drops of milk, tasting the life-giving nectar her body contained. "It's sweet." His words held an element of surprise, and he smiled up at her, entranced by the look of confusion she wore.

"I didn't know…" she whispered, her eyes widening as she watched him flick his tongue once more against another drop of her milk.

He lifted himself above her and touched his tongue to her mouth. "Taste it." The droplet moistened her lip and her tongue darted out to snatch it.

A smile twitched reluctantly at one corner of her

mouth and she blushed anew. "I'm not sure that was proper of you."

"What we do in our bed is always proper, Erin," he said quietly, suddenly solemn, as if this moment were of exceeding importance. "Your body is wonderfully made, sweetheart, and when you married me, you gave me permission to claim it as my own. You belong to me now. And I belong to you."

Her mouth trembled and then stilled, her lips pressing together for a moment. "I want to belong to you, Quinn. I thought for so long that…well, that's not important now."

Her eyes had darkened, just for a moment, and he wondered at the shadows of the past that had visited their memories on her. He yearned to forever banish the thoughts of Damian Wentworth from her mind, to flood her being with so much joy and pleasure that the past would be buried for all time.

"Nothing is important but this," he said, tasting her, touching her, taking her mouth with his in a caress that was welcomed with a sigh of acquiescence. She opened to his seeking, needing no urging as she allowed his kisses full sway. His tongue found hers, and he felt the minute hesitation, then the restrained movement as she allowed his exploration.

She was virgin flesh to his touch and Quinn was exalted by the knowledge. Whatever her marriage had done to her, it had not damaged the innocence of her response, the eagerness with which she returned his caress. Her hands left his hair—her fingertips seeming reluctant to release the grip they had taken—and then moved to his shoulders and she tugged at him.

"I want to touch you, Quinn." Erin's whisper was breathless and he felt the damp movement of her lips against his as she spoke. Again his flesh surged, thrusting against her, and she shifted beneath him, her hips rising from the mattress.

He lifted himself over her, resting on his forearms, mesmerized by her beauty. Her hands spread wide on his shoulders, then moved slowly to his chest where her fingers tugged at the dark hair that curled in a wide triangle. She brushed inquisitive fingertips across his nipples and he shivered, closing his eyes as he savored the sensation she brought him.

"Quinn?" He thought he would never tire of her voice whispering his name, and he smiled as she repeated the single syllable. "Quinn?"

"I don't know how long I can wait, Erin." His voice sounded hoarse to his own ears as he offered his words of apology. "I don't think you'd better do that anymore."

"This?" she asked, her hands sweeping slowly over his chest again.

He shivered. "Yeah, that."

Her mouth curled in a satisfied smile and he growled, deep within his throat, his need overcoming his patience as she teased him once more, her fingertips taking new liberties.

His kiss captured the curl of her lip, ventured beyond and traced the edge of her teeth, delving even deeper to discover the secrets of her mouth. Her moan of pleasure was accompanied by the slide of her arms around his back, and her hands clutched at his waist, as if she anchored herself against the tide of pleasure he brought to her.

He rolled with her, his arms urging her body to meld with his, one hand sliding to cup her bottom, relishing the firm curve of her hip and thigh beneath his fingers.

His mouth left hers and he tasted the tender skin of her throat, her shoulder and breast, his tongue and teeth testing the resilience of her flesh.

Erin moaned, her fingers kneading his back, and he gloried in the sound of her passion. His touch slowed, gentling as he sought the hidden secrets of her woman's flesh, and then he swallowed a sound of exultation as his touch gave proof of her desire.

He had vowed to bring her joy, had promised himself the gift of her pleasure. Now his own needs were put aside, almost forgotten as he worshiped the woman he'd taken as his wife. He wooed her, praising her for the beauty of her form, whispering words of encouragement as he brought her to the edge of completion. His hands caressed her, his fingers sought her pleasure in a hundred ways, and his kisses pressed her ever closer to fulfillment.

She cried out, a muffled sound that pierced his heart, and he opened his eyes, rising above her as she met his gaze with eyes that reflected his. ''Quinn!'' Her cry was frantic, as if she sought a goal she could not attain, and he covered her mouth with his own, his manhood urgent against her. She trembled in his arms, then opened to him, urging him to seek the haven he'd denied himself for too long.

She clung, as if her very life depended on the warmth of his flesh, the movement of his body against her. ''Quinn!'' The entreaty was whispered again and she lifted herself, offering entrance, entwining her limbs with his, straining to capture that part of him that promised a pleasure beyond bearing.

And then he was there, stretching her, filling her, bringing her once more to a knowledge of her own womanhood.

Erin groaned aloud. She'd known the touch of a man's hands, the weight of a man's body on hers. Yet never had she known this purity of love, the joyful acceptance that made two bodies into one flesh.

She could only whisper his name, her whole being alive with his presence, his arms enclosing her as his manhood claimed her depths with a sweet invasion. Gone was the terror of the past. Forgotten were the harsh reminders of another's hands. Only the fresh, pure knowledge of Quinn Yarborough's possession filled her mind and heart as she knew the primitive exaltation of belonging to the man she loved.

The letter came on the stagecoach from Denver, and was hand delivered by Tater Folsom just before noon. Erin scanned the envelope, her curiosity on edge as she read the return address.

Louis Hardiman, Special Investigator. What a special investigator in Denver wanted with Quinn was a mystery she stood no chance of solving, she decided. She stifled the urge to hold the envelope up to the light. Even if she could see through the heavy paper, whatever was written within was none of her business.

Or was it?

It was because of her that Quinn had come to Denver and made inquiries of people there. And it made sense to think that one of those persons who had led him to Pine Creek might have been Louis Hardiman.

Reluctantly she placed the envelope on the kitchen table, leaning it on its edge against the sugar bowl. From there it drew her eyes like a magnet, and it was with a sense of heartfelt relief that she heard Quinn at the back door.

"Dinner's about ready," she sang out, careful to ignore the envelope that had demanded her attention for almost an hour. "Wash up and I'll fix our plates, Quinn."

He shrugged from his coat and hung his hat over it near the door. "Sheriff wants me to consider working with him, Erin. What do you think?" He made a production of rolling up his sleeves as he walked toward the sink.

She glanced at him over her shoulder, her hands busy with a pan full of cornbread. "Is that what you want to do?"

Quinn leaned over the washbasin, working up a layer of suds and scrubbing at his hands. "Come pump some water for me, will you?" he asked.

Erin nodded, stepping to his side. She pushed the handle down, then allowed it to rise, feeling the surge of water as it rose through the small pitcher pump, watching as it poured forth to rinse Quinn's hands.

He leaned against the sink, drying his hands on her dish towel, watching as she scurried back and forth between table and stove. "I want to have my own place, Erin."

She halted abruptly, a plate in each hand. "Here? Here in Pine Creek?"

Quinn shook his head. "No, not here. This is just a place to winter. And before I say any more about it, I think we need to talk."

"You don't have to worry about me, Quinn. I'm not especially attached to this place. The only thing holding us here, as far as I'm concerned, is finding out about making sure Robert is legally ours." She placed the two plates on the table, then stood back, eyeing the food she'd prepared.

"I think that's it. Slumgullion and cornbread go pretty well together. I'll just get the coffee."

Quinn's brow furrowed. "Slumgullion? Is this something new?" He peered at his plate. "Looks like goulash to me."

Erin served the coffee and slid into her chair. "It's beef and tomatoes and whatever else you can find to put in it. Alice gave me a couple of quarts of tomatoes she canned from her garden, and some macaroni she bought from the emporium. That's about all I had, besides onions. I guess you can call it whatever you want to, so long as it tastes good."

"Smells all right to me," Quinn said agreeably, bending to kiss her cheek as he circled the table to his own chair. "I've learned to enjoy most any kind of food over the past few years."

He sat down and lifted his spoon, only to eye the letter that faced him from in front of the sugar bowl. "What's this?"

"It came a while ago. Tater brought it from the general store when he picked up the sheriff's post. He said we probably should start checking on general delivery every few days, in case we get mail."

Quinn slid his finger under the flap and opened the letter. "No one knows we're here, so far as I know." He glanced down. "Except for Louis Hardiman, I guess." He scanned the single page quickly, then put it aside.

Erin picked up her fork and began eating, her eyes straying to the abandoned letter as she chewed. "Is it important, Quinn?" she asked finally, her curiosity getting the better of her.

"In a roundabout way, I guess," he answered, reaching for a piece of cornbread. He buttered it carefully, frowning as if it took an immense amount of concentration.

"Is it about me?" She felt a flare of anger at his reticence, and chewed with vigor.

"Mr. Hardiman says someone's been making inquiries about both of us in Denver. Joel Guinan got wind of it in New York and asked Louis to notify me that a detective's been nosing around, and that Ted and Estelle Wentworth have left the city for an extended trip."

"They're coming here?" Erin asked, fork in midair as she awaited the answer. Her appetite was gone, washed away in the flood of anxiety that spread throughout her being.

Quinn shook his head. "He didn't say that. Matter of fact, he didn't offer them any information, either in person or by way of the detective they seem to have hired." He lifted his fork to take another bite, and Erin eyed him with impatience.

"How can you just sit there and eat when I'm being hunted down like an animal?" Her voice was harsh, and she caught her breath in a sob as she pushed away from the table.

Quinn shot her a glance that stopped her as she would have risen to her feet. "Just stay put, honey. Getting all in a dither won't help a thing," he said quietly. "And this food won't be fit to eat when it's cold. Sit back down."

His tone of voice left no room for argument, and Erin sat on the edge of her chair. Never had he given her an order before; but he was telling her what to do now, and in no uncertain terms. She relaxed the grip she'd held on the sides of her chair and watched as Quinn cleaned his plate.

"You don't look very concerned," she said with a tinge of accusation coloring her words.

He lifted an eyebrow and shrugged. "No sense in worrying about it until something happens. We don't know if Ted has found out where we are or not. And if he does follow me here, I can't see that he's gonna be able to do much to harm either of us."

"He'll be angry that I managed to hide, and they'll both accuse me of terrible things when they find out that my baby—" Her voice broke, and her hands buried themselves in the folds of her dress.

"Your baby died, Erin, and no one could have been more upset about that than you were. I can understand that they'd be unhappy about it. That was their last link to Damian, and when they find out that the little fella didn't make it, they'll have a fit about it. But it isn't going to do them a bit of good. All of Ted Wentworth's money can't bring that baby back, any more than money spent on a grand education and fancy tailoring could make a man out of Damian."

She blinked back tears, facing him with a look of sorrow that had become familiar to him over the past months. Only when Damian's name was mentioned did that blend of misery and distress color her visage.

"I'd like to erase that look from your eyes once and for all," Quinn muttered, his quick anger a surprise. "I think you're still afraid of him, aren't you?"

Erin shook her head. "No, not of him, but of what his parents can still do to me. You don't understand, do you, Quinn? Ted really feels I had something to do with his son's death. What if he accuses me? What if the police come after me? What will happen to Robert then?" She got to her feet, and her gaze swept the edges of the room as if she sought escape.

"They won't hurt you, Erin. I'll see to it. You're my wife now." Quinn's hands clenched, and his temper rose as he considered her fears. "So far as I know, the cause of Damian's death was never disputed. If Ted wanted to cast doubt on you, he'd have done it then. And if the authorities were after you, I'd have known it by now."

"How?" She tossed her head and her mouth tightened. "You know, you've never told me all the details of how you found me. How many investigators did you involve in the hunt for the missing widow, Quinn? And how, pray tell, did you plan on hauling me back to New York?" Her voice was shrill as she shot her queries at him.

He shook his head dismissively. "All that's in the past, Erin. You know very well I wouldn't have tried to force you to do anything. Whose side do you think I'm on?"

"Well, it must have cost Ted a pretty penny to hunt me down. He's going to want blood before he's done. I'd lay money on that. And private investigators don't come cheap. How much was I worth, Quinn?" As if all the anger and fear and outrage of the past months had exploded in one grand display, Erin faced him across the room. Her skin was pale beneath the flush of passion on her cheeks, her eyes blazed with an icy blue flame and her breasts lifted and fell with each breath, as if her lungs could not expand enough to contain the anger she exhaled with each breath.

"How much were you worth? Shall I tell you, wife of mine?" Quinn's teeth were bared as he laughed with a savage inflection that allowed his own feelings an outlet. "You were worth every penny Ted Wentworth paid me. But it ended up coming out of my own pocket. I've already had a voucher sent to his bank for the amount of my retainer. I gave him back every bit of my advance monies. I haven't made one red cent on this venture, lady."

His hands fisted against his hips as he bent toward her. "All I managed to do was chop your wood, tend your stock, deliver your child and end up with a crease in my head for your benefit. Now, you tell me what that was worth!"

Erin's mouth opened, then closed, one hand covering it as if she would hold back the words that might issue forth. Her nostrils flared as she inhaled, and she trembled visibly, the flush of anger overcome by a pallor that washed all color from her skin.

"I didn't know I had cost you so much," she managed finally, her hand spreading wide across her breast as she backed from him. "I've been quite a drain on your bank account, haven't I?" Her head bent low, but her voice vibrated with pride. "I beg your pardon, Mr. Yarborough, for all the trouble you've suffered on my behalf."

"Ah...hell, Erin! Cut it out!" As fast as his anger had infused him, as rapidly as he'd loosed his thoughtless words on her ears, he repented, shaking his head in regret.

"No..." She stepped back again, coming to a halt against the wall as Quinn approached her, his hands outstretched.

"You know I don't regret anything I've done," he said quietly, as cautious now of her unnaturally calm demeanor as he had been of the riotous frenzy she'd unleashed only minutes past.

"Don't you?"

He shook his head. "No. I regret nothing except my failure to keep you safe. I married you because—"

"Yes," she hissed, her head lifting as she interrupted him quickly. "Why did you marry me? For the child? Or was it because you thought I would provide you with a degree of entertainment during the long…" Her eyes closed, and she shook her head. "Even that didn't work to your benefit, did it? I couldn't even…I wasn't worth much to you as a wife, was I?" Her mouth pouted with the words, and she looked away, turning from him.

"Have I complained?" he asked, lifting his hand to touch her hair, his fingers tangling in it. He saw the small movement she could not hide, the flinching of her shoulder from his touch, and he cursed beneath his breath.

"Don't ever do that to me." His words were steel, wrapped in a harsh whisper that brought her whirling to face him. "Don't draw back from my touch. I've never given you reason to fear me, Erin."

"Even now?" Her eyes defied him. "You look like you could shake me or worse." Her jaw was clenched, and her shoulders drew back in a gesture of defiance he could only admire.

"You don't want to hear what I'd like to do to you right now, Erin Yarborough." He gritted the words out between his teeth.

"I'm sure I've heard it before. I know what comes next. Remember? I've been there."

"Not here, you haven't." He noted her wince as his callused fingers tugged at her hair, and he ignored it. He heard the smothered protest as he swept her into his arms, his actions pressing her face against his chest. And when he carried her up the stairs to the bedroom beneath the eaves, his arms held her firmly.

He placed her in the center of the bed that had held them only hours before, the bed he had prepared for her just last night. Now he stood over her looking like a man intent on proving a point. His hair was ruffled, his jaw set stubbornly, and his eyes were glittering beneath lowered brows.

She should have been afraid. She should have been running for dear life toward the door, intent on escape. And yet, she watched him.

His fingers worked deliberately at the buttons of his trousers, until the denim fabric hung precariously on his hips. "If you make any noise you'll wake the baby," he said in a low voice, nodding at the dresser drawer where Robert nestled.

A flush of desire outlined his cheekbones, and his nostrils flared as he bent over her. "Are you afraid of me yet, Erin?" His whisper was ominous and his gaze swept across her bosom, even as his hands touched the buttons that protected her modesty.

She felt the rapid beat of her heart beneath his fingers as he uncovered the lacy border of her chemise. His index finger edged the plump rise of one breast, then the other, and Erin closed her eyes, aware that her body responded to his touch. He laughed beneath his breath.

"Look at me, Erin." His finger stilled and she drew in a breath, shaking her head.

He sat on the edge of the bed, then rolled to lie beside her, and she was aware of the outdoor scent of him, the masculine aroma of his skin as he drew her into his embrace. Her nose touched his chest, the curls brushing against her mouth, and she turned her head away.

Quinn rose over her, holding himself on one elbow, the other hand brushing her hair from her cheek. "Look at me, Erin," he repeated. "I want to see the fear in your eyes."

Chapter Seventeen

Her lids rose slowly, her eyes appraising him as he watched her. "I'm not afraid of you, Quinn Yarborough. If you think I'm going to beg for mercy, you're sadly mistaken."

He lowered his head, his whisper taunting her as he brushed her mouth with his. "One day I'll hear you beg, sweetheart. Maybe not now, but one day you'll need me as much as I need you."

"Beg you for what?" she asked, careful not to allow him entrance to her mouth as she spoke, holding her lips taut.

An amused gleam tempered the darkness of his gaze. "I can't wait to show you," he answered, a husky tension underlying his words. His hand tugged at her dress, pulling it up to expose her legs, and her own fingers tangled with his, wrestling for possession of the garment.

"It's the middle of the day, Quinn Yarborough."

"I'm well aware of that." He grasped her wrist and moved the offending hand over her head, where, with very little effort, he managed to capture it, shifting to hold her in place. His thigh was heavy, keeping her leg immobile, and she grumbled loudly, wiggling against him in vain.

"Shh...you'll wake the baby," he whispered, exaggerating the words. His hand went back to the hem of her dress, lifting it to her waist. She lay beneath him, frustrated by his high-handedness, yet intrigued by the sensations those same shenanigans were producing in her body.

His nimble fingers untied her drawers and he stripped her of them, his hands moving with impudence over her legs as he pulled the cotton fabric down, stripping her of her house shoes as he went. And then those same fingers took a tingling path once more, finding their way back to the supple skin that covered her belly. They spread wide, flexing against her skin, teasing her with the promise of pleasure.

She rose instinctively from the mattress as his wandering fingertips touched her, as if her errant body sought closer contact with the hand that dared to claim her most intimate secrets as his own.

This was not the gentle lover of the night, the tender husband whose only thought was for her care and pleasure. This man, who touched her knowingly, who lavished hot, wet kisses upon her, who whispered words she had never heard into her ear, was another side of Quinn Yarborough she had not dreamed existed.

He was demanding, willing her response, his hands and fingers agile as he discovered tender flesh that deserved his attention. He was thorough, lifting her legs, murmuring appreciation for the slender length of her calves, brushing his mouth against her knees as he hovered over her.

And then he watched her through narrowed eyes as

he brought his male flesh to that place he had so carefully readied for his taking.

Quinn clasped her hands, spreading her fingers with his, joining them together symbolically. He sought and found the softness of her desire, then bent to kiss her, accepting her low cries into his mouth. He filled her, stretched her, became a part of her, and still she was left wanting. There, there…just beyond her grasp.

Erin lifted her hips, twisting, seeking that elusive pleasure. He withdrew slowly, leaving her empty and yearning, and she cried out, only to hear his words in her ear as he surged against her once more.

"Do you need me?" The whisper was rasping, his breathing harsh, and again he retreated, holding her still beneath him, hesitating for moments before he returned to her, slowly filling her with the entire measure of his manhood. "Is this what you want, Erin?" he asked, his words breathless against her hair.

"Yes…yes." Caught in the whirlwind, she rushed to meet whatever it held in store. She sobbed, writhing against him. Her arms enclosed him, her face buried against his shoulder, her cries of completion urging him in incoherent whimpers. And then he thrust within her a final time, his voice guttural as he called her name in an urgent plea.

"Erin…ah, baby!" He was heavy, pressing her into the mattress, and she gloried in it. He was male, strong, vibrant, and just a bit arrogant. She smiled secretly at that thought. He'd pushed her deliberately, she realized. He'd forced her to face her fears and recognize their absence in this bed they shared.

Quinn's anger had not frightened her. She had not retreated from his virile male strength, nor had she bowed to his taunts. He'd held her captive and yet, had she feared him, had he sensed panic or horror at his touch, she knew he would have given way. Even in his strength, she recognized the care and concern he lavished upon her.

And now her heart lifted with the knowledge of freedom gained. No longer would the specter of Damian Wentworth haunt her with its memory of cruel deeds and harsh treatment at masculine hands.

"I love you, Quinn." She'd said the words silently before. Now she lavished them upon him, repeating them as she scattered kisses wherever she could reach. "I love you!" Her whisper was tinged with a sob, and she brushed her tears against his shoulder.

"Don't cry, baby!" He lifted himself on his elbows, and his hands framed her face. "You know I love you, sweetheart. I can't stand to cause you pain. Don't cry."

"You haven't. You know you haven't hurt me, Quinn." She swept her hands up the length of his back, pressing against his shoulders. "Kiss me...please kiss me."

He lowered his head, his mouth taking sweeping possession of hers. Bestowing words of praise, Quinn whispered his love against her brow, breathed it against the tender skin of her throat and dropped countless kisses wherever his lips touched.

"I think I loved you first when you held my baby in your hands and breathed into his mouth, Quinn," she told him, cradling his head against her breast.

"Did you? I'd have given my soul at that moment to bring life to your child, Erin."

"You've done more for me than any other person in my life. I feel inadequate sometimes, as if I have nothing to give in return."

"Oh, but you have," he told her.

"You mean...this?" Her hand swept his back, pressing him against her body.

He shook his head. "No, I knew we'd come together in time. But more than that, I wanted your trust. I needed you to trust me enough to love me, and know I'd take care of you. I wanted you to depend on me without wondering if I'd ever turn on you, or use my strength against you."

"I know better than that," she said. "I think I've always known."

"Maybe. I was afraid it would take a while. I probably shouldn't have pushed you. You know, downstairs and just now." He closed his eyes and bent his head. "More than anything else, I needed to know you love me, Erin."

"And now you know."

He nodded, lifting his eyes to meet her gaze. "Now I know."

The snow had melted, turning the yard and street into a sea of mud. Only a hard frost had rescued Erin from losing her boots on the way to the emporium this morning.

On her way home Erin stopped at the sheriff's house, where Robert had stayed during her shopping expedition. Alice smiled, her arms reluctantly turning her charge over to his mother, and Erin then made her way to the small house. She had begun to call it home, settling in nicely, after less than two weeks. Quinn had teased her, accusing her of nesting, like the early bluebirds that perched on the fence every morning.

She put away her supplies, elated at her good fortune, having the general store right at her fingertips. Living in town had a lot to be said for it, with a friendly neighbor just steps away, and Quinn getting involved with the lawmen. A good way to keep his ear to the door, so to speak, he'd told her.

Having him go off every morning made her feel like a real housewife, something she'd never been acquainted with in her life. The switch from pampered lady of the manor to the sole occupant of a primitive mountain cabin had been a shock. Tending house with everything so handy revealed to her daily just how much she had been missing.

"I could get real used to this," she sang to Robert as she placed him in the small crib Quinn had bought for the baby's use downstairs. He'd watched her carry the dresser drawer down the stairs and frowned. Within a half hour the crib had replaced the drawer and taken one more chore from Erin's shoulders.

Robert's eyes closed and he yawned widely, bringing a thrill of joy to Erin's breast. "What a sweetheart you turned out to be, you precious lamb," she crooned, covering him with his quilt.

She had bread to mix and set to rise and supper to consider. Quinn had told her not to expect him for dinner at noon, so she'd given him a towel with cheese and crackers wrapped inside to tide him over. For that she'd earned a hearty kiss and a whisper of thanks.

It was well past noon when Erin heard someone stomping their feet on the porch. Sheriff Mason wore a look of solemn concern when he appeared at the kitchen door, and she knew a moment of terror. Something was wrong. As sure as the sun rose every morning, her intuition told her that her bubble of happiness was about to burst.

She should have known that the simple joys of living with Quinn and Robert in this house were too good to last, Erin thought wistfully as she opened the door to the lawman.

"What brings you out this morning?" she asked, mentally crossing her fingers, hoping for the best.

It was not to be.

With a shuffling of feet and much clearing of his throat, Henry Mason entered the kitchen, closing the door behind him. "Afraid I've got some news you're not gonna like to hear, Miz Yarborough," he muttered. He removed his hat, running his fingers through his hair, looking exceedingly uncomfortable to Erin's eye.

"You might as well tell me," she said stoutly, girding herself for whatever might come. If only Quinn...

"There's a lawyer fella coming from Denver to see you. He's been hired by some folks from New York City, name of Wentworth. Anybody you know?"

She nodded. "They were my first husband's parents."

His brow furrowed. "Thought your name was Peterson. Would have sworn that was what I heard."

Erin had the grace to blush. "I used that name. I left New York after my husband died, and I really didn't want his parents to find me, Sheriff."

"Looks to me like they went to a lot of trouble, young lady. Is there something else I should know?" His eyes held a challenge she could not refuse.

She lifted her hands in a silent appeal, her throat dry. "I was running from them, and pregnant when I arrived here. With their grandson. They wanted the child, and I didn't want them to have him. It was as simple as that."

"So you bought that old miner's cabin up the mountain and set up housekeeping, all on your own. I wondered what in tarnation you were doin' there, with winter comin' on."

She sat down at the table, her knees feeling as if they

might fail her. "No one questioned me a whole lot. I bought provisions at the emporium and supplies at the livery stable for my animals. People were kind."

"We don't ask a lot of questions out here. Never know when a person has something to hide, and so long as he's not breakin' the law, we kinda like to leave folks to themselves. But, to tell the truth, ma'am, I surely didn't know you were in the family way when you set off up that mountain, draggin' that cow and with a box of chickens tied on your packhorse." He laughed aloud. "You were some sight to behold. I remember thinkin' you were a spunky lady."

"Why is the lawyer coming here now?" Erin asked bluntly. Better to know the worst right off, she figured.

"Well, now that I know a little more about things, I begin to understand the issues. He's talkin' about taking custody of your child."

She felt cold fingers of fear slide up her spine, radiating to the tips of her fingers. "What makes him think anyone would have the right to my child?"

Sheriff Mason hung his head and sighed. "I think I better sit down for this, ma'am." He pulled out a chair and sat across the table from Erin. "It seems they found records in Denver from the hearing here in Pine Creek. Don't know what they were after, going through things at the courthouse, but the judge's findings were right there for them to see."

"What does that have to do with the baby?"

Henry Mason cleared his throat. "It seems the lawyer and the folks who hired him don't think you're a good candidate for motherhood, what with you shootin' that miner a few weeks ago. They're bringing a piece of paper along that says they've been granted custody of their grandson."

"But Robert isn't their grandson." Erin stood up abruptly, sending her chair toppling.

"Yes, ma'am. You and me both know that. It's only gonna be a matter of time before we clear it all up, I'm sure. I just hate to see you havin' to face such a thing."

"Where's the judge? Will he be here, too?"

Sheriff Mason shook his head. "He won't be back for another week. We only get him comin' around once a month. Unless there's reason for it."

"Isn't this reason enough?" Erin asked, pacing to the window and back. Her heart was pumping at a rapid pace, and the need to see Quinn was uppermost in her mind. "Where did you send my husband?" she asked.

"Aw, they had a fuss up at the mining camp. Couple of fellas shootin' at each other. I pinned a badge on Quinn and told him to bring both men back down. Figured they could cool their heels in jail till next week. Probably both of them will be ready to behave themselves by then."

"When is this lawyer coming?" She walked to the window again, as if watching for Quinn would bring him home to her more rapidly.

"Might be on the evening stage from Denver," Henry Mason allowed. "The letter came yesterday, and Tater didn't pick up the mail from the emporium till this morning."

From near the stove a fretful cry caught her attention. Erin turned, her footsteps quick as she reached Robert's side. He was fussing, kicking at his blanket, and, from all signs, more than ready for his midafternoon meal.

"Mama's here," Erin crooned, lifting him to her shoulder. She jiggled him in her arms, stilling his impatience, and turned back to the sheriff.

"Do I have to see him?" Beneath her, her legs trembled, as if she had walked a very long way and desperately needed a place to rest. The rocking chair seemed a likely spot and she headed there, aware of a wave of dizziness that brought perspiration to her brow.

"Say, now! You feelin' all right, ma'am?" Sheriff Mason asked, abruptly rising from his chair. "You look a mite peaked, Miz Yarborough. You're not comin' down with something, are you?"

She shook her head. "I'm fine. I'll be better when Quinn gets back." She rocked Robert in her arms, aware that his whimpering, as he nuzzled at his fist, would soon develop into a full-blown cry for his dinner.

The sheriff nodded, clapping his hat into place, tugging up his trousers by the belt and heading for the door. "I'll just leave you to it, ma'am. I'll let you know what's goin' on as soon as that lawyer fella shows up."

Erin nodded, rocking harder. She was trembling, fearful of shedding the tears that were gathering. Just when things were at their best, just when she'd finally found a home and a modicum of security in her life...

With a final nod, the sheriff left, closing the door behind him, and Erin fought the urge to search for the key that would lock it against intruders. Thus far, they had settled for latching the door at night. Now she felt that even this haven was not secured against whatever Ted and Estelle Wentworth had set in motion.

The hotel was brimful to the eaves, what with its usual patrons, and now the occupants of the evening stage taking up residence. Quinn watched from the door, reluctant to track across the lobby with his muddy boots. The sun had come out today, once more turning the streets to a miry mess; even though he'd scraped his boots against the edge of the boardwalk, he was still dragging dirt on his soles.

"Deputy? What can I do for you?" The owner of Pine Creek's largest establishment bustled to the door where he waited, and Quinn gestured at his feet.

"I spent the best part of the day tramping around in the mining camp. I'm afraid I'm a mess from one end to the other, Mr. Bogart. I'm just wondering if I can buy one of those fancy cakes from the dining room to take home with me tonight."

Mr. Bogart's eyes twinkled and he rubbed his hands together gleefully. "Going to surprise the missus, are you? Well, you can't do better than one of our Devil's Food Delight double layers, Deputy."

Quinn stepped inside the lobby, careful to stay on the rug by the door. "I'll just wait here, if you'll ask one of your ladies to fetch it for me."

Mr. Bogart hurried off to the hotel kitchen and Quinn leaned against the door molding, careful not to touch the flocked wallpaper. He was bone weary, what with hauling back two rascals who'd come within inches of killing each other, making the mine owner madder than a wet hen. Wayne Tucker had hated to lose two more workers, but better that, he'd said, than having another mess like the last one.

Home was sounding pretty good to Quinn's ears about now, and the thought of the woman he'd left there was enough to make him wish Mr. Bogart would step lively and let him be on his way.

At the desk a woman in full regalia, up to and including a fur of some sort wrapped around her neck, was announcing her presence in angry terms. Must not have the fanciest room available, Quinn thought with a grin.

"My dear sir, the name of Wentworth means something in civilized parts of this country."

It was all he heard, but it was enough to stand him bolt upright, his eyes scanning the couple before the desk. "Damn, if it isn't Ted and Estelle!" Delivered in an undertone, his exclamation failed to reach the pair, and Quinn was tempted to skin back out the door before he was spotted.

"Here you go, Deputy." Mr. Bogart approached, carrying a box tied with string. Quinn had hoped to produce some startling results with that cake. Now it had lost its value and he accepted it glumly, after tilting his hat over his eyes.

"Thanks, Mr. Bogart. I'll stop by and settle up tomorrow."

The hotel owner shook his head. "No sirree, you won't, Deputy. We like to take good care of our lawmen here in Pine Creek. This one's on the house." He beamed brightly, nodding as Quinn turned to the door.

Casting one last glance at the weary travelers standing by the desk, he ducked out the door and headed home.

Erin was in the kitchen, the table was set and something on the stove smelled like a gift from heaven. Quinn opened the door and offered the cake. "Hold this, honey. I want to take my boots off outside."

She accepted it with a nod, placing it on the table as he slid his boots off and carried them inside. Her eyes were red rimmed, her mouth pressed in a tight line, and Quinn knew without being told that she was already aware of the proximity of the two people who comprised her worst nightmare. Even the man who had forced her to pull the trigger on the shotgun had not imposed his presence on her dreams as had Ted and Estelle Wentworth.

More often than he wanted to remember over the past weeks, he'd awakened to find Erin tossing and turning in her sleep, muttering and half crying at the demons who filled her nights. He'd held her and cherished her through those times, all the while reviling the Wentworths for what they had done to her fragile emotions.

Now he held out his arms to her and she came to him gladly, fresh tears welling.

"Oh, Quinn! There's a lawyer here who's talking about taking custody of Robert. I don't understand how he thinks he has any right to him, but the sheriff came and told me I'll have to at least see him in order to clear it up."

"We'll see him, honey. You're not alone in this." Quinn held her close, rocking her in his arms. "There's more news, Erin," he said quietly, wrapping his arms tightly across her back as she jerked against him.

"What? What else?" She was pale, trembling and near collapse.

Quinn sat down in a chair and turned her to sit in his lap. "Ted and Estelle are here, in Pine Creek. I just saw them at the hotel."

Erin shook her head. "I don't want to see them, Quinn."

"I expect you're going to have to, like it or not, honey. We'll have to get the doctor to sign a legal paper stating that Robert is not the Wentworths' grandson, and that should be the end of it."

"That's about what the sheriff said," Erin whispered, nodding in agreement. "Will it be that simple?"

"Don't know why not. Estelle isn't going to give up easy. We know that. But once she sees the baby, she ought to be able to tell that he doesn't resemble Damian in any way, shape or form, except that he's a boy." If he'd thought to gain a smile from her with that last remark, he was disappointed. "Ah, shoot, sweetheart! It'll all work out, and in a couple of months we'll start looking for a home somewhere away from all the bad memories."

"I wish I were as sure of that as you are." She sighed, settled her head against his shoulder and slid her arms around him. "I love you, Quinn."

His arms tightened their grip and he brushed his mouth against her forehead. "You don't know how happy that makes me, honey. It just about makes it all worthwhile."

"I fixed supper for you," she whispered. "Are you hungry?"

He chuckled. "Does a bear sleep all winter? Yeah, I'm hungry. Those crackers and the cheese lasted till the sun was high in the sky. Not near long enough."

Erin rose from his lap to stand between his thighs, her fingers lingering in his hair. "I'll be all right now. I think just knowing you're here with me was what I needed."

"I'm here. I'll always be here. We'll scout up the sheriff after supper and get things rolling."

"He said the judge won't be back in town till next week. I was hoping we could get some paperwork together for adopting Robert before all this happened."

Quinn went to the sink and rolled up his sleeves, then scrubbed at his hands in the washbasin. "Let's eat. I can think better on a full stomach."

Erin's dreams were chaotic, involving Estelle and a shotgun that refused to fire, a madman intent on wrenching Robert from her arms and Quinn looking the other way. She awoke to find herself locked in Quinn's embrace, sobbing her fears aloud.

"I'd have killed her. And after I shot Russ Hogan I'd have sworn I'd never pick up a gun again." Erin shivered convulsively. "I was going to shoot her!" she whispered loudly, aghast at the hatred she'd felt so vividly. "I never thought I was capable of so much anger, Quinn. Even when Damian...even then, I couldn't have deliberately hurt him."

He rocked her in his arms, his big hands soothing her, his words a salve to her fears. "A woman defending her child is like a mama bear protecting a cub, Erin. All teeth and claws, willing to fight to the death."

She trembled in reaction as the dreams washed over her mind, opening her eyes in the darkness to banish the tendrils of horror. "I want it all over with," she sobbed, her hands fisting against Quinn's chest.

"Soon, sweet. Soon."

"I'm going over to see the sheriff, honey," Quinn said quietly, tugging his hat into place.

Erin watched from the doorway, the baby asleep in her arms. His crib was near the stove and she placed him there, tucking him in with gentle touches before she responded to Quinn's announcement.

"You won't be far from home, will you?" She hated the trace of fear her words conveyed, and bit at her lip.

"No. I'm only going to talk to him about getting Judge Beal here before Monday. I think we need to have this over and done with." He eyed her, taking her measure in the sunlight that streamed through the windows. "I don't think you're going to stand up under much more pressure, Erin."

Her chin tilted and she gritted her teeth against the fear she had allowed to surface. "I'm stronger than I look, Quinn. I'll be fine. And I won't even load the shot-gun,'' she said smartly, lifting an eyebrow as she spoke.

He relaxed visibly. ''You won't have to. Ted Went-worth's a sensible man, for the most part. I have a notion that Estelle has pushed this whole matter all along. I'm going to talk to him right after I see Henry Mason.''

Chapter Eighteen

"**Y**oung lady," Judge Beal intoned, his gaze focused on Erin. "I hadn't thought to see you in my court again so soon." He leaned back in his chair and surveyed the group of people seated before him. "This had better be worth my inconvenience, folks," he announced. "I wasn't due here for some time and I've had to rearrange my schedule accordingly. The trip was not pleasant."

He banged his gavel with vigor. "This court will come to order."

From a chair across the room a distinguished-looking gentleman rose, then approached the judge with a sheaf of papers in his hand. "I'd like to present this for your approval, Your Honor," he announced. "It represents the interests of my clients, Mr. and Mrs. Ted Wentworth."

Judge Beal looked up over the top of his glasses. "And who might you be, sir?"

"Attorney-at-law, Martin Morris, sir."

"What's all this?" Judge Beal asked tartly, motioning at the papers lying before him.

"A petition to the court for the custody of the Wentworths' grandchild, who is now in the possession of his mother.''

Judge Beal's eyebrows rose inquiringly. ''And what is the purpose of this?''

The lawyer cleared his throat. ''The court in Denver, after viewing the public records, decided that the notoriety of said mother and the conditions under which she has chosen to live are not conducive to the best interests of the child.''

''Is that so?'' He peered at Erin, rested his gaze briefly on Quinn beside her, and then looked back to the papers at hand. ''These folks here are your clients?'' he asked, waving his hand at Ted and Estelle.

''Yes, sir.''

''Ma'am?'' Judge Beal turned his attention to Erin again. ''Where's this baby these folks are wanting to take away from you?''

''They have no grandson, Your Honor,'' Erin said quietly, silently battling the fluttering, rapid beat of her heart.

''That's a lie!'' Estelle blurted, rising to her feet, her face contorted with fierce emotion. ''She has my grandchild, and she's not fit to raise my son's—''

Ted tugged at her arm, sheer force propelling her back into her chair, and bent to whisper loudly in her ear. Estelle subsided, but her complexion remained crimson, and Erin's heart continued to beat at an astonishing rate.

''Where is the grandchild in question?''

Erin rose and walked to stand before the judge. ''My baby died just minutes after he was born, five months ago, sir. He's buried next to the cabin I was living in at the time.''

''Any proof of this?'' he asked, his manner more kindly as he watched Erin.

"Quinn?" She looked over her shoulder, and Quinn rose to stand beside her. "Your Honor," she continued, "my husband buried the baby."

"He's not her husband. He's the man we hired to find her!" Estelle cried shrilly, struggling against the hold Ted had on her arm.

Judge Beal tilted his head to peer at Quinn. "You married to this girl? Seems to me we had this conversation before, didn't we, young man?"

Quinn tried to suppress a grin and failed miserably. "Yessir, we did, when Erin was brought before you, and I left the deputy behind to follow her."

The judge cleared his throat. "You prepared to swear that this girl's baby died and was buried, young man?"

Quinn nodded, gripping Erin's elbow as she swayed. She felt a surge of nausea well up within her as her knees weakened. Quinn's hand left her arm to snake around her back, and she leaned against him with relief.

The Denver lawyer stepped forward again. "These people have in their possession a baby boy, according to my sources, Your Honor."

"That true?" the judge asked, turning once more to Quinn and Erin.

She nodded. "The doctor was to be here, but he had an emergency. He sent the baby to me when his mama died and no one could feed him. He can tell you, sir. We want to adopt him," she said in a whisper.

"We require proof of that, Your Honor," the lawyer announced.

"She's lying! That's my grandchild!" Estelle cried, her rage overcoming her best attempts to remain silent. She was livid and visibly trembling, and Ted was hard put to restrain her.

"My wife is suffering terribly from the loss of our

son, Your Honor," Ted said above Estelle's tantrum. "She is not responsible for her behavior today."

"Where's the doctor?" Judge Beal asked loudly. "We need to get to the bottom of this whole mess, it seems to me."

"I'll fetch him," Tater Folsom offered from the back of the room.

"Do that!" Judge Beal was rising now, and Quinn led Erin back to their seats. The gavel banged loudly and Judge Beal nodded firmly. "Y'all just stay right where you are while this court recesses for as long as it takes to get all the parties in one room."

"Estelle will never get over this, will she?" Erin asked, leaning heavily on Quinn's arm as they climbed the steps to the sheriff's house. From within, the wails of a baby could be heard, and Erin's breasts began tingling as her milk made its presence known.

"Estelle is a sick woman," Quinn pronounced. "Ted Wentworth has his hands full. I don't know what he's going to do with her, but the trip back to New York tomorrow should be a dandy."

Alice opened the door, one arm filled with a squirming, blanket-wrapped bundle, her smile wide and relieved as she welcomed them into her kitchen. "He's been workin' on pitchin' a fit for almost ten minutes now, Erin. Hope you're prepared for him."

Erin made a face, feeling the pads she wore beneath her chemise dampen against her skin. "More than ready, Alice."

"I'm going to leave you here, honey," Quinn told her. "I want to talk to the sheriff for a few minutes, and then I need to make sure that Ted Wentworth understands why I had to return his money. He needs to know a few things that I don't think he's aware of.''

''All right.'' Erin's gaze turned to the buildings that ran the length of the main street of Pine Creek. ''I'll go on home with the baby after I feed him.''

''You'll be fine.'' Quinn's smile was reassuring as he dropped a quick kiss against her forehead.

Robert's cries were angry, his small face screwed up in a reddened mask of rage, and his arms and legs kicked, fighting free of the blanket. His plump legs pumped vigorously, exposed beneath the flannel gown he wore, and his fisted hands punched the air in time with his howls of frustration.

Erin took him in her arms and settled at the kitchen table, one hand unbuttoning her dress as she soothed him with phrases he ignored.

''There, there, sweetheart,'' she whispered, guiding him to the source of his nourishment. He hiccuped loudly, then his mouth enclosed her nipple with enthusiasm and he nursed, his hand clutching her index finger, his eyes closed tightly.

''Somethin' about a baby that just nudges your heart, ain't there?'' Alice said softly. ''That young'un sure is lucky to have you, honey.''

''Not nearly as lucky as I am to have him,'' Erin said, looking up at her. ''You know, I almost feel sorry for Estelle Wentworth. She really thought she would find her grandchild here, and now she has to go home empty-handed.''

Alice sat down, after fetching her cup of coffee, and leaned both elbows on the table. ''Tell me everything that happened. From start to finish. Here I sat, watching that blessed baby, and I missed all the excitement.''

* * *

"And the Wentworths will be leaving on the noon stage tomorrow for Denver," Erin finished. "The doctor told the judge that Estelle is suffering from delusions brought on by grief and an inability to know the difference between reality and what she perceives to be the truth."

"She sounds like a sick lady to me," Alice said promptly. "I think I'll be relieved when she's gone, and you can get back to normal again."

Erin buttoned her dress, the baby sleeping on the table before her. "I'm going home, Alice. Quinn should be home soon, and I've got supper to think about."

"Is Quinn heading out with Henry in the morning?" Alice asked. "There's something going on at Silver River Camp that needs looking into."

Erin nodded. "He said Tater is going to make sure the Wentworths get on the stage." She pulled on her coat and picked up the sleeping baby. "Thanks again for watching him, Alice."

She should have locked the door. As soon as the knob turned, the moment the wooden panel moved inward across the kitchen floor, Erin gave voice to the thought.

"I knew I should have locked that door. I suppose I didn't think you'd have the nerve to walk into my house uninvited, Estelle." She faced the woman who had been her mother-in-law, and in a flash she recalled her dream.

"I dreamed about you," Erin said slowly, moving to shield Robert from the other woman's gaze.

"A nightmare, I would assume," Estelle retorted, her eyes scanning the room, her demeanor filled with an unnatural calm.

"Yes," Erin admitted, her fright surfacing as she

wished desperately for Quinn's presence. "You've caused me more than one bad dream, you know."

"I certainly hope so. You made my son's life one long horror, with your nagging and complaining all the time. And then driving him to drink there at the end. You weren't happy until you killed him." The vicious words poured forth in a shrill litany as Estelle's control gave way, her hands waving in rhythm with her accusations.

Erin watched her closely. Once more Estelle Wentworth's facade of elegance was lost in an outpouring of vengeful anger. The woman who held a prominent place in society in New York City was clearly beyond reason.

"I didn't kill Damian." It seemed the most important accusation to answer. The rest of Estelle's notions were, in part, true. Erin had, after the first flush of romance wore off, nagged at Damian when he went out gambling, coming home drunk. She had complained when the bill collectors came to the door, demanding money for the frivolities he bought for his women.

She had not, however, killed the man. And for that she would never take the blame.

Estelle's eyes narrowed, and she faced Erin across the kitchen table, her long, carefully manicured nails stabbing the air as she gestured wildly. "You were there when he fell. You saw him roll down those stairs. You saw him hit the marble floor in the foyer, and you did nothing to save him. You never shed a tear." She leaned across the table and her whisper was scathing.

"I'll warrant it was your hand that made him lose his balance. I intend to prove that you killed my son."

Erin shook her head. "You know the court deemed it an accidental death. He was drunk."

Estelle ignored her denial. "I'll file a suit against you.

Once I take my grandson back to New York, I'll have you put in jail."

"Your grandson is dead, Estelle. We've already gone through this." There was no pretty way to phrase it, Erin decided. "Do you hear me? My baby came too early and died, just minutes after he was born."

Estelle smiled cunningly, and Erin shivered at the sight. The woman's eyes widened as she looked around the kitchen. "Where do you have him hidden? I know you have him here. There's his blanket on the rocking chair, and his clothes drying on the rack."

"I don't have your grandson, Estelle. The baby here is an orphan that Quinn and I took in. His father died in a house fire, and his mama died birthing him." Erin moved to head off Estelle's advance as the woman walked around the table.

There was no stopping her. She shoved Erin from her path and hurried to the doorway that led to the rest of the house. Then she turned, catching sight of Erin as she moved to stand in front of the crib.

Estelle's eyes lit again with that crazed look as she bent her head, peering past Erin's skirts. "Ah...is that where you thought to hide him? How foolish of you." She marched forward, her arm outstretched and stiffened, pushing Erin from her path.

Erin staggered, hitting the table and overturning a chair. She righted herself, only to see Estelle pull a small gun from her pocket. A wave of dizziness engulfed her and she shook her head, unable to believe her eyes.

"Don't make me shoot you, Erin," she warned. "And don't make the mistake of thinking I won't do it. You deserve to die, you know." Her eyes were glazed, her mouth working with convulsive movements, and Erin was struck with the knowledge that Estelle Wentworth had truly begun to lose her mind.

"What are you going to do?" she asked quietly, amazed at her own sense of composure. Robert's well-being was of the utmost importance. And that Estelle meant the baby no harm was obvious.

"Why, what does it look like?" Estelle asked archly. "I'm going to take my grandson home with me." She bent over the crib, the gun still pointed in Erin's direction. "Would you just look at him. The very picture of his father, with that beautiful dark hair. I'll warrant his eyes are the same color as Damian's, too, aren't they?"

She shot Erin a look of scorn. "You really thought to fool me with your story, didn't you? Maybe that small-town judge believed you, but I'm smarter than that. Did you think I'd swallow such a foolish tale? Orphan child, indeed! This boy is a Wentworth, through and through."

Awkwardly, intent on holding her weapon as she worked, Estelle picked up the baby, easing him into her left arm, pulling the blanket over his head. "I'll just cover you up nice and warm, my darling," she said, her words a crooning singsong. Passing the rocking chair, she snatched the second blanket, tossing it over the sleeping child, snagging it with the barrel of the gun she held.

She frowned, her concentration broken, and edged the gun free, tossing a triumphant look at Erin. "You thought I couldn't do this, didn't you? You probably thought you could fool me. Well, I'll have the last laugh, young woman. You took my son from me. You won't have the same chance with my grandson. That stage-coach will be here in a few minutes. Ted is carrying the baggage down to the hotel lobby right now, in fact. We'll be gone before you know it."

Erin felt frozen to the floor. Any movement on her part could force Estelle's hand, and the thought of that weapon being fired set her teeth on edge. She watched as Estelle opened the door and stepped out onto the porch. The glance she shot at Erin seethed with hatred, and her words were a warning that could not be ignored.

"I'll see this baby dead before I let you have your hands on him again. Mark my words, young woman. Don't tempt me."

The door closed and Erin sank to the floor, her legs giving way, her heart beating so rapidly, she thought it might burst from her chest. "Oh, God! Oh, God!" The words were a litany, a prayer with no answer forthcoming, it seemed.

Quinn was off with Sheriff Mason, and even though Ted might do battle with Estelle, the thought of Robert being in the midst of the conflict was too horrible to consider.

Erin struggled to her feet, grasping her coat and donning it quickly. She scorned the buttons, instead pulling it together across her breasts as she eased the door open. Over a hundred feet away, Estelle hurried between the bank and the hotel, bent over the baby in her arms like a hovering angel.

Demon, more likely, Erin thought mutinously. She set off, her mind racing as she followed the path Estelle had taken. Reaching the corner of the hotel, she stopped, leaning to peer toward the entrance. Only two elderly gentlemen met her gaze, and she hesitated.

Facing Estelle in the lobby was not an option. No doubt the gun was loaded, and deep in her heart Erin was certain that Robert was not at risk, as long as she did not make her presence known.

"Erin." It was an almost silent whisper, and her eyes

closed in relief. From close behind her, she felt the warmth of his body, and then his hand rested against her shoulder and she swallowed convulsively.

"Quinn!" She moved only a matter of inches and her back was met by the strong, tall body of her husband. Her head tilted back and she whispered his name again.

"It's all right, baby. I'm here. We'll take care of it."

"How did you know?"

His voice was flat, without emotion, softer than a whisper. "I didn't...not for sure, anyway. I just had a feeling, about ten miles out of town, and I turned around." His hands gripped her shoulders tighter. "I shouldn't have left you until they were on that stage."

His voice promised retribution as he drew Erin back into the space between buildings. "Don't worry. I'll get Robert away from her. You stay here."

"She has a gun."

"I'm not surprised. It's the only way she could have taken him from you." His big hands pressed Erin against the side of the hotel, and his voice was harsh. "Don't move. I don't want her to see you."

Erin bit at her lip and nodded. Arguing with him would only be futile at this point, she decided. She was not equipped to tangle with an angry Quinn. His eyes were dark and cold, intense with an emotion that went beyond simple anger. And yet he was controlled, his body moving with a lithe, rippling ease as he rounded the corner.

Erin held back the moan that nearly slipped past her lips. Her body trembled in the wintry sunlight. A horse neighed not far away, and a woman's laughter rang out from across the street somewhere.

Then the sound of jingling harness and rolling wheels

caught her attention, and she heard the rumble of a vehicle approaching.

The stage to Denver. It must be almost noon, and Ted would be waiting with their luggage in the hotel lobby. The big, boxy carriage filled the narrow opening just feet away and Erin crept closer to the corner of the building as the stage came to a stop before the hotel.

Voices intruded, several men calling back and forth, then two ladies walked past her hiding place. Without hesitation, she fell into step behind them, only to see the hotel doors open just ahead.

Ted Wentworth appeared, his eyes searching the sidewalk, his features tense. Behind him, Quinn was framed in the doorway. Around the far corner of the hotel Estelle appeared, a serene smile upon her face, her uplifted hand still holding the small gun.

"Ted!" she called brightly. "Come see what I have!" She hurried toward him and his head turned a bit, until he met Quinn's gaze.

"Don't let her see you," he warned in a whisper.

Quinn nodded, stepping back from Erin's view as she kept slow pace with the two women she followed. They drew to a halt next to the front window, and she backed against the white siding next to them.

Ted hastened to Estelle, reaching for the baby she carried against her bosom. "Let me see," he said brightly. And then, as she smiled and relaxed her hold, he attained his goal. One hand rolled the blanket-wrapped child into his possession, while his other hand enfolded her fist, pointing the gun at the sky.

Her finger squeezed the trigger in an automatic movement and the sound was swallowed in the scream that accompanied it. A piercing howl of anguish followed her first shriek of anger, and Estelle Wentworth dropped to the wooden sidewalk as if she had been the recipient of the lone bullet. Her body crumpled limply, and Ted stood over her, the harmless gun in one hand, a wriggling bundle in the other.

Quinn burst from the doorway and was met by Erin's own headlong rush as her feet skimmed the boardwalk. His big hands snatched Robert from Ted's arm and handed him to Erin. She enclosed him, bending her body to shelter his, turning away as she hovered over him as if to shield him with her own flesh and bones.

"Ted? Is she...?" Quinn looked down at the crumpled form at his feet.

"The shot went straight up, Quinn," Ted said quietly, his voice toneless. He slipped the gun into his pocket and bent to his wife. "Estelle, get up."

She mumbled beneath her breath, and Quinn felt a chill as he heard the disjointed words. Ted lifted his wife, gently placing her on her feet, holding her erect. The once formidable society woman was rumpled and disheveled, her eyes blank, her mouth slack, and Quinn's anger died.

"I'll help you get her on the stage, if you like," he offered, then stepped back as the other man shook his head. "Can you handle it, Ted?" Quinn spoke softly, still at hand should Estelle's condition change.

"I told you yesterday I feared she was out of control," Ted said in a low voice, "but I didn't think it would go this far." He slipped his arm around her waist and took her weight upon himself. His eyes were dull with pain as he met Quinn's gaze.

"I shouldn't have let her talk me into this. I knew she was...becoming unhinged. I suppose that's the nicest way to put it. Losing Damian broke her heart. She loved him."

The stagecoach driver left the hotel and a horn sounded, announcing the vehicle's imminent departure. "Are your bags on top?" Quinn asked.

Ted nodded. "The manager took care of it, I'm sure."

The crowd that had gathered stood aside, as if unwilling to intrude while Ted helped his wife toward the open door of the coach. Erin shrank against the front wall of the hotel watching the couple pass by, and Ted cast her a long look of regret.

Quinn helped lift Estelle onto a seat and saw Ted settle next to her. The coach was crowded, and they were the subject of apprehensive glances from the other passengers, but Ted ignored them and offered his hand to Quinn.

"Tell Erin…" The older man glanced from the doorway into the sunshine that flooded the sidewalk. Erin watched from her spot near the hotel door, her expression somber, a ray of sunlight catching her, illuminating her fragile features.

"Tell her…tell her I'm sorry. For all of it. I knew all along she was the innocent party. I said things…" Ted shook his head and leaned back in the seat.

"I'll tell her," Quinn murmured, jumping to the ground as the horn sounded again. He closed the door and stepped back, watching as the vehicle lumbered away, the horses breaking into a trot within seconds.

Erin stood at his elbow. He caught her scent even before he turned, felt the warmth of her presence and welcomed it with a smile as he swiveled to face her.

"I won't even scold you for not staying put," he said softly, his gaze admiring as he scanned her face. She was pale, but the strength of the woman he'd married shone through the anxiety of the past few minutes. Her eyes were calm, meeting his with a warmth he welcomed.

"Let's go home," she whispered, and he nodded his agreement. His arm slid around her waist as they walked. The crowd, not unaccustomed to a stray gunshot, had already dispersed.

The sun and wind were drying out the mud, he noticed, catching Erin's weight against himself as she stumbled over a rut. Her grip tightened on Robert and he wailed a protest.

"You're squeezing him, honey," Quinn told her with a chuckle.

"He's really all right, isn't he?" she asked, peering down at him, parting the blanket, the better to see his face. He squinted up at them in the sunlight, his mouth opening as he uttered another protesting wail, and then his fist flailed in the air and he caught sight of it. His eyes narrowed, and with a look of intense concentration he lowered his hand to his mouth and commenced sucking on the protruding thumb.

Erin laughed aloud, a carefree sound that melted the last vestige of ice around Quinn Yarborough's heart. He'd allowed his emotions to become remote—lest fear take control of his actions—and had known that he must set aside his own safety for the protection of Erin and the child. He'd become that frozen man, that hunter, for those few moments, only to succumb to the laughter of this woman.

Never again did he want to be the stalker, the pursuer. He'd entered into the chase for the last time. His heart lifted as he considered that thought. He'd found the sweetest bounty of all, in the arms of this bright-eyed creature who walked beside him.

Closing the gate behind them, Quinn snatched her up

in his embrace, his arms holding mother and child against his chest. The steps were mounted, the kitchen door opened and closed behind them, and he stood in the warmth of the small home Erin had created for their benefit.

She watched him, her mouth twitching as if she held back laughter, and he ducked his head to plant a kiss upon those rosy lips.

"It's finally over, isn't it, Quinn?" she asked, her cheeks rosy now as she responded with refreshing candor to his caress.

He shook his head. "No, it's not over, sweetheart." Lowering himself to a kitchen chair, he shifted her to his lap and opened the blanket, the better to see the child they held between them.

"It's not over. It's just beginning."

Epilogue

Sweet Valley, Wyoming
1880

The woman sat on a quilt beneath a tree just beyond the side porch of the ranch house. A young boy leaned against her side, a book in his hand, and at his feet, a toddler curled beneath a corner of the quilt, as if it had been clutched in his hand and he had rolled with it in his sleep.

Quinn Yarborough watched from horseback, sweating beneath the summer sun, his face and hands deeply tanned, his narrowed eyes intent on the trio before him.

"There's Pa!" A loud whisper announced his presence, and Quinn slid from his mount, tilting his hat back with one long finger as he watched the dark-haired boy spring to his feet. He ran quickly, his small face eager, his arms upstretched, and Quinn bent to catch him in his arms, lifting him high against the blue sky.

"We was reading a book, Pa!" Robert told him, his voice ringing out with enthusiasm. "Joey went to sleep, but Ma and me read the whole story."

Quinn's gaze focused on the woman who gained her feet with awkward movements. Gone was the slender form, the ease of motion she was accustomed to. Instead she walked with one hand at her back, the other resting on the curve of her advanced pregnancy.

Erin met his gaze, and her eyes lit with a message he never tired of reading within their depths.

"You all right, honey?" It wasn't what he wanted to say, but that would wait until later.

"I'm feeling sort of achy," she answered, a message emerging in the tone of her voice.

"What do you think?" he asked, his gaze sweeping her length, noting the hesitation in her step.

Her smile was radiant. "I think you're going to be up till all hours tonight, Quinn Yarborough." And then she halted, the hand on her belly tensing as she closed her eyes.

"How long's that been going on?" His long strides carried him to her side, and he lowered Robert to the ground. His arm circled her back. "Do you want me to carry you?"

She shook her head. "I want you to send one of the hands to fetch Roseanne. I'll need her before long."

He nodded. The next ranch was an hour's ride. Within minutes after that, Roseanne, who was an old hand at this, would be on her way, probably toting her own newborn with her. "I'll help you into the house, honey," he offered.

Erin shook her head. "Just send for Roseanne. I want to sit on the porch for a while. I need to watch Joey while he sleeps."

At that, the little boy beneath the corner of the quilt rolled over and lifted his head. "Mama?" He sat up and rubbed his eyes, then rose and headed in her direction.

Quinn scooped him up and delivered a loud kiss against the rosy cheek.

"Your mama's gonna be busy today, scout. How about takin' a walk with your pa." The two-year-old wrapped his arms around his father's neck and nestled against his shoulder, as if it were a familiar resting spot.

"I'll help you up on the porch, Mama," Robert offered, lifting his hand for Erin to grasp.

"Thank you, sweetheart," she said, her eyes tender as she scanned his youthful beauty. He'd been her salvation from the first. There was about him a sensitivity to her moods, as if he were privy to her needs even before she knew them herself.

"I love you, Mama," he told her gravely, lending his shoulder for her balance, as if they had walked thus before today.

The hours went swiftly, as she had known they would. With the arrival of Roseanne, Erin had gone to her bed, aware that her time was almost upon her. Tater Folsom, who had followed them almost five years ago from Pine Creek to be their ranch foreman, tended to the boys in the big sitting room. Quinn was by her side, his hands soothing and comforting as she labored to bring forth his child.

And then the waiting was over. A soft whimper met her ears, matching her own smothered gasp. Then it escalated in seconds to a cry of outrage as the pink creature in Roseanne's hands flailed her arms and legs.

"It's a girl, Erin," her friend said with a laugh. "She's strong. Look at her kick!"

"Let me have her," Erin whispered, leaning on her elbows to see better.

Roseanne nodded. "Just let me tie the cord. Here, Quinn. Take the baby."

He rose from his place beside Erin, and his big hands almost enveloped the squirming babe. Roseanne tied off the pulsing cord in two places and cut it halfway between, then wrapped a soft flannel around the plump infant.

"Here," Quinn said gruffly, placing her in Erin's waiting arms. The glaze of tears dimming his sight was apparent to the woman who shared the baby's weight with him for a second. Then Erin held her daughter to her breast, gazing down at the blinking eyelids, the damp, dark hair, the mouth that worked as if seeking sustenance, and the hand that clutched at her mother's finger with amazing strength.

"Elizabeth Rose," Erin said softly, lifting her gaze to his. "Is that all right with you?"

Quinn nodded, kneeling by the bed once more. "Oh, yes." His words were husky, his vision clearing as he beheld the woman who was his very heart and life. The bounty of love he'd been gifted with. Sweet bounty...

* * * * *